BLIND MAN'S BUFF

BLIND MAN'S BUFF

Florence Ryerson
AND
Colin Clements

Why do I yield to that suggestion
Whose horrid image doth unfix my hair
And make my seated heart knock at my ribs,
Against the use of nature?

Macbeth

COACHWHIP PUBLICATIONS
Greenville, Ohio

For

O. O. McIntyre

Blind Man's Buff, by Florence Ryerson and Colin Clements
© 2023 Coachwhip Publications edition
Introduction © Curtis Evans

First published 1933
Florence Ryerson, 1892-1965
Colin Clements, 1894-1948
CoachwhipBooks.com

ISBN 1-61646-567-0
ISBN-13 978-1-61646-567-4

Ryerson and Clements Do Murder
Curtis Evans

As the decade of the Thirties dawned in the United States the author of the bestselling Philo Vance mysteries, S. S. Van Dine (pen name of critic and author Willard Hunting-ton Wright), strode over the mystery fiction landscape like a monocled colossus, his five detective novels, the most recent of which was *The Scarab Murder Case* (1930), having sold over ten million copies and been translated into twenty-two languages. To be sure, the hard-boiled boys of American pulp fiction, such as Dashiell Hammett, who had recently hit it big with *The Maltese Falcon* (1930), had Philo and his creator in their pitiless gunsights and would soon enough shoot them down, so to speak. Yet for now that posh, g-dropping, cosmopolitan aesthete and gentle-man amateur sleuth, Philo Vance, was still Big Man on the murder campus. When the cousins Frederic Dannay and Manfred Lee began successfully publishing mysteries as Ellery Queen in 1929, they used Van Dine's books as their model. There were other, lesser known Van Dine imitators as well who published their first detective novels in 1930, just a year behind Ellery Queen, including two collabora-tive teams: Roger Scarlett, pen name of partners Dorothy Blair and Evelyn Page, and Florence Marie Ryerson (1892-1965) and Colin Campbell Clements (1894-1948), a pro-lific spousal writing team who co-authored novels, plays and film scripts. Like Roger Scarlett, Clements and Ryerson only ever published five detective novels and their mysteries were soon mostly forgotten; yet their mysteries, like Scarlett's, are now being revived for modern-day readers charmed, like an earlier Depression-era generation, by the baroque splendors of the Van Dine school of Golden Age detective fiction.

As stated Florence Ryerson and Colin Clements published only five mystery novels, these being *Seven Suspects* (1930), *Fear of Fear* (1931), *Blind Man's Buff* (1933), *Shadows* (1934) and *The Borgia Blade* (1937), the first four of which, the Jimmy Lane series, bear the greatest impress of Van Dine. (*The Borgia Blade* is a standalone.) For Ryerson and Clements, mysteries were just the proverbial drop in the writers bucket. The couple wed in 1927, not long after Clements, Director of the Little Theater in Memphis, Tennessee, met Ryerson, a scenario writer for MGM Studios, while out in California. After their marriage Clements settled with Ryerson in Hollywood, where he also wrote for the film business, though playwriting remained his first (and most lucrative) love. Ryerson had the more notable screenwriting career, working on scripts for the mystery thriller films *The Canary Murder Case* (1928) (based on the Van Dine bestseller), *The Mysterious Dr. Fu Manchu* (1929) and *The Return of Dr. Fu Manchu* (1930), (with Charlie Chan portrayer Warner Oland as the nefarious Asian mastermind), *The Crime of the Century* (1933), *The Casino Murder Case* (1935) (Van Dine again, albeit adulterated) and the operatic mystery *Moonlight Murder* (1936). She is best known, however, for being one of the credited scriptwriters (there were many who stuck a finger in the pie) of *The Wizard of Oz* (1939).

Working on *The Canary Murder Case* led to Ryerson meeting S. S. Van Dine himself, and the two became friends after Ryerson, in Van Dine's eyes, rescued his book from the clumsy handling of what he bluntly termed "Hollywood morons." Observes Van Dine's biographer John Loughery of Ryerson: "She wasn't the usual studio hack," even having actually read the book on which the film was based. Ryerson worked with Van Dine to iron out the unsightly wrinkles in the script, deleting "sentimental love scenes," a "gratuitous car chase" and a "stock villain." She "was happy to do battle with the studio bosses for her new friend and saw to it that a workable script was ready by the summer [of 1928]. In September the movie went into production with a screenplay more appealing to everyone."

A few years later in 1931, Van Dine, accompanied by his second wife, came out to California to work with Ryerson on the script of the mystery film *The Blue Moon Murder Case*, which, unfortunately, was scrapped, later emerging in 1933 as the much altered film *Girl Missing*. "Ryerson gave a dinner in honor of the Van Dines and treated them to a lavish weekend at Palm Springs," notes Loughery. Sadly Ryerson and Van Dine later had a falling out over the script of *The Casino Murder Case*, filmed at a time in the mid-thirties when Van Dine's stock as a film property was falling, the hottest thing in mystery films now being not celibate gentleman sleuths like Philo Vance but rather wisecracking couples like Nick and Nora Charles, introduced by Dashiell Hammett in his popular detective novel *The Thin Man* (1934).

Both Philo Vance and Nick Charles in fact were played by William Powell, symbolizing Van Dine's diminution of status relative to Hammett. Ryerson and her scripting partner Edgar Allan Woolf first hit upon the idea of "Hammettizing" Van Dine by introducing Myrna Loy, who played Nick's wife Nora, into the Philo Vance series as the love interest of Vance, who would still be played by William Powell. Thus the pair managed to outrage Van Dine, who loathed the character Nick Charles, deeming him plebeian and vulgar. In any event Powell opted out of the project, letting it be known he had tired of playing Vance. "I know Bill is glad the [S. S. Van Dine murder mysteries are out of his life]," Hollywood gossip columnist Louella Parsons confided to her readers. Ultimately Hungarian-born Paul Lukas was cast as Vance (a rather bizarre choice as Vance is decidedly an Anglo-American type), with a young Rosalind Russell playing his wisecracking love interest. Van Dine washed his hands of the whole affair, just making sure he collected his check.

While Ryerson ultimately may have bastardized Van Dine's work, the Jimmy Lane mysteries that she wrote with Colin Clements were very much modeled after the Philo Vance tales. The four books are narrated by Jimmy Lane's self-effacing attorney and old college chum Philip Carter, recalling the narration of the Philo Vance mysteries by Philo's self-effacing attorney and old college chum Van Dine. All four books, like many of the Van Dine mysteries, are infused with outré atmospheric elements, particularly *Fear of Fear* and *Blind Man's Buff*, the two novels in the series reprinted by Coachwhip. *Fear of Fear* involves spiritualism and eastern mysticism, while *Blind Man's Buff* takes place at a mansion on a storm-isolated island, complete with a creepy family tomb, wherein lies interred (or so they say) the family's deceased eccentric patriarch. Both have involved plots, including house plans, artist illustrations, family trees and tabulations. Assuming Van Dine ever read either book, he should have been pleased to see his own influences in them.

* * * * *

Fear of Fear, which carries a dedication "*For our friend WILLARD HUNTINGTON WRIGHT and his friend S. S. VAN DINE*," might well have been titled, had Van Dine written it, *The Spirit Murder Case*, or perhaps *The Jasmine Murder Case*. It opens with Jimmy Lane's literary chronicler Philip Carter explaining why now "the time has come to tell the truth about the murders on Russian Hill." The events in the tale take place primarily at three adjacent Victorian row houses in the San Francisco neighborhood of Russian Hill, wherein reside an interconnected group of people: Harlan Grant, a famed spiritualistic medium; his brother Colonel Grant, late of India; Chanda Steeb, the colonel's beautiful daughter; Otto Steeb, her scientist husband; Singh and Lalah, Indian servants to Harlan Grant; and Dr. Waverly, a physician friend of the Grants.

Somewhat reminiscent of Earl Derr Biggers' Charlie Chan novel *The Black Camel* (1929), an actress, Norah Fallon, comes to Jimmy Lane, Hollywood scenarist, playwright, ex-journalist and recent solver of a Hollywood murder mystery (see *Seven Suspects*), complaining that she is being blackmailed by Harland Grant. Soon she and her boyfriend, scientist Richard Stoddard, are implicated in Grant's locked room murder at his home on Russian Hill and Jimmy is called upon to get the couple off the hook. That he does, though not until he has confronted more murders and considerable bamboozlement and hoodoo. (Speaking of the latter, readers are reminded that Ryerson and Clements' portrayal of Jimmy Lane's unsubtly nicknamed man, Friday, while regrettable, is of its time.) The *Sacramento Bee* was impressed, declaring "it will be a wise solver of mystery detective puzzles who will guess the right answer."

Blind Man's Buff takes Jimmy and Philip to New York, where they receive a telegram from novelist Lucia Conroy, with whom Jimmy is collaborating on a play, imploring them to come to her ancestral mansion (complete with mausoleum) on Sycamore Island, where the Conroy clan has made its annual gathering. Upon their arrival at

Sycamore Island the pair is plunged, along with the Conroy clan, into a nightmarish series of slaughters reminiscent of S. S. Van Dine's *The Greene Murder Case* (1928), as a storm cuts them off from outside aid. The cast of characters is a large one indeed, with no fewer than nine Conroy connections, a housekeeper and a caretaker, giving ample scope for both a ruthless murderer and puzzle-solving readers.

Buff is an atmospheric and creepy tale indeed, owing a not insignificant debt to another "Edgar Allan" besides Ryerson's screenwriting partner Edgar Allan Woolf, a man by the name of Poe. "This is one great yarn," proclaimed the Camden, New Jersey *Morning Post*. Reflecting on the escalating body count in their detective novels, Florence Ryerson recalled humorously: "[W]e had to top ourselves each time in gore. The first story only killed one person. The second killed three. And then it got to be a kind of slaughter house."

Ryerson composed the first drafts of all the mystery novels, dictating them into a Dictaphone, from which written transcriptions were made. Colin Clements then would read them, making revisions. "We have found that it to pays to dictate," observed Clements, his eye as ever on the saleable market. "It somehow seems to move faster—and if there's anything a modern-day detective story has to have, it's speed."

* * * * *

Speed of production characterized the career of the two authors. Among other thing the couple wrote over one hundred one-act plays, which, although not staged on Broadway, proved quite lucrative during the Depressions years. "Fact is," boasted Clements, "I understand that 365 nights a year somewhere in the world, at least one of our plays is being produced." One of their many plays, *Through the Night*, was a three-act inverted mystery dramady that was tried out in Hollywood in 1939 and produced in both London and Glasgow to great success, with debonair English actor Esmond Knight taking a well-praised sinister turn as the play's treacherous killer. (Nearly a half-century later he would appear in British television's 1987 adaptation of Agatha Christie's final published Miss Marple mystery, *Sleeping Murder*, starring Joan Hickson.) "The appeal of the piece lies in the unravelling of the crime by the characters," pronounced a delighted Scottish reviewer. "There is bright and sparkling dialogue filled with true American wisecracks." Declared a similarly impressed American reviewer: "Chuckles, chills, and a whirlwind finish. When the Ryerson-Clements team twists a plot it stays twisted up until 10:29 P.M., and then unravels so fast you are amazed to find not a single loose end."

The husband and wife also enjoyed a pair of non-criminous successes on Broadway. *Harriet*, a drama about *Uncle Tom's Cabin* author and abolitionist Harriet Beecher Stowe starring Helen Hayes in the title role and staged by future famed film director Elia Kazan, ran for over a year and 377 performances at Henry Miller's Theater in 1943-44. Catching a wave of patriotic fervor, *Harriet* became the authors' biggest hit and was even praised by First Lady Eleanor Roosevelt. Another play, the romantic comedy *Strange Bedfellows*, ran for six months and 229 performances in 1948, surviving Clements, who was stricken with a heart attack during an out-of-town tryout in Philadelphia and never lived to see the play make it to Broadway.

Florence Ryerson survived her partner of over two decades by seventeen years, passing in 1965 at the age of seventy-two. During their heyday as a power writing couple in the late Thirties and Forties, the spouses resided and wrote in the San Fernando Valley at their domicile

Florence Ryerson

the Shadow Ranch, a historic structure still standing today. Petite, sloe-eyed and crowned between the wars with a bob of black hair, Ryerson certainly had not needed a man to achieve success, though Campbell clearly made a congenial writing partner for her. The daughter of Charles Dwight Willard, a progressive Los Angeles journalist and booster and secretary of the Municipal League, and Mary MacGregor, she graduated from Pasadena High School and for three years attended Radcliffe College, where she was deemed a "brilliant young writer." However, in 1914 she unexpectedly married Harold Ryerson, youthful president of Ryerson Manufacturing Company and her late father's assistant in the Municipal League, immediately after the wedding sailing away with him for a honeymoon on his recently purchased yacht. The yacht notwithstanding, however, love turned. The couple had one son, Hal, in 1915 before Harold left Florence for another woman in the early 1920s. Florence began publishing short stories the year of her son's birth and in 1926, a year before she wed Colin Clements, she was hired by MGM as a script-writer, where she quickly made the grade.

Tall, fair and handsome, Colin Clements was born in Omaha, Nebraska, the son of William Clements, a native Cornish cattle driver, and Ada Swanback, an adventurous nurse of German and Dutch derivation. (After she and William divorced, Ada later practiced her profession in the frozen wilds of Alaska.) A 1917 graduate of the University of Washington, Clements, or "Clemmy" as he was nick-named, also attended the Carnegie Institute for Technology and George Pierce Baker's playwriting class at Harvard and worked as a play-reader, actor and stage manager for Stuart Walker's Portmanteau Theater, a traveling reper-tory company which performed plays in the homes of patrons using an ingeniously designed portable stage. ("The Theater That Comes to You" was its motto.) Described as

Colin Clements

a "he-man" in spite of his artistic temperament, Clements soon proved a restless globetrotter, serving as a lieutenant in the U. S. Army after American entry into World War One in 1918, plunging into humanitarian relief efforts in Armenia upon the conflict's cessation, and even, before his eventual return to the States in 1922, spending a stint with the Rumanian National Theater in Rumania, where he staged plays for Queen Marie. Between 1922 and his marriage to Florence Ryerson five years later, he directed little theater companies in Gloucester, Massachusetts, Santa Barbara, California and Memphis, Tennessee.

A frequent collaborative writing team of varied and prodigious talent, Florence Ryerson and Colin Clements affably proclaimed to the English press, at the time of the debut of their play *Through the Night* in 1940, that they "have had no professional jealousies in twelve years of happily married life." This equable and able entertaining couple deserves to be better remembered than they are today. Perhaps the reprinting of a pair of their Thirties Van Dinean detective novels by Coachwhip will help accomplish this.

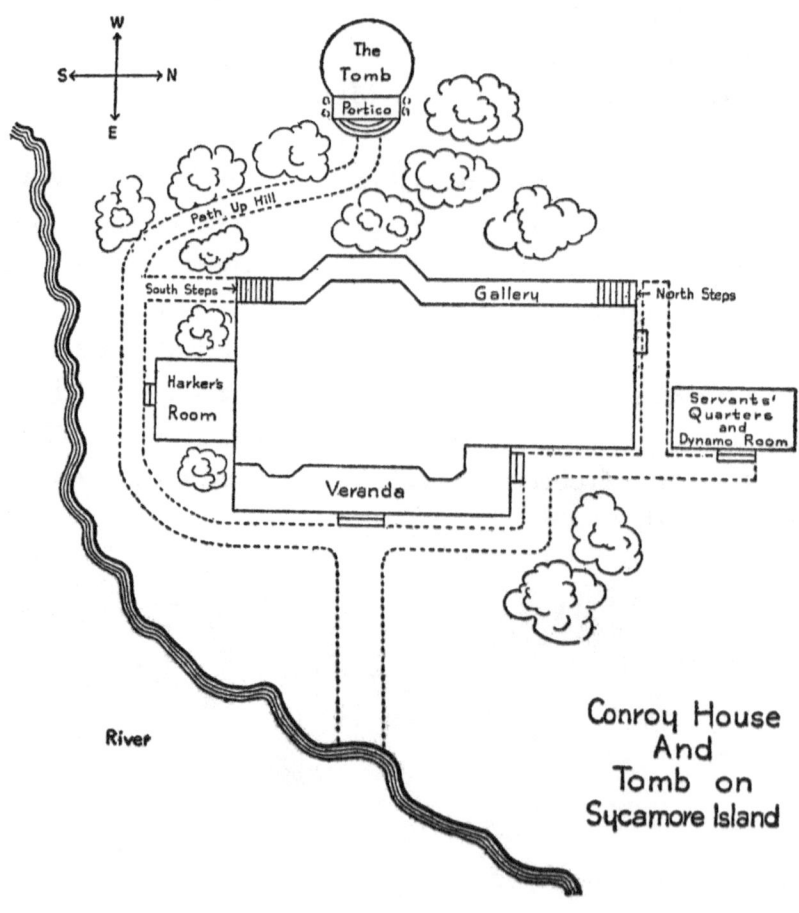

Conroy House
And
Tomb on
Sycamore Island

Those Concerned in the Murders

Jimmy Lane

Philip Carter, *who tells the story*

Lucia Conroy, *a novelist*

Lee Conroy, *her twin-brother, a composer*

Mrs. Prill, *their housekeeper*

Dr. Mark Dietrich, *Lucia's cousin*

Connie Dietrich, *his wife*

Count Roberto Patri, *another of Lucia's cousins*

Tony Patri, *his half-brother, a painter*

Douglas Conroy, *another cousin, a broker*

Judith Conroy, *their aunt*

Hagar Conroy, *a great-aunt*

Henry Harker, *a caretaker*

Truffles, *Aunt Hagar's spaniel*

Note

Since to reveal the true identities of those
who were concerned in the tragedy of "Sycamore Island" would cause unnecessary pain,
I have, at the request of Jimmy Lane, altered
the locale and used fictitious names throughout the following chronicle.

                                Philip Carter

Chapter 1
A Telegram Arrives

SYCAMORE CITY 1930 SEPT 16 A M 8 02
JAMES LANE
    HOTEL ALGONQUIN NEW YORK NY
NEED YOU DESPERATELY STOP IF YOU
LOVE ME COME AT ONCE STOP BRING
NORTHWEST MOUNTED
                    LUCIA CONROY

The telegram was brought to us while we were breakfasting in our rooms. Jimmy Lane read it with a puzzled frown, then passed it across the table.

"Now what does she mean by that?" I asked, astonished.

"Hanged if I know. But whatever's happened, you can bet your bottom dollar it's serious. Lucia wouldn't drag us across three states on a false alarm."

He took the telegram from me and reread it, muttering "desperately" and "if you love me" half aloud.

Resignedly I swallowed my coffee and prepared for the worst. Jimmy is incorrigible in his pursuit of adventure. He insists that he is in search of material for books and plays, but I have noticed that it is usually a woman who draws him on. It was to save Diana de Silva that he undertook the Lopez mystery. Nora Fallon's red hair and green eyes involved him in that dreadful affair on Russian Hill. Now came this call from Lucia Conroy.

There was no sentiment involved. Whatever the telegram might seem to imply, Lucia was not Jimmy's beloved.
She was, we both knew, engaged to her cousin Douglas
Conroy. That "if you love me" stuff was merely by way
of strengthening her appeal. The rest of the message was
easily decoded. My legal name is Philip Carter, but "The
Northwest Mounted" has been Jimmy's nickname for me
ever since our college days, when I spent rather more time
than I could afford in hauling him out of difficulties with
pretty ladies, with irate townsmen and with the Dean.

In one form or another that has been my job ever since.
Jimmy's lack of respect for constituted authority is equaled
only by his superb disregard for the law, and I am constantly following in his wake, playing a legal Sancho Panza
to his Don Quixote.

You have doubtless guessed by now that Jimmy Lane is
James Lane, *the* James Lane, author of *Naughty Nan, The
Priceless Girl,* and half a score of other successes. His usual
stamping ground is California, but at the time of Lucia's
telegram he was in New York, busy with what he termed
his "fall hatching of drama."

I was equally busy, with his contracts.

Between rehearsals Jimmy had been collaborating with
Lucia upon a play. Lucia was a writer, too, a novelist with
what the critics termed "brilliant promise." Her books had
brought in more praise than money so far, I gathered, and
Jimmy's offer to help her adapt one of her romances to
the stage was a godsend. All through August they slaved
steadily upon the first two acts, and were rounding the
third into shape when Lucia made her startling announcement. She must drop her work and go away for a month.

"But you can't stop now," Jimmy protested. "If you're
pining for a summer resort we'll pack up Mrs. Prill and
motor down to Atlantic City."

Lucia firmly declined Atlantic City; she must go to her island, and she must, moreover, be there promptly on the fifteenth of September.

"You see," she explained, "all the family will be there."

"I didn't know you had any family except Doug and your brother."

"Oh, I've lots," vaguely. "Aunts and cousins. We own an island together, and we always meet there at this time of year. No matter what we may be doing we drop it and go."

Go she did, upon September thirteenth, a fine prophetic date in view of what happened later. That was on Saturday. Tuesday the telegram arrived, and Thursday we stepped out of the train at the little river station nearest to Sycamore Island.

Lucia was waiting on the platform with her brother, Lee. For thirty-six hours Jimmy and I had been hazarding wild guesses as to what had happened to Lucia and why she needed us so desperately. We had pictured her in almost every condition of mind and body except the one in which we found her. The little wretch was smiling, actually smiling, and her greeting had all the cheeriness of a hostess welcoming casual week-end guests.

"So glad you could get away," she bubbled. (Lucia is distinctly not the bubbling type.) *"Do* let Lee tend to your luggage. The family are all dying to meet you."

It was like stepping on a top step that wasn't there. Like turning on a warm shower; and finding it icy. Jimmy and I both goggled at her. Then, simultaneously, we jumped to the same conclusion—she didn't want to talk in the presence of Lee.

Lee Conroy was Lucia's twin, but they were as different as day and night. Although she, in her middle twenties, was slim and trim as a schoolgirl, Lee had allowed too many women and too many drinks to blunt the edges of his youth. He had Lucia's fair curly hair and large gray eyes combined with a slight, poorly knit figure, which made him appear weak and ineffectual. Jimmy assured me that he wrote surprisingly good music, or, rather, he would have written it if he had not been so sunk in dissipation. As it was, he turned out an occasional piece of work, just enough to keep up a pretense of industry. Lucia both mothered and spoiled him, feeding his doubtful talent at the expense of her own; this I gathered from the caustic comments of their housekeeper, Mrs. Prill.

Mrs. Prill acted as a sort of Cerberus for Lucia. She was a grim, spare woman of sixty with snapping black eyes, wide-set upon either side of a monumental nose, a Scotch covenanter sort of nose assertive as the prow of a ship. When Lucia and Lee had escorted us to the boathouse at the end of the village street, we found her seated in the stern of the launch, surrounded by baskets and bundles of provisions. That Lucia had planned this, I felt sure, for Lee was running the engine, and, without Mrs. Prill, we might have talked in privacy. As it was, Lucia kept up a gay stream of inconsequential chatter about the weather, the trip, and the play. In the end, I moved up toward the engine and sat down beside Lee.

The island was three miles from the town, he told me, and belonged exclusively to the Conroy family. Lee seemed to have some grievance against their custom of meeting there. Why he should have stayed, or, indeed, why he should have come at all when he felt so bitter about it, I could not imagine.

"The cursed old place is worse than a tomb," he growled. "Matter of fact, there is a tomb there. Grandfather's. I wish to God somebody'd strangled him at birth!"

"Then you wouldn't be here," I pointed out, and he laughed harshly.

"Small loss! Which goes for the rest of the Conroys, too. We'd all be better off at the bottom of the sea!"

That was his general line of cheery conversation from the time I joined him until we swung into the harbor at Sycamore.

I wish I might say that some subtle sense sent a premonitory chill down my spine at first sight of the island. Jimmy Lane, were he recounting the affair, would give at least a paragraph to that chill, and a second to the dark foreboding which accompanied it, with a vivid and Poesque description of the strange, tortured shapes of cypress that lined the water, and the melancholy shadows of the gum and magnolia trees beyond. As a matter of fact, I felt nothing but pleasant relief as we drew up to the small dock and stepped from the launch into the midst of what Lucia called "The Conroy Clan."

She introduced them casually, beginning with Dr. Mark Dietrich, a tall thin man in the late thirties, with hair already graying at the temples. In spite of the heat, he was dressed meticulously in a suit of dark blue flannel. He wore a neat straw hat upon his head, and a pair of gold rimmed *pince-nez* was perched upon his nose and anchored by a black ribbon. There was something pedantic about him, something dry and detached. I was not surprised to learn that he had given up general practice and gone in for research.

Beside him was Connie Dietrich, a small, vivacious blonde in a bathing suit and shorts. Her wide blue eyes and curly, pale gold hair gave her such an air of childish innocence that one almost failed to notice her sensuous mouth and the discontented droop at its corners. She was so young that it was something of a shock to learn that she was not Dr. Dietrich's daughter but his wife.

Roberto and Antonio Patri—"'Berto and Tony," Lucia called them—were brothers. Both were tall, dark, and handsome in a foreign sort of way. When they spoke, their perfect, not to say colloquial, English was strangely incongruous. Only 'Berto the elder, had a slight foreign intonation.

"'Berto's a Count when he's in Italy and working at it," Lucia told us. "But we don't hold it against him. He went to Oxford, and Tony to Yale—so they've lived it down."

That explained the slang. But why the title? And why Italy? I glanced across and found Jimmy wearing the same expression of bewilderment that must have been mine.

"Don't try to get us all straight at once," Lucia advised, "or you'll go jittery. Just figure we're cousins, except when we're aunts and in-laws. We're all part of the Conroy clan. Even the ones who have different names." She looked around, and demanded: "Where's Judith?"

"In the house," Connie said. "Aunt Hagar's been throwing one of her fits."

"Oh, Lord," Lucia groaned. "Is she still at it?"

"Louder—*and* funnier," Tony told her.

There was but one house on the island, I found, a huge rambling building of weathered shingles, situated rather strangely at the foot of a sharp rise which completely cut off air and light from the rear windows. The doors and shutters were painted a blue-green, and the roof had once been the same shade. Now, roof, house and shutters were all so mottled with lichen, so spotted with mildew and fungus, that the whole structure seemed part of the tree-covered hillside beyond.

There was no garden about the house, only a tangle of swamp maple, sycamore and locust, festooned with wild grape and raspberry vines. On the low hill, the trees were much larger, with a look of great and gloomy age. Here there were cypress and gum trees, a huge magnolia and an orchard carefully tended. In the center of the circling cypress was a small building of stone, which shone deathly white against the dark background.

"That's grandfather's tomb," Lucia told me. "Cheerful, isn't it? Just the ornament for a summer place." Her words were flippant, but her tone was somber and, as she looked up the hill, I saw there was no laughter in her eyes.

We had reached the house and were climbing the steps when I caught the sound of a voice raised in violent imprecation. It was a strange voice, almost inhuman in its harsh stridency. The tone was so loud that it might have come from the throat of a man, yet there was an hysterical quality about it which was feminine.

"Aunt Hagar brightening her little corner," Tony explained.

As we stood in the gloomy shadows, listening to that horrible voice, I had my first feeling, not of premonition, but of vague uneasiness and distaste. I did not want to climb the steps and enter the doors of that somber house. I wanted to leave the island, to return to New York.

Then I remembered that Lucia had sent for Jimmy and the Northwest Mounted. She had said that she needed us desperately. It was too late to turn back now.

CHAPTER 2
WE LEARN ABOUT SALLY

"Admit that I fooled you," Lucia said. "Admit that you thought I was in trouble and came galloping down to the rescue like a couple of blooming Launcelots."

"I admit it," Jimmy growled. "What then?"

"Why then . . . you're going to stay a week—two weeks—and have a grand vacation. You can swim, and fish, and play tennis. We'll get to work and finish the play. . . ." Lucia was sitting on the grass under the magnolia tree on the hill, where we had finally cornered her alone. Jimmy had demanded an explanation of her telegram, and she was giving it with the impishness of a gamin that has played a successful prank on its elders. "We'll finish the play," she told him, "and you'll have a rest in the bargain."

"So that's why you sent the telegram?"

"That's why. I knew it'd fetch you!"

"You're lying, my girl," Jimmy told her. "And doing it damn' badly." She gasped at that, and before she could recover: "Better start fresh, and give us the truth. You owe it to us, you know."

"Yes; I suppose I do." She paused to select a cigarette, partly, I thought, to recover her poise, then: "You're right; I *was* lying, Jimmy. I hated to admit what a fool I'd been. Fact is, I let myself get stampeded into a panic."

"Just what," Jimmy asked, "stampeded you?"

"It doesn't matter now. I was wrong—and I apologize. If you'll stay I'll make it up by giving you a good time."

"You're going to tell us what frightened you," Jimmy said firmly, "It wasn't just a little thing, Lucia. It was something that gave you a bad shock, and you're still worried. Look at your hand."

We both looked. The fingers with which she was holding a match to her cigarette were shaking.

Lucia surrendered. "All right. I'll tell you. It's about Mark's sister—my cousin Sally. She killed herself last year."

"Killed herself?"

"Yes. Here on the island. At least, we think so. We were never quite sure that it wasn't accident! No," she contradicted herself, "that isn't the truth. It couldn't possibly have been an accident."

"Why do you say that?"

"Because she never took that medicine alone. It was always prepared for her."

"She died of an overdose of medicine?"

"Yes, chloral hydrate. But she wasn't the sort to commit suicide, not Sally!" There was real anguish in her cry, and Jimmy leaned forward to pat her shoulder comfortingly.

"See here," she said, "there's no use your tearing yourself to pieces. You'd better tell us, the whole story. To begin with, how old was Sally?"

"Five years older than I—and oh, Jimmy, she was a darling. Not erratic like the rest of us. Just dear, and sweet, and kind. After I left home and went to live in New York, I looked forward to the summers just because I knew I'd have a month with Sally. Last year I was so anxious to see her that I came down a week ahead—and then she couldn't come. She'd been ill, and the doctor made her stay in the hospital. When she did arrive, we weren't expecting her, and I'd gone off on a silly boating trip with some friends. By the time I got back she was dead. . . ."

Lucia was dabbing at her eyes with her handkerchief, and Jimmy pounced before she could regain control.

"What makes you think she was murdered?"

"Murdered?" She looked up, shocked. "I didn't say—"

"No; but it's evident you've been thinking it."

There was silence while Lucia considered this. She had ceased crying now, but her hands were moving in her lap with a little wringing gesture that betrayed her emotion. In the end, she nodded reluctantly.

"Yes; I did think she was murdered. But only for a little while."

"What gave you the idea?"

"Something I found in the novel she was reading when she was taken ill. Nobody looked at it last year. It was just picked up and put back in the library. When I got here Monday, I happened to open it. I found something scrawled in the front."

"You mean a note?"

"Not exactly. It was just one word, so illegible I could hardly read it. It was—" Her voice failed, and she tried again. "It was 'murdered.'"

"'Murdered'?" Jimmy echoed. "You're sure of that?"

"Yes. She'd been intending to write some notes, and had her fountain pen. It was scrawled with that. She must have lost consciousness before she could finish."

"Where is the book?"

"Mark has it. You see, after I found the thing I was desperate. When Sally died there wasn't a soul on the island except the family, and the servants, of course. If anyone gave her that poison, it must have been one of us. I felt I couldn't talk to anyone here, so I sent you that telegram. Then I realized Sally was Mark's sister. I'd no business telling a thing like that to an outsider without first going to him."

"And Mark persuaded you it was suicide?"

She nodded. "When I showed him the note he agreed with me that Sally had written it, but he felt it didn't mean anything—because she'd been in a delirium."

"Mark took care of her?"

"Yes; he and Mrs. Prill. They both said she was out of her head almost from the first, and might have had any sort of delusion, even that some one had murdered her."

"Do you think it was delusion?" Jimmy asked suddenly, and she flinched.

"What can I think? It's impossible to believe it was an accident. The bottle was kept in the medicine chest upstairs. It was plainly marked, and Sally never took it unless she had a bad headache. Then, only when Mark fixed it for her. She didn't say anything about having a headache that afternoon, just that she was tired from her trip and was going to lie down on the swinging seat at the glassed-in end of the veranda. Everyone else was bathing, or asleep upstairs. Suddenly they heard Sally laughing in a horrible, crazy sort of way. They ran down to the veranda, and found her out of her head. The book was lying on the floor, and there was a glass, about a quarter full, of tea-punch on the table beside her."

"Was the drug in the punch?"

"Yes. Mark tested it and found a quantity of chloral. There was sherry in it, too. He says if some one doctored it the alcohol would have disguised the taste of the drug."

"Where did she get the punch?"

"We don't know. Malinda, the cook, made up a big pitcher of the drink at noon and left it in the ice box. That's in the butler's pantry, right next to the veranda where Sally was sitting. She may have got it for herself. Or some one else may have brought it to her."

"Anyone could have taken the drug from the medicine chest, I suppose?"

"Yes; anyone. I've asked questions since, and, as near as I can find out, every member of the family was in and out during the time Sally was on the veranda."

"Did you have the medicine bottle tested for finger-prints?"

"No; because there wasn't any bottle. I mean, we were never able to find it after her death."

"How did Mark explain that?"

"He thought she'd poured an overdose into the punch and then thrown the bottle into the river."

"Did he think she had a reason for killing herself?"

"No!" Lucia cried protestingly. "He couldn't think that—no one could."

"Perhaps her illness—" Jimmy began.

But she negatived that. "It was just a bad appendix. Serious, but nothing lasting. While she was in the hospital she wrote me the happiest letters. All full of plans for the summer. The day she arrived, they say, she was even gayer than usual. Laughing. Joking. Teasing everyone." Lucia was close to breaking down again, and Jimmy inter-posed a hasty question:

"You say there was no one on the island at the time, except the family?"

"And the servants. They've all been with us for years. It couldn't have been one of them, Jimmy. It couldn't have been anyone in the family, either. You don't know them yet, but when you do, you'll see."

"I'm sure I shall." His voice was as soothing as though he were speaking to a frightened child. "I don't doubt Mark is right. After all, he's the one best qualified to judge—a doctor and Sally's brother."

"Oh, Jimmy!" It was a gasp of pure relief. "If I could only believe that. . . ."

"Of course you can believe it." (For the life of me I couldn't tell whether or not he was sincere.) "You've let

yourself get hysterical over this business, Lucia. Made a
bogy out of nothing. No doubt Sally had some worry you
don't know about. She thought her illness was serious;
she'd had an unfortunate love affair; or was just depressed
from sickness, and took an overdose in a moment of mental aberration."

"Yes," Lucia spoke in an odd, thoughtful way, as though
her mind were busy with something else, "that's possible."

"Hell, girl, it's not only possible, it's probable. In any
case, worrying won't help. Will you promise to put it out
of your mind?"

"I'll only too glad to forget," she sighed.

"Good!" Jimmy rose to his feet and stretched luxuri-
ously. "How about a swim? Let's start that vacation you
promised."

"You mean," delightedly, "you're going to stay?"

"Of course I'm going to stay. Only, I warn you, I don't
intend to think a serious thought for the next two weeks."
He was grinning as he spoke, his cheerful, pleasant grin
that crinkled the corners of his gray eyes and disclosed
square, white teeth. To look at him, one would have said
he had not a thought in the world beyond the pursuit of
amusement; but, as Lucia turned to lead us down the hill,
I caught a second glimpse of his face—and I wondered.

CHAPTER 3
THE CONROY CLAN

The week that followed was full of long, lazy, sunlit days in which we slept and boated and bathed. Usually we swam when the tide had gone out. The island was situated at the mouth of a river, and enough salt came in at the flood to make it brackish. We were forced to keep careful watch, for the waters returned with a rush, and the wave—"bore," they called it—was frequently three or four feet high.

The house was over a hundred years old, Lucia told us, although her family had owned it only a quarter of that time. It was a comfortable, rambling place with a broad veranda, high-ceilinged rooms and spacious hallways. There had once been a front and back parlor, but the partition had been torn out between them, making a huge living room. Back of this was a library and, on the other side of the entrance hall, a finely proportioned dining room.

The service wing was at the north; it contained a butler's pantry, breakfast room, kitchen and screened porch. The second floor centered about a square upper hall which was so large that it was used by the family as a sitting room. Seven bedrooms were upon this floor, and three above, all of them roomy and comfortable, although those at the back were darkened by the overhanging hill and by a gallery which ran the full length of the house.

The servants' quarters were with the dynamo room in a separate building near the kitchen wing; and an office, entered from the garden, was on the south.

The Conroys were all busy with their own affairs and I saw them only a few hours a day, which was just as well. Taken in larger doses they might have been overpowering. To begin with, they were all remarkably good looking, with regular features and a subtle air of race and breeding. Dr. Mark Dietrich, the oldest of the cousins, was grave and self-contained; but the rest were volatile and given to prankish changes of mood. *En masse,* they gave the effect of lightness, yet I had a strange feeling that their gaiety was all upon the surface.

There was, at one end of Sycamore Island, a swamp, where Lucia took me one day to see the butterflies. It was not a loathsome place full of mud and quicksand, as I had expected, but a spot of uncanny beauty where the jade-like foliage hung above many-colored fungi, and where strange flowers sent forth an overwhelming perfume. At night, she told me, there were fireflies, and that weird light called *ignis fatuus.*

Looking back, I can see that the Conroys were not unlike that swamp, for their surface brilliance and charm, their easy mirth and impudent high spirits covered an abysmal morbidity.

They were a friendly, informal lot, with apparently no sense of time or convention. Night was as day to them, and until one or two in the morning they were running back and forth, up and down stairs, or into each other's rooms. Jimmy, for reasons of his own, laid himself out to be charming, and within a few days we were on first name acquaintance with all of them.

There were six of the cousins: Lucia Conroy and her twin-brother Lee, Dr. Mark Dietrich, and the brothers

Roberto and Antonio Patri. The sixth cousin, Douglas Conroy, appeared two days after our arrival. He was Lucia's fiancé, a broad-shouldered, red-haired young giant with the quick, easy movements of an athlete. As a matter of fact, he had been on the football team at college and had never given up his interest in the sport—one of those "old boys" that may be seen rooting themselves red of face and hoarse of voice at every game from September to January. An amiable Babbitt, given to solemn and bromidic pronouncements, in the best after-dinner-speaker style, he was something of a duckling among the Conroy swans.

How Lucia could ever have fallen in love with him was a mystery. I suppose it must have been the attraction of opposites. Instead of literature and the arts, his interests were quite simple—football and tennis, hunting and fishing. Almost every day he disappeared at dawn with a rod or a gun, and the Conroy table was continually loaded with fish and game.

Neither of the Patris cared for sport. Tony, the younger, was an artist, and a good one, but I rarely caught him at work. Any exertion was anathema to him, any physical exertion, that is for his wits were bright enough. He had an eye for absurdities, and his caustic and impudent tongue spared no one. Yet it seemed to me that Tony, for all his airy humor, was not happy. There was a strained look about his eyes, and his indolence had a certain quality of defiance, which was most exaggerated when Doug was present. He claimed the mere sight of Doug's boundless energy exhausted him—and after two or three days of his cousin's robustiousness I gained a certain sympathy for Tony's point of view.

While Tony loafed about with a paint box, which he rarely opened, 'Berto—Count 'Berto—amused himself by carrying on a flirtation with his cousin-by-marriage, Connie Dietrich, in full view of the family and her husband.

What Dr. Mark Dietrich thought of this affair we had
no way of knowing. From all appearances, he was too deep-
sunk in his work (the correlating of laboratory notes for a
book) to notice his wife's flirtation.

During the greater part of the day Lucia and Jimmy
worked on their comedy. Intermittently they appeared
from the library and played tennis, usually with Tony or
with Doug, who took a childish delight in beating them
all. Why, I could not imagine, since they were fearful dubs
at the game.

Lee never played tennis. In fact, he did almost nothing
except lie in a half-stupor on the veranda, or grouse about
the food and drink, especially the drink. I gathered that
there had been some sort of a family conference on his
case and the cousins had agreed to cut down their usual
consumption of alcohol. Tea-punch with a trace of sherry
was allowed, claret or port at dinner, and hot mulled wine
before we went to bed; but no whiskey, no gin, and no
brandy. The decree threw Lee into a frenzy of angry protest. Once he took the launch across to the mainland and
returned with a demijohn of "white mule." It was Tony and
'Berto who discovered him, took the jug away, and poured
its contents upon the ground. After the row which ensued,
Lee withdrew still farther into his sulky detachment.

The only other members of the family, outside the
sextette of cousins, were Aunt Hagar and Judith Conroy.
Judith was an aunt, as well as Hagar, but she was only five
years older than Mark. A tall woman, beautiful in a haggard sort of way, with exquisitely chiseled features and a
slender figure. Her black hair was graying at the temples,
and her dark eyes had that tragic look of futility which one
sees in the faces of women who have been betrayed by life.

Poor Judith. That was the adjective which was always
coupled with her name by the family, and before long I
found myself thinking of her in the same pitying fashion.

Poor Judith sang superbly in a rich contralto voice that was as smooth and soft as velvet. She had planned to go into opera in her youth and had studied in Rome; but her father, old Nathan Conroy, had forced her to return home, and since then she had been in virtual slavery, first to his whims, and later to Aunt Hagar, who made of her a nurse, companion and servant.

Of all the old ladies I have ever known, Aunt Hagar Conroy was the most actively unpleasant. Old ladies, particularly great-aunts, should be small and plump and gentle, with pink skins and silver hair. Aunt Hagar was and had none of these things. Although she was over seventy, her hair was dyed an unnatural purple-black, and her eyebrows were broad bands of jet that almost met over her heavy nose.

Once she had been a beauty, of the stately, full-busted type that was so admired in the '70's, and the cruelty and arrogance with which she had queened it in her youth still remained. From the remarks made on the day of our arrival I had taken it for granted she was an invalid, but nothing could have been farther from the truth. Her attacks were not of illness but of wild, uncontrolled rage. Twice during the first week of our visit she went into tantrums. Both were occasioned by some fancied slight, for Aunt Hagar demanded the center of the stage, and if she considered herself neglected would go to any length to gain attention.

"We're always hoping she'll burst a blood vessel," Tony told us with his impudent frankness. "Or that the old heart'll blow up. Mark says it isn't so good."

We were sitting about on the veranda in the lull that followed the storm of Aunt Hagar's latest temper. Mark had quieted the old lady with a sedative, and Judith, looking drawn and white, had joined us.

"I can't stand it much longer," she burst out in a rare attack of bitterness. "In a few years I'll be fifty. Mark and

Connie will have children and I'll be Great- Aunt Judith before I've had a chance to live!"

Lucia moved over and slipped an arm about the other's shoulders.

"You won't have to stand it much longer," she comforted. "Everything will be different after next month."

Jimmy had been sitting, deep-sunk in a wicker chair, his eyes apparently half closed, but I knew that he had been studying them all, as he had studied them ever since the day Lucia told us her story about Sally. Now, he started slightly and opened his eyes with an effect of lazy interest.

"What's going to happen next month?" he asked.

"Grandfather's money's to be divided. We're all going to get our share."

"Talking about that cursed money again?" Lee demanded from the swinging seat. "I'm sick of the sound of it."

"Not too sick to grab yours, I'll bet," Tony gibed, and Lee snapped back:

"Well, I've earned it. Spending ten summers in this stinking hell-hole with a bunch of incipient maniacs—"

"Hush!" Lucia cried sharply, and Tony drawled:

"Even in your cups, remember you're a Conroy and a gentleman."

Lee rose from the seat, muttering angrily, and shambled off into the house.

Lucia looked after him, troubled.

"I wish I knew what to do about him," she mourned. "I thought a month away from New York might help, but he's still getting liquor somewhere, and he's worse than ever."

"What he needs," Doug said sententiously, "is a stiff course under a good trainer. Ten miles walk every morning, tennis, boxing—"

"And setting up exercises," Tony finished. "Don't you ever get tired of playing that record?"

"Exercise is a darned good thing," Doug argued. "So is hunting and fishing. Quiets a man's nerves. Makes him sleep. You'd be a lot better yourself if you go to bed before midnight."

"And jumped out with the rosy-fingered dawn. No thankee. Not to shoot a lot of harmless dickey birds!"

"If you'd ever tried it—"

"He has tried," 'Berto interrupted from the steps, where he was sitting with Connie. "Before we went to Scotland last fall I sent him to a shooting gallery every day in hopes of keeping him from disgracing me, but at the end of a month he still couldn't hit a barn door."

"I'm not shooting barn doors." Tony was plainly annoyed, and an instant later he burst out: "If you're so afraid I'll disgrace you, why don't you give me what I've got coming and not keep me dangling?"

'Berto answered angrily in Italian, and for a time they wrangled; then Lucia hammered upon the floor with her heel.

"Stop that quarreling!" she commanded. "It's disgusting."

Tony apologized. "Sorry. We weren't rowing really. It just sounds worse in Italian."

But from the look he threw at 'Berto I doubted his statement. Also, I happen to know a little, a very little, Italian, enough to distinguish the words *"denaro,"* and again, *"denaro."* That is to say, "money."

Jimmy Lane had been drinking in all the talk, filing it away in his mind for future reference. I had expected him to follow up the question of the grandfather's will, but he let it drop, fearing, I discovered later, that any undue interest might put the family on its guard. He was anxious, at that time, to lull the suspicions of everyone, even of Lucia, who seemed to have accepted his pronouncement as to Sally's death with pathetic trustfulness.

Yet nothing which might have a bearing on the case escaped him. All that I have given here was taken from copious notes made at the time in a shabby loose-leaf notebook which had been with us on many strange adventures. It will be understood that, there were many other conversations and incidents recorded, but at Jimmy's suggestion I have culled only those which proved of importance later on.

The other happening of interest upon that day was a violent row between Mrs. Prill and Henry Harker.

Harker was a sort of combined caretaker and handy-man who watched the house and grounds the eleven months of the year when the Conroys were absent from the island. During the month of their residence, his duties seemed to be tending the flowers and trees on the hill, doing odd jobs about the place, and running the dynamo, which furnished electricity to the house and tomb.

He was a grotesque figure, dwarfed and misshapen from some illness or accident which had bowed one leg and distorted his shoulders, but in no way seemed to have affected his strength. His arms were long, with prehensile hands that hung away from his body when he walked. His head was bald, and his eyes a pale, watery blue, the whites slightly bloodshot. One eyelid drooped, and the corner of his thin, cruel mouth went up to meet it, which gave him a strange, sly look. With his bald head and the hanging wattles at the sides of his cheeks, he resembled nothing so much as a buzzard, a fact which was pointed out, unflatteringly, by Mrs. Prill during their verbal encounter.

This took place while the family was at dinner. The side window of the dining room looked out across the veranda to the service wing, where Mrs. Prill and Henry Harker were eating. Because the other servants were colored, the two had their meals in the breakfast room, beyond the butler's pantry. We had frequently heard their voices raised in argument, but never had it been so violent as now. We gathered that Mrs. Prill was accusing Harker of something which he furiously denied. In addition to calling him a buzzard, and a miser, she declared he would willingly strangle his own mother for a dollar.

Henry's replies were largely unintelligible, but once he called her a meddling old busybody, and once he offered an excellent price for her tongue, cut out and laid upon a platter.

"Oh, for heaven's sake, somebody go out and choke him," Lucia begged, and 'Berto departed through the swinging door.

An instant later his voice came sharply from the breakfast room. Harker must have offered some impudence, for the Count, all Latin at the moment, flew into a sudden rage.

"*Dios mio!* You dare speak to me like that, a dog of a servant?"

Harker's answer was furious but inaudible, and 'Berto went on: "A little more of that, my friend, and there will be no money for *you* next month."

"You can't stop my getting it!" Harker snapped, and 'Berto laughed unpleasantly.

"Is that so? Well, how about last November?"

There was a sudden silence, then the caretaker's voice, less assured: "I had a bad tooth. It had to be pulled."

"Did it take a month?"

There was a snarl from Harker and the sound of a scuffle. Mrs. Prill came hurrying into the dining room and said that Harker had attacked 'Berto with a knife from the table but that the Count had twisted his wrist and disarmed him.

From Jimmy Lane's notes I quote the prophecy with which she finished her recital:

"'He's got the best of him this time,' she said ominously. 'But he'd better look out. That Henry Harker's no better than a snake, and if Mr. 'Berto isn't right careful he'll wake up some morning and find himself with his throat cut!'"

CHAPTER 4
"PLENTY OF CORPSES"

Henry Harker was not discharged. After the row with 'Berto, I had taken it for granted that the Conroys would get rid of him. But no, the next morning he was still there, moving sulkily about the garden on the hill. Casually, Jimmy made inquiries and found that Harker's position depended not upon the family, but upon a trust company that was handling the grandfather's estate.

"He has to stay to take care of the tomb," Lucia explained. "It's in the will."

"Was he your grandfather's servant?"

"Not exactly a servant. He was a foreman on the plantation. When grandfather sold the place and came here, he brought Henry with him. He's been on the island ever since."

That was all we learned either about Harker or the will. Lucia seemed reluctant to talk about it, I thought, and her replies were evasive. Jimmy could not press her further without arousing her suspicion. I sometimes wonder whether, if he had insisted upon following that lead at once, it might have changed the course of events later on. Useless, now, to speculate. At the time, there seemed no need for haste, and every reason for moving slowly, cautiously. Jimmy Lane had not known the Conroys three days before he realized that their pride of family would outweigh their sense of justice, and that if he was ever to learn the truth about Sally's death he must discover it unaided.

The day he questioned Lucia was the twenty-fifth. At breakfast she announced that the town at the mouth of the river was holding a barbecue to celebrate the completion of a new levee. The colored servants had been promised a holiday and were leaving at ten, in time to avoid the bore.

"Of course they won't be back until dawn," she said, "and of course they'll all get riotously drunk, but Malinda has cooked plenty of provisions and Mrs. Prill will look after us while they're gone."

After breakfast we all strolled down to the boathouse and saw the servants off on the launch. The day was peculiarly sultry, with a low-lying haze like golden smoke. Beyond the river's mouth the sea was a blazing blue, hard and smooth as steel. Not a breath of air stirred. It was too hot to work, too hot even to think, and lunch was brought, by Mrs. Prill and Henry Harker, up the hill to the lawn under the great magnolia, where it seemed a trifle cooler than below.

Since the happenings of that afternoon, unimportant as they seemed at the time, had a definite bearing upon later events, I shall give an account of the few hours that followed.

For a time we lolled about lazily upon the grass. 'Berto, dressed in immaculate white, was sitting near Connie, who seemed to be sulky about something and did not make her usual flirtatious replies to his banter. Judith was watching them curiously, I thought, but Mark was either unconscious of any undercurrent, or deliberately ignored it.

Lucia was sitting against the trunk of the tree. She was wearing a gay pajama outfit of jade-green silk, and her hair was bright gold against the black bark. Tony had brought up a new sketch-pad, purchased in the town across the river, which he unwrapped and laid out across his knees. For a time he attempted to sketch Lucia, but the crayon slipped from his damp fingers and he abandoned all pretense of work.

Lee was lying along a broad limb of the tree, like a panther; in a patch of lush grass below him, Jimmy Lane gave a really superb imitation of a worm. Nearby, Aunt Hagar sat in a garden chair, absorbed in a murder mystery, while, beside her, Truffles lay sleeping.

Truffles deserves a whole paragraph to himself. He was an ancient and obese spaniel of rusty black and white. Belonging originally to Lucia's grandfather, old Nathan Conroy, he was officially the property of Aunt Hagar, but for some inexplicable canine reason his heart belonged to Henry Harker, and he was continually disappearing in search of his idol. Since Aunt Hagar insisted each time upon his being found and brought back, he kept the house in a constant turmoil. To-day the heat seemed to be affecting him and he was content to remain comatose at his mistress' feet.

Doug, too, was less vigorous than usual. He made one or two worthy attempts to persuade the rest of us to play tennis or go swimming, but his voice lacked its usual insistence, and after a time he dropped down upon the grass and unfolded the newspaper which had come with the morning supplies.

"Any news?" Jimmy asked idly, and 'Berto groaned. "Don't ask that," he begged, "or we will have to listen to the football scores."

"Too early for football," Doug informed him. "It's the World Series just now. Anyway, there's no news." Tossing the paper aside, he took out his handkerchief and mopped his brow. "Whew, but it's humid!"

"It isn't the humidity, it's the heat," Tony observed with great solemnity, and while Doug was ponderously explaining his mistake 'Berto started a three-sided literary argument with Lucia and Jimmy Lane. Gradually the rest of the family were drawn in, and, since most of them were bi-lingual—Mark, Tony and 'Berto spoke three languages —the discussion covered a good deal of territory. Hemingway and Colette, Joyce and Saint-Exupéry, Angioletti and Virginia Woolf. The names flew thick and fast, blurring a trifle in my ears as I began to grow drowsy. Only Aunt Hagar, absorbed in her mystery story, Connie, and Doug took no part in the discussion.

Doug was lying, now, with his head in Lucia's lap, playing with the hand which wore his engagement ring. As the beautiful stone flashed in the light, I dozed off and slept until a loud report startled me into wakefulness.

It was Aunt Hagar's book, which she had closed with a bang and hurled against the tree by my head. "Wretched drivel!" she was raging. "Swindling cheat!"

The family chuckled. Aunt Hagar's fondness for murder stories was one of their chief amusements, and this was by no means the first time she had burst out.

Jimmy reached over and picked up the book.

"Just what form of skin game is it?" he asked.

"Unknown murderer," she snapped. "Man shot on page twelve. Along about a hundred and forty you're told the murdered man once had a brother who quarreled with him and went to Borneo in 1885. On page three hundred and fourteen you discover *he* did the killing. I'd like to lynch him," she added savagely. "I mean the author."

"Don't blame you," Jimmy agreed. "I hate to be stung that way, myself."

"So do I." Doug sat up, suddenly interested, now that the talk had dropped to his mental level. "What I say is, it's just the same as though the author had stolen two dollars out of your pocket. Something ought to be done about it. I mean, writers oughtn't to be allowed to cheat like that."

"Why not take it up with the League of Nations?" Tony drawled. "International Code for Detective Fiction."

"With the death penalty for infringement," Jimmy chuckled; but Doug took it quite seriously.

"What would you put into the code?"

"Plenty of corpses," boomed Aunt Hagar ghoulishly. "I won't be dragged through three hundred pages for one measly murder. And plenty of chills."

Doug protested: "But not too many. There's got to be some comic relief. Like Lord Peter Wimsey. A bit of a laugh now and then—"

"—is relished by the best of men," Tony finished. "All that I ask is that the murderer be prominent in the story, or, at least, that he be mentioned often enough so that there's no chance of my forgetting him."

"And he must do *all* the murders," Jimmy declared firmly. "No running in double harness, no playing with accomplices, no finding one corpse hanging in the attic and the other in the back yard, then discovering that it was mere coincidence."

All of the family were interested now. The absurdity of the idea seemed to appeal to them, and only 'Berto failed to contribute suggestions. He had moved nearer to Connie and was tapping her hand with a scarlet hibiscus blossom, watching her averted face with amusement which held a hint of cruelty. Jimmy, too, had thrown himself heartily into the discussion, but I had the feeling he was not entirely ingenuous, that there was some purpose hidden behind his words.

Doug was saying earnestly, "Then the murderer mustn't be a servant, unless it's an old retainer who's practically one of the family."

"Like Prillie," Lee suggested. "Or Henry Harker. There's a swell killer for you!"

"Above all, the writer mustn't hold out any clews—"

"He mustn't forget to mention that gramma's false teeth were found on the back stairs—"

"And that the scalp of a red-headed woman was under the piano—"

They were all talking at once, and Jimmy summed up their scattered suggestions. "In short, the International Code should run something like this: 'Detective stories must have plenty of blood, chills and humor. All clews must be plainly stated; all murders must be committed by one character, and that character must have an established place in the story.' Does that cover everything?"

"Beautifully," Lucia agreed. "It makes me want to write one."

"Why don't you?" Jimmy asked. "Where could you find a better background than this? A low-lying, mysterious island with a ghost-ridden house—"

"Stop him!" Tony protested. "The hackles are rising at the back of my neck."

But Jimmy went on: "An ancient tomb surrounded by twisted cypress, a family all hating each other—"

"Oh, come," Doug protested.

"Strictly in the story," Jimmy explained. And to Lucia: "Whom would you murder first?"

"I don't know." She looked around. "Of course I'd have to pick someone a lot of people had it in for."

"Like me," 'Berto suggested with a sardonic flash of his white teeth. "That is the truth," he added. "There are one, two, three people here who would be glad if I were dead. That does not count those of you who would gain if I was not there next month when the money is divided."

There was a little rush of protest. "It's ridiculous!"

"Absurd!"

'Berto drew out a cigarette and spoke with the faint hint of mockery which spiced all of his talk.

"It is not absurd, and you know it. Only, you will not admit the truth. There is hardly anyone in the world whose death would not benefit someone."

I caught a sudden flash in Jimmy's eyes, but he lowered them again as he asked casually:

"Then why aren't there more murders?"

"Because men are cowards. They are afraid to kill."

"But look here," Doug protested, shocked, "you're all wrong. It isn't cowardice that keeps us from murdering, it's morals. 'Thou shalt not kill,' you know."

"And 'Honesty is the best policy,'" Tony groaned. "Spare us your pearls of thought! You're not addressing a Chamber of Commerce meeting."

Doug flushed and opened his mouth as though to reply angrily, then changed his mind and muttered something about pearls before swine.

'Berto laughed. "You see? For one moment Doug would have liked to murder you, Tony. Only he did not, because he was afraid. As for you and me, if we had lived in the days of cave men, you would have long since picked up a rock and hit me on the head so that you might have my money and my title."

"I don't doubt it," Tony agreed cheerfully, and Doug was about to burst forth again when Jimmy asked:

"Whom would *you* murder first, Judith?"

Before Judith could answer, Aunt Hagar broke in with a shrill, high cackle: "Me! She'd like to put me out of the way because I'm old, and sick, and helpless."

The idea of the old harridan in the role of a martyr was too much for the family. Several of them laughed aloud.

Aunt Hagar's face flushed darkly.

"You hate me," she said, "all of you! And I hate you!" She was about to fly into one of her rages when Jimmy interposed diplomatically.

"Whom would *you* pick, Miss Conroy?"

"Don't call me 'Miss Conroy,'" she snapped, "Call me 'Aunt Hagar.' You do it behind my back. Might as well do it to my face." And added with such ferocity that we all jumped: "I'd pick Roberto. He may be a Conroy on his mother's side, but I don't like his Italian manners and morals. Next, I'd kill Connie."

"Why Aunt Hagar!" Connie widened her blue eyes and tried to look unutterably hurt.

"Yes, I would, too; before you disgrace us; and next—"

But she was not allowed to go on. Several of the Conroys seemed to feel that too many family skeletons were being dragged out of the closet, and tried to change the subject.

Jimmy suggested guilelessly: "You don't seem to be getting anywhere on your story, Lucia. Too many conflicting opinions." And to the others: "Why don't each of you write the story as you think it should be written?"

"That's an idea," Tony exclaimed, and 'Berto agreed.

Even Lee brightened. "Why not start a pot for prize money? A fiver apiece?"

Doug said: "Make it ten and I'll join."

"We're not bloated bondholders like you," Lee complained, but Doug protested he hadn't a chance of winning.

"I'm not clever like you chaps. Just a hard-headed business man."

In the end, under the Machiavellian management of Jimmy Lane, ten dollars was agreed upon, and a limit of five thousand words put on the stories. The contestants were to abide by the rules which had been formulated earlier in the day. At 'Berto's suggestion it was decided that

all the stories should be handed in anonymously, and then
read aloud. A secondary prize was to be given for the one
who came nearest to guessing the authorship of each.

Jimmy firmly declined to enter the contest upon the
grounds that he was needed to hold the stakes and read the
stories. I gathered that he preferred to have me out of it,
too, so I pleaded laziness.

"Let's say that the stories must be in by eight o'clock
tomorrow night," Lucia suggested. "That will give us over
twenty-four hours. Anyone ought to be able to dash off
a yarn in that time." She stopped, astonished. "Will you
hear me talking about dashing? In weather like this!"

"But it's not 'like this' any more," Tony pointed out.
"It's really cool."

And so it was. While we had been talking, the sun had
dropped toward the horizon until now, it stood a ball of
flame above the dark rim of the coastline. A breeze, faint
but plainly perceptible, was moving the branches of the
trees and scudding a low bank of clouds along the eastern
horizon.

The Conroys looked at each other with raised eyebrows.

"You know what *that* means," Judith said, and Lucia
groaned.

"Only too well. Of course it *would* come now, with the
servants all on the other side."

"Perhaps it won't start to-night," Connie said hopefully.

"Didn't you ever notice an equinox?" Tony asked. "Why,
you giddy little optimist, in two hours you won't be able
to hear your own thoughts—if any," he added, *sotto voce*.

"By midnight the river will be a mill race," Lucia continued. "We'll be lucky if we see the servants within the
next three days."

"You mean," the truth of the situation was bearing in
upon Jimmy Lane for the first time, "that we're going to
be cut off completely from the mainland?"

"Completely. We're marooned. No fresh milk, no mail, no bills. . . ."

"No morning paper," Tony added. "Doug'll love that. He'll miss the World Series."

"And nine chances out of ten, no electricity. In a storm the generator usually goes on a strike."

"'Usually?' Do you mean this happens often?"

"About two years out of three. It's Ol' Man Equinox." Tony broke off as a gust of wind, stronger than the last, struck the branches overhead and set his sketch-book and the paper in which it had been wrapped aflutter.

Lucia scrambled to her feet, followed by Judith and the others. Tony gathered up his papers, and Doug prevented the news-sheets from blowing away. Singly, and in groups of two or three, we wandered toward the hill path, our odd assortment of costumes already insufficient to protect us from the growing chill.

By the time we reached the house, the breeze had stiffened, and the sun had dropped until it was a gout of blood behind the misty horizon.

We were not to see its face again until we had looked upon real blood.

CHAPTER 5
THE GAME OF BLIND MAN'S BUFF

All evening the wind grew stronger until the old house was shaken by the assault of ten thousand dark furies that shrieked and raged and lashed themselves into frenzy among the branches of the trees. The cypresses on the hill above were bent almost double and streamed out over the cliff like tattered banners, while the gum trees rocked and moaned and clashed their metallic leaves in constant warfare. Although there was no rain as yet, the sky was filled with ominous clouds that rolled in from the east, now covering, now disclosing the moon. In the fitful light we could see the river, churned by the contending wind and tide into a maelstrom of black plunging water and white foam.

Hope of the servants' return having been abandoned, we ate a bountiful meal prepared by Mrs. Prill and served, sulkily, by Henry Harker. After coffee we adjourned to the living room, where Doug built a roaring fire in the grate.

Tony, lying full length on the divan, watched him derisively. "What would we do without our Douglas?" he queried. "Just a little boy scout . . . always doing his good deed."

"Well, what I say is," Doug accepted the compliment with becoming modesty, "when you're doing anything, you might as well do it right."

"And 'Virtue is its own reward,'" Tony gibed, then burst into a ribald improvisation to the tune of *Onward, Christian Soldiers,* which he delivered in a sweet, mocking tenor. In the middle of it Judith sat down at the piano and began an accompaniment, her lovely voice blending with his. Mark brought his 'cello from a corner, and Lucia drifted over to her harp. Without apparent effort, *Onward, Christian Soldiers* resolved into *Swing Low, Sweet Chariot,* which in turn gave place to Homer Grunn's *Indian Nocturne* and part of the César Franck *Symphony in D Minor.*

I believe I have, until now, said nothing about the Conroys' talent for music. They were really an amazing lot, able to turn their hands to anything. "Jack of all trades, but unable to get the jack out of any of them," was Tony's version. In nothing was their casual facility more striking than in music. Judith both sang and played; Tony had a fine voice; Mark could perform upon either the violin or the 'cello, while 'Berto played the piano as well as Judith, or better. He came in presently and slipped down on the bench beside her, making a duet of the accompaniment. While the wind beat a wild tattoo in the trees and screamed on the hill above, they finished the, César Franck and swung into opera. Some of what they played was new to me; some I recognized: a bit of the fire music and *Ride of the Valkyries,* an aria from *L'Amore dei Tre Re,* another from *Manon,* and then, quite irrelevantly, Tschaikowsky's *Nut Cracker Suite* and a surging, turbulent thing which Lee told me was Palmgren's *Sea.* All of it they played with a wild swing, a diablerie that was weirdly beautiful and not a little mad.

It was Jimmy Lane who asked, more to test them, I think, than because he believed it possible, whether they could play any of Stravinsky's *Sacre du Printemps.* Lucia threw up her hands and dropped out; but Judith and

'Berto swung into the diabolic rhythm of the *Dance of the Adolescents,* and Mark followed with his 'cello.

In the midst of it, Doug burst out: "Oh, for Pete's sake, give us a rest! Can't you play something that isn't a dog fight?"

'Berto brought the dance to a brilliant close and grinned at Mark over the top of the piano. "Let us play something for Cousin Doug," he suggested, *"The Rosary . . .* or, wait, I have it!" He began *Hearts and Flowers,* improvising wickedly with saccharine runs and trills that were subtly insulting. I half expected Doug to heave a chunk of firewood, but no, he sank back upon his heels on the hearth rug and smiled contentedly.

"That's more like it," he said. "It's got some tune to it."

"Doug doesn't know anything about music, but he knows what he likes," Tony confided to us solemnly.

"I don't like only lowbrow stuff," Doug protested, "I often turn on the radio and listen to really good music. Such as—"

"Selections from *Carmen,*" Tony suggested.

"Anitra's Dance, and Mendelssohn's *Spring Song,*" someone added.

"Yes; good music," Doug agreed, and listened with unsuspicious gratification to 'Berto, who was giving an inspired burlesque of Offenbach's *Barcarole.*

Lucia had taken no part in the baiting of Doug, and I thought she looked a trifle annoyed. Now, she slipped her arm about his shoulders in one of her rare moments of affection.

"Come on, old darling," she said, "we've got to get busy on our stories. It won't hurt the rest of you to do the same," she added tartly, and there was a general murmur of agreement.

It was at that moment Aunt Hagar first missed Truffles. He had followed her in from the dining room, we all remembered, and had been lying asleep upon the pillow by her side. Now he was gone, not only from the room but from the house. After a fruitless search of all three floors, Aunt Hagar began to show signs of hysteria, and Doug said he would look about the grounds. Mark and I offered to accompany him. Tony stretched, and drawled that since it seemed to be "Kind to Dumb Animals Week" he would go along.

All of us were certain that the dog was with Henry Harker; but when we reached his room, which was the office at the south end of the house, we found no sign of Truffles. The wind was still shrieking and howling. The thought of facing the blast made us cringe; but, as Tony pointed out, the storm was mild compared to what we might expect from Aunt Hagar. We continued our search. The island was small, less than six acres in area, and most of it had been cleared, so that it seemed impossible for even a dog to escape observation.

But after an hour we were obliged to admit defeat. The spaniel was not in the boathouse, the servants' quarters, nor the tomb. We were cold. We were tired. We were cross. And to top our annoyance, we found, when we returned, Truffles whining at the front door.

As we swooped down upon him and carried him into the house, the rain began. First a few drops, flung spitefully against the windowpanes, then more and more until there was a steady downpour that beat upon the roof with the persistence of African drums. I have heard of medicine men in the jungle who send their victims mad by the sustained rhythm of voodoo drums, and after the fearful time that followed I can easily believe it. Never, during the entire three days of horror, was that steady and ominous roar to cease for long. It might die away, momentarily, but only to return, increasing slowly . . . slowly . . .

until strained nerves gave way, until anything, even murder, seemed justifiable.

All the next day, while the storm raged over the sea, the river and the island, the Conroys wrestled with their stories. The conversation at breakfast and lunch dealt entirely with medical matters. As the only doctor in the crowd, Mark Dietrich was besieged with questions ranging from the length of time it would take *rigor mortis* to set in to the gruesome details of death by prussic acid. In self-defense, he finally brought two books on toxicology from his room and left them in the library.

By eight o'clock that night all the stories were finished and deposited in a small red leather chest in the hall. When Jimmy and I came down the broad staircase we found the others preparing for a game of blind man's buff. I had never seen the Conroy clan in such high spirits. The shadowy room, with the firelight playing over the polished furniture, the wind and rain outside, seemed to have reminded them of other days when the equinox had kept them, as children, indoors, and they had romped through the spacious old house. Now, they were laughing and reminiscing as they pushed back the furniture and prepared for their infantile sport.

What followed was gone over in conference so often, later on, that I am able to give an accurate account. All the Conroys were present; and all of them took part in the game of blind-man's-buff, with the exception of Aunt Hagar, who was seated in a chair by the fire with Truffles wheezing at her feet.

Henry Harker and Mrs. Prill had gone to their rooms somewhat earlier in the evening.

Tony was selected as "it." In accordance with the Conroy custom, instead of a blindfold being put over his eyes, all the lights were turned off, which left only a fitful flicker from the living-room fire and a reflected glow on the wall of the stair-well from the upper hall.

"Tony'll count a hundred, by fives," Lucia explained. "Then if he catches anyone and guesses who it is that fellow must post a forfeit."

"The things you'll have to do to redeem those forfeits will be nobody's business," Tony warned. "All ready?"

"Ready," they called cheerfully; and Tony turned to hide his face against the mantel, small-boy fashion.

"Five . . . ten . . . fifteen . . . twenty. . ."

For a good half hour the game ran its noisy course through the dark rooms of the lower floor. At the end of that time there was an imposing row of forfeits on the table in the living room, and everyone was breathless from running and from laughing.

It was Mark who ended the game. Dropping down on the divan he gasped: "The rest of you can go on if you like, I'm through."

Lucia turned on the lights.

"Shall we read the stories first or redeem the forfeits?" she asked, and Aunt Hagar said firmly:

"Let the forfeits wait; I want to hear the stories."

Jimmy brought the red chest from the hall and opened it on the table.

"There are nine manuscripts," he said. "I counted them before the game. That means ninety dollars in prize money for the lucky fellow who wins."

"Don't say 'fellow'!" snapped Aunt Hagar. "It may be a woman."

"It may at that," Jimmy agreed, and began to read the first story.

It was called *Death in the Attic*. A short affair with a clever twist at the end. Since neither this nor the eight which followed were of importance, I shall not go into detail, except to say that they varied greatly, ranging from extreme cleverness to the hopelessly banal. Several writers had chosen the island background, but none had used the Conroy family, finding the idea, they confessed later, too gruesome when put into effect. Many of the manuscripts were brief. One was an improper but amusing verse, one was a short short-story, and one a pointless limerick. With the time it took to read and guess the author of each contribution, the hours passed; it was after one when Jimmy Lane picked up the last manuscript.

"This ends it," he said a trifle wearily.

Lucia looked puzzled. "Wait a minute. I thought you said there were nine? This makes ten."

"Ten?" Jimmy recounted the manuscripts. "You're right. It's the tenth. I could have sworn there were only nine."

"There are only nine of us," Lucia pointed out. "Aunt Hagar, Lee, Mark, Judith, Doug, Tony, Connie, 'Berto, and myself. By the way," she glanced about, "where is 'Berto?"

"Upstairs probably," Tony said impatiently. "He'll be back. Let's get on with the reading."

Tony had been nervous and tense all evening. The remembrance of his quarrel with his brother came into my mind, and I was wondering whether, perhaps, the prize money meant more to him than to the others when Jimmy picked up the last manuscript.

"'*Murder in the Conroy Clan,*'" he read.

Lucia exclaimed, and Connie giggled.

"Some one *did* have nerve enough to do it!"

"Hush!" trumpeted Aunt Hagar.

"'*The first of the Conroy murders,*'" Jimmy continued, "'*occurred Friday evening, September twenty-sixth, upon Sycamore Island.*'"

Again some one gasped, and was immediately suppressed by Aunt Hagar, who pounded upon the floor with her foot for silence.

"*In any other family, the fact that a murder was committed at such a time and in such a spot might have been remarkable; but the Conroys were a strange brood, with strange blood flowing through their veins. Under their assumption of cousinly affection was a hidden undercurrent of passion and unnatural hatred.*'"

"Wait!" Doug sat up in sudden protest. "I don't think we ought to go on with this."

"Why not?" Aunt Hagar inquired tartly.

"Because it's in rotten taste, that's why! It's indecent to read a thing like that before strangers."

"Jimmy and Phil aren't strangers," Lucia argued. "Anyway, it's just a story."

"Yes." Tony grinned at Doug over Lucia's head. "Better look out or you'll give them the idea it's the truth."

"All right . . . have it your own way. But just the same, I don't like it." Doug dropped, grumbling, into his corner of the divan.

"'—*undercurrent of passion and unnatural hatred. . . .*'" Jimmy went on, while the Conroys listened with breathless intentness.

The story was clever, with a cruel and searching frankness in its description of the Conroy family. In careful detail it related the conversation which had taken place on the hill the day before, and told of the coming of the storm. Nothing remarkable in this, you will see. Audacious, perhaps; and, as Doug said, not in the best of taste, but nothing that any one of the family might not have written. Followed an account of the evening we had just passed. Beginning with dinner, it described the retirement to the various rooms until the manuscripts, were finished, and the family coming down stairs and dropping their several contributions in the red leather chest. All of it, might easily have been foreseen; nevertheless, it gave the whole thing a feeling of uncanny authenticity.

Out of the darkness Judith spoke. "How much more is there?"

"Only two pages," Jimmy answered, and she sighed with relief.

"Thank goodness. It's getting on my nerves."

"I'll hurry the rest," he promised.

"'*The stories were all in the red box, and the family were about to gather around the fire when someone suggested a game of blind man's buff.*'"

"What ?" There was a gasp, and everyone sat forward.

"You're not reading it," Lucia accused. "You're making it up."

"No." Jimmy looked as astonished as any of us. "I give you my word, it's written here."

"But that story was handed in before we played the game."

"Oh, go on! Go on!" Aunt Hagar's voice was shrill with excitement. "Don't keep us in suspense. What's next?"

"'*Through the great, echoing house, from darkened room to darkened room, the Conroys romped joyously. To have heard them laughing you would have said that all was friendliness, all amity. And yet, somewhere in the shadows, Death was lurking.*'"

A quick breath ran around the circle, and Connie Dietrich gave a little cry, but Jimmy did not stop.

"'*When the game ended and the players returned to the living room, one member of the family was missing. So intent were they upon the reading of the stories that his absence passed unnoted. Only one of the group, the murderer, knew that Count Roberto Patri lay on the floor of the breakfast room, his shirt covered with blood, a gaping wound in his throat, and a gory knife at his feet.*'"

Again Connie cried out. (Someone said quickly: "Don't be silly, it's only a joke.") "I don't like it," she half sobbed.

Doug said: "If you ask me, I think the whole thing's rotten."

"Nobody asked you!" This from Aunt Hagar. And to Jimmy: "What comes next?"

"Nothing. That's the end."

"Where's 'Berto?" Connie would not be denied. "You've got to find him. I'm frightened." Her teeth were chattering, and I think all of us were in sympathy with her agitation, for Mark said quickly:

"I'll go look."

"I'll go with you," Jimmy volunteered.

"Not me," said Tony. "You'll find it's just a hoax."

Lee, too, made no move, but Doug rose to his feet and I followed.

The four of us passed through the darkened dining room to the butler's pantry, turning on lights as we went. The door between the pantry and the breakfast room was locked. A startled look passed between Mark and Doug. Without speaking, we hurried into the kitchen. Throwing open the door of the breakfast-room, we entered and turned on the light.

Stretched on the gay carpet of braided rags was 'Berto Patri. His coat had fallen back, disclosing a shirt that was dabbled with scarlet stain; his wrists and ankles were bound with rope, and at his feet lay a long, thin knife, its once shiny blade clotted with dark and thickened blood.

Chapter 6
We Enter the Tomb

How long it was before our senses accepted the evidence of our eyes, I cannot say. Even after Jimmy Lane had gone forward and knelt down beside the body, with Mark, I still had the feeling it was, that it must be, some macabre joke, that 'Berto would presently sit up and laugh at our horrified faces. Doug seemed to share my feeling.

"He can't be dead," he mumbled. "He can't! He can't!"

Mark looked up from his examination. "He *is* dead. His throat has been cut from ear to ear."

Suddenly Doug was overtaken by nausea, and staggered to a chair.

"Take some water," Jimmy directed. "Or wait. Here's some brandy." He rose and picked up a bottle that stood on the table, carefully using his handkerchief. Just as he was about to pour the liquor into a glass, something seemed to arrest his attention. For a moment he stared, then put down the glass and threw a napkin over it.

"Sorry," he said. "You'll have to take water, after all."

Mark was finishing his examination. "There's no doubt of its being murder." (For the life of me I could not tell whether it was a callous lack of emotion or iron self-control that kept his voice steady.) "The throat has been cut from right to left, and his hands are tied."

"But it's impossible—" Doug was beginning, when Lucia called from the butler's pantry:

"Mark! Doug! Why is this door locked?

"Stop her," Jimmy said quickly. "She mustn't come in here. You take charge of her, Doug. And of the other women."

"All right." If Doug drew himself somewhat groggily to his feet and went out through the kitchen. We heard his voice in the pantry, and Lucia's muffled cry, then the swish of the swinging door as they went toward the front of the house.

Unconsciously, Jimmy Lane assumed command. "We'll have to lock the windows and doors. Nothing must be touched until the police arrive."

Mark protested: "But that may be several days. We can't leave the body lying here all that time."

Jimmy considered for a moment, then agreed. "I suppose you're right. Is there room for it in the tomb?"

"Plenty of room."

"Good. We'll move it there. But first I want some photographs. There was flashlight powder left over from the pictures we took the other night. Do you mind getting it, and the camera?"

The instant Mark was gone, Jimmy began moving about, studying the room. The windows were closed, but not locked, the blinds drawn down even with the sills. The door from the butler's pantry was locked on the inside; a second door, at the farther end of the room, opened into a windowless supply closet, which he investigated without making any discovery.

The table had been cleared after the evening meal, and was spread with a checked red and white cloth. It contained nothing except a pitcher of water, a bottle of brandy, and the glass which Jimmy had covered with a napkin. Two or three chairs that were used for meals were standing back against the wall, and an oak settle near the kitchen door held a pillow and a folded blanket. The only object of real interest in the room was a saucer, which stood upon a shelf at one side. This contained a piece of cheesecloth, stained with scarlet. Jimmy studied the saucer and cloth attentively, then again bent over the body.

After a moment he called in a low tone: "Come here, Phil, and see what you make of this."

Reluctantly I joined him and looked down. As I have said earlier, 'Berto's shirt was dabbled with blood, which had soaked down through his collar and tie; the rug beneath him was also stained, and the last spurt of the jugular vein had spattered the floor. In the hours since 'Berto's death, this blood had coagulated and darkened until it was deep carmine, edged with brown; yet on the lower part of the shirt it was still bright crimson.

Jimmy was frowning as he touched the cloth with his finger. "That's not blood," he affirmed. "It's some other liquid."

"What can it be?"

"God knows." He was inspecting. 'Berto's wrists and ankles, which were tied with a double twist of rope. "That's clothesline, plain enough, Probably any amount of it in the kitchen. And that knife looks like a carver." He broke off as Mark returned with Lee, who was carrying the camera and tripod.

I think I have never seen such horror as was stamped upon Lee's face, sick horror combined with livid fear. For a moment he stood in the doorway, his eyes fixed not upon the body but on something across the room. Before I could discover what it was, Mark came forward and stood between us.

"I brought Lee," he said, "to operate the flashlight."

"Very well. I'll set up the camera." Lee handed over the tripod, then crossed the room. Something in his movement was furtive and I watched him curiously. What was

drawing him over to the table? Suddenly a light dawned. It
was the bottle of brandy, of course. He had his hand upon
it when Jimmy's voice sounded sharply:

"Put that down!"

Lee's face went white. "I just wanted a little drink."

"You don't need another."

"What do you mean?"

"You know what I mean," Jimmy told him. And to me:
"Take that bottle and the glass to our room. No; don't
touch them with your hands. Use a towel."

"If you think you'll find my finger-prints on them—"
Lee began. "You know damned well you will. I just picked
up the bottle."

"But not the glass. Take the stuff away, Phil."

Five minutes later I came down the front stairs and
into the living-room, where the remaining Conroys were
gathered. The women, as a whole, were taking it bravely,
I thought. Aunt Hagar was still seated by the fire, her
witch-like profile silhouetted against the blaze. If she had
felt any emotion at 'Berto's passing, she had conquered it
with inhuman fortitude; there was no sorrow in her face,
only wild excitement.

Lucia, crying quietly, was on the divan. Tony was beside her. Although his face looked white and strained he
gave me the impression, fleeting but none the less positive, of a man who is not so much sorrowing for the loss
of a brother, as harassed by some overwhelming anxiety.

Judith was on the other side of the hearth, half lost in
the shadows. She seemed to be keeping herself under control with difficulty. The shaking of her hands, the twitching of her lips betrayed her suffering.

Connie, alone of them all, was giving her emotions full
sway. She was under the care of Mrs. Prill in the library,
and from time to time her voice was lifted in an outburst

of wailing sobs which the others seemed determined to ignore.

Doug had gone for Henry Harker. When they appeared, the caretaker was protesting against the plan of putting 'Berto's body in the tomb. He insisted that it should either be left where it was or locked in the cellar. His arguments became so vehement that, in the end, Doug lost patience and ordered him to hand over the keys with a sharpness that forced a reluctant obedience.

It was a full hour before Jimmy Lane was finished with his photography, and Mark his examination of the body, which was then carried up to the tomb through the pouring rain.

The tomb was brightly lighted. Indeed, it was always lighted at night, a provision having been made in the will of Nathan Conroy that the dynamo should be kept running winter and summer. With its wet white marble reflecting the glow of half a dozen hidden globes, the place shone through the darkness of the surrounding trees like a vast phosphorescent bubble.

It was round in shape, built on the plan of a small Roman temple, with curving steps and a covered portico. To left and right of the doors were bronze panels, done in bas-relief, the design half hidden by a row of potted cypress trees. The doors themselves were of heavy carved wood, banded and morticed with metal. As they swung open I saw that the whole structure was merely an entrance hall, with steps at the rear which descended to a crypt below.

Henry Harker led the way down the steps, a scarecrow figure in his flapping oilskins. We laid our burden upon an improvised bier, and, while Jimmy Lane and Mark attended to the last details, I looked curiously about the underground room. It was fifteen feet square at least. The floor was of cement, and the walls of plaster, except at

the far end, where blocks of marble covered the entrance
to the vault. Above low doors of wrought metal were the
incised words:

NATHAN CONROY
1845-1920
NON VIXIT QUIS POST MORTEM NON VIVIT

Upon our return to the house, we found all the family
assembled in the living room drinking coffee which had
been brewed by Mrs. Prill.

Jimmy waited until she had retired, to serve Harker in
the kitchen, then put down his cup.

"No use procrastinating," he said. "We'd better go into
this matter while it's fresh in our minds. In the first place,
you're sure there is no way of communicating with the
mainland?"

"Absolutely sure," said Mark. "We've only the rowboat
and the canoe. It would be suicide to try to cross either
of them."

"At least that will prevent the murderer from escaping,"
Jimmy remarked. "But it also makes it impossible to report this to the authorities."

A quick glance passed among the Conroys.

"Must you report it as murder?" Judith asked. "I mean,
are you certain it wasn't suicide?"

"More than certain," Jimmy said grimly.

"But couldn't it have been accidental?" she persisted.
"Surely he might have fallen on that knife."

Lee seized upon her words feverishly. "Yes; that must
have been it. 'Berto came into the room in the dark and
stumbled on the rug. The knife was on the table and he
fell across the blade."

Jimmy started to answer sharply, then controlled himself
and turned to Mark. "You examined the wound, Doctor.

Would you say there was any possibility of its having been caused accidentally?"

"Not the slightest," Mark said positively. And to the others: "We couldn't persuade a coroner's jury to accept that story, even if we fooled ourselves." There was a faint sigh of disappointment, and he went on, in his unemotional voice: "One thing the murderer can do. He can spare the family the disgrace of a trial in court."

"What do you mean?" Judith asked in a low voice.

"He means suicide," Aunt Hagar cackled.

Mark nodded somberly. "That's exactly what I mean. If the one who did this thing will come to me quietly, I will give him something that will put him to sleep without pain."

Without pain. Would that have described Sally's death, I wondered. And was the drug Mark promised, to be drawn from the same bottle? I glanced at Jimmy, but he was watching the Doctor.

Mark stood with his back to the fire, facing the circle. His eyes were moving about, resting upon each in turn—Judith, Aunt Hagar, Doug—until they reached Lee, who sprang up wildly.

"Don't look at me like that!"

"Lee!" Lucia cried warningly, but he was beyond control.

"He's trying to make you think I did it. The filthy swine! He's saying that about suicide so when he poisons my coffee you'll think I killed myself. That's what he's planning. You can see it in his face. Look!"

He did not need to enjoin us to look. Simultaneously we turned and stared at the Doctor, who was standing unmoved, an expression of slightly scornful amusement upon his face.

"So that's my idea, is it? What possible reason could I have?"

"Because you killed 'Berto yourself. You killed him because he was making love to Connie."

"That's a lie!" Connie snapped to her feet. "'Berto never made love to me."

"Never?" Lee laughed unpleasantly.

"No . . . never . . . *never!*" Connie was facing Lee upon the hearth rug. She had lost her look of baby-softness, lines had sprung to life at the corners of her mouth and eyes; her voice was no longer caressing but had a cruel, rasping quality. There was something horrible about the sudden transformation of the pink and white girl, with her lisp and slightly saccharine sweetness, into this ugly termagant. It showed in a blinding and unnerving flash what havoc is wrought by fear. "I tell you I didn't care anything about 'Berto," she shrilled. "And he didn't care anything about me."

"Then why," Lee demanded, "were the two of you making love on the veranda at two o'clock Wednesday morning?"

"It wasn't two o'clock! It was only a little after one, and we weren't making love, we were quarreling."

"Quarreling?" With her hooked nose, her unwinking, predatory eyes, Aunt Hagar reminded me of a hawk dropping upon its prey. "What were you quarreling about?"

Connie turned sullen. "Never mind. It's nobody's business. Only, Mark hadn't any reason for killing him."

"But perhaps *you* had!" Lee suggested, and she flew into a rage.

"It was you who killed him! 'Berto told me you'd wanted to stick a knife into him ever since he took your liquor away."

"Stop!" Lucia jumped up and brought her hands together with a sharp slap that was as startling as an explosion. The two swung about, forgetting their anger in their astonishment. "Haven't you any decency? Quarreling at a time like this!"

Lee looked a trifle shamefaced and sat down. Connie too subsided; and in the ensuing quiet Jimmy Lane spoke.

"Look here, we won't get anywhere at this rate. It'll just lead to confusion and hard feeling. Why don't you let Phil and me take charge? This is a ticklish business at best, but it'll be easier for us because we won't be swayed by sentiment."

There was a long, pregnant silence with only the crackle of the fire and the dreary beating of the rain. It seemed to me that the circle of faces had hardened and blanked into masks, tragic masks, that concealed fearful thoughts. In a flash, the suspicion that had haunted me all evening became a certainty. The Conroys did not want to know who had committed the murder. Left alone, I felt sure, they would have made some attempt to hide the truth from the world, have invented an accident, or sunk 'Berto's body and reported him drowned. Our presence on the island forced them to make at least a decent gesture toward uncovering the murderer, but they resented the necessity.

Jimmy answered their unspoken thoughts. "There's no use hoping you can hush this thing up. Not a chance in the world. But if you'd rather wait for the police—"

"No," Lucia spoke with a little gasp, "not the police! Anything but that. We'd rather you took charge."

The others murmured their assent, and Jimmy asked soberly, "You'll do as we say? I mean, of course, within reason?"

"We'll do as you say." The promise was given around the circle; but there were, I felt, mental reservations. They would do as we said, so long as obedience did not jeopardize the safety of brother, of husband, of wife.

It was then, for the first time, that I fully realized the peculiar horror of their position. In most murders there is a chance that the crime has been committed by some outsider, but here there was no such possibility. Even the faint hope that there might have been some stranger on the island was eliminated by the search we had made for Truffles the preceding night. Every foot of the island had been combed; and the idea of anyone crossing the raging river since that time was too absurd to be considered. The Conroys knew, we all knew, that the murderer of 'Berto Patri must be one of those who lived under the lichen-spotted roof of the old house.

Something of this was evidently passing in Jimmy's mind when he spoke again. "After all, it isn't absolutely certain that he was killed by one of the family."

"You mean," Doug asked, "Henry?"

"Henry, or Mrs. Prill."

"But that's absurd! Impossible!" Lucia and Judith cried out simultaneously.

"You find it easier to believe that it's one of the family?" Jimmy asked, and, as they dropped back, aghast at their own implication: "I'm not saying either of them killed 'Berto. I'm merely pointing out that all of us on the island, even Phil and myself, would be considered suspects by the police until we had proved our innocence. We had better follow the same plan."

He drew a blue copy-pencil from his pocket; and, knowing his methods, I rose and looked for some scratch paper. There was a pad on the table with a list some one had made earlier when trying to guess the authorship of the stories. In a clear, firm hand was the roster of the Conroy clan.

1. *Aunt Hagar.*
2. *Judith.*
3. *Mark.*
4. *Connie.*
5. *'Berto.*
6. *Tony.*

7. *Lucia.*
8. *Lee.*
9. *Doug.*

To this Jimmy added four names.

10. *Henry Harker.*
11. *Mrs. Prill.*
12. *Philip Carter.*
13. *James Lane.*

"Thirteen," he said softly. A little chill went over the group as he drew his pencil through 'Berto's name. "And now there are twelve." For a space he studied the page, then: "As a general rule, it's best to look first for the motive, next for the opportunity. In this case I think we'll reverse the procedure and see who could have had the best chance of committing the murder. To make things easier, we'd better have a rough sketch of the ground floor."

"Now," he said as he finished the drawing, "as near as I can make out, 'Berto was murdered some time during that game of blind man's buff. We know that he did not appear after the lights were turned on, and it's a pretty safe bet he would have joined us if he had been alive. What we've got to discover is who could have gone into that room during the game."

"That takes in all of us, I'm afraid," Mark said, and Lucia agreed.

"I was in there myself at the beginning of the game."

"So was I," Connie confessed. "And Lee came in as I left." She glanced maliciously at Lee, who glared back.

"I did go in," he told Jimmy, "but I stayed only a minute."

"Long enough to take a drink?"

"Well . . . yes." He glanced defiantly at the family. "I had a bottle of brandy hidden in the supply closet. But how you knew—"

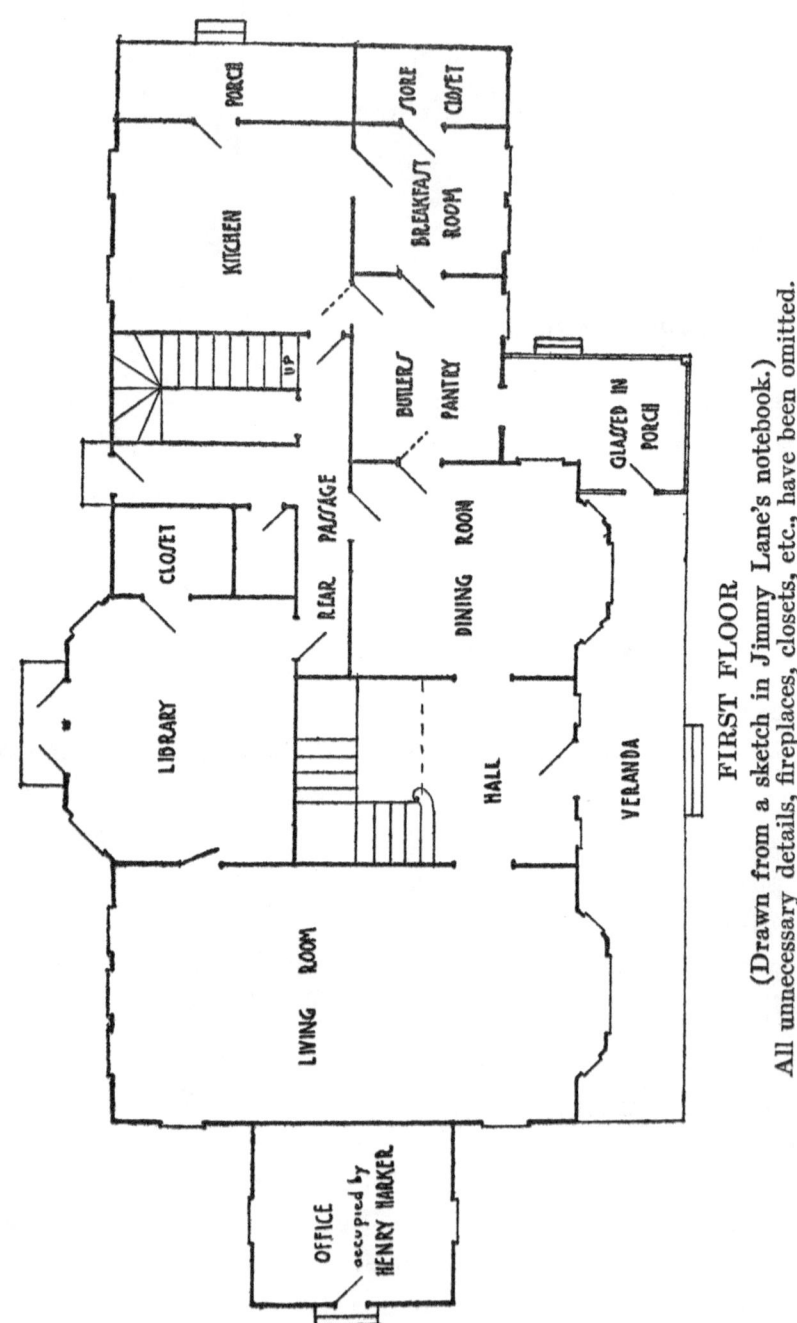

FIRST FLOOR

(Drawn from a sketch in Jimmy Lane's notebook.)
All unnecessary details, fireplaces, closets, etc., have been omitted.

"Smelled it on your breath," shortly. "Also, you were a little too anxious to muss up that bottle with finger-prints. Did anyone come in while you were there?"

"Yes; 'Berto. He came in from the kitchen. And there was some one with him. Would you like to know who it was?"

"You know we would," Jimmy snapped.

Lee laughed mockingly. "So would I. I'd give a lot to know. But at the time, I didn't want anyone to catch me taking that drink, so I sneaked out through the butler's pantry."

"Without seeing who was with him?"

"Yes. But I did hear something. 'Berto said, 'Look out, or you'll hurt some one with that knife.'"

"Good God!" Doug gasped, and Judith asked incredulously:

"You mean 'Berto knew the other had a knife?"

"He must have known."

"I meant to ask about that knife," Jimmy interposed. "Do any of you know where it came from?"

"Of course," several chimed at once, and Lucia explained:

"It's the game-knife from the drawer in the kitchen cabinet. Henry keeps it as sharp as a razor."

"So Harker knew where to find it, eh?"

"Of course he knew. We all knew."

"In that case," Jimmy sighed, "it doesn't get us anywhere. Now who else went into the breakfast room tonight?"

"I tried to get in," Doug spoke up, "but the door was locked."

"What time was that?"

"Around eight-thirty, I should say."

"Did you hear anything?"

"No. But there was a crack of light under the door. I thought Prillie must be using the room so I went away."

"Speaking of Mrs. Prill," Jimmy said thoughtfully, "do any of you know where she was during the game?"

"Prillie was in her room," Lucia told him. "I saw her go up, just before we started to play."

"She might easily have come down the back stairs."

"Yes. But why on earth—"

"We don't need to go into motives. We're checking on opportunities. Prillie goes down on the list. How about Harker?"

"He was in his room when I went to get the keys for the tomb," Doug testified.

"But he could have walked along the outside of the house and slipped in the back door while we were playing that rotten game." His eyes lighted suddenly. "We can look for footprints."

"Too late now. We've all been tramping in and out." Jimmy returned to his list. "Besides Harker and Mrs. Prill, I suppose we'd better say that anyone in the game could have slipped into the breakfast room. That leaves only Aunt Hagar."

"But she was sitting by the fire," Judith said.

"How do you know I was?" Aunt Hagar's voice was tart.

"Because I saw you, dear. Everyone saw you."

"Then everyone's wrong. I got up twice. Once to lock a window, another time to get a drink of water from the butler's pantry."

"The butler's pantry?" Jimmy was suddenly interested. "Have you any idea what time that was?"

"Yes; it was twenty minutes after you started that silly game. The clock had just struck the 'half hour' so it must have been about eight-thirty-three or -four when I decided to get a drink." There was a smirk on her face, as though the thought of being the center of interest, even for a moment, gave her satisfaction. Deliberately she prolonged the suspense. "There was a faint light in the hall, but the dining room was as dark as pitch. I was just crossing to the pantry when I ran into some one." Again she paused and looked about, gathering her audience. "It was a man," she said thrillingly. "He grabbed me—and kissed me!"

CHAPTER 7
FORFEITS

"Kissed you?"

There was a gasp, then half-hysterical laughter.

"Whoever it was must have recognized you," Jimmy suggested.

"No," grimly. "It's a long time since anyone in the family has kissed me like that."

"What did you do?"

"I laughed out loud. Couldn't help it." She gave a reminiscent chuckle. "And he let me go."

"You don't know who it was?"

"Haven't the faintest idea."

"Though it doesn't seem of any particular importance now," Jimmy mused, "it may prove of value later. Which one of you was it?"

To our astonishment no one spoke. For a full minute we stared at each other, then Jimmy repeated, a trifle sharply:

"I asked who kissed Aunt Hagar. Surely the man who did it can have no objection to telling." Still there was an abysmal silence; and, in the end, Jimmy shook his head. "It must be more important than I thought, though I can't, for the life of me, see why. We'll pass it up for the present." He turned to Aunt Hagar. "What happened next?"

"Well, after I'd been kissed," she seemed to savor the word, "I went on groping my way toward the pantry, in the dark. I finally got my hand on the swinging door and pushed it open." Again she paused to enjoy our tense interest. "I pushed it open, and found some one washing his hands in the pantry."

"Washing *his* hands?"

"It might have been *her* hands," Aunt Hagar amended. "It was so dark I couldn't tell whether it was a man or a woman. All I know is, that some one was washing at the sink, and when the door creaked, he, or she, left in such a hurry that the water was still running and the damp towel lying there."

"Towel?" Jimmy turned quickly. "Will you look for it, Phil?"

I hurried out to the butler's pantry. But there was no towel in sight. When I returned to report, Jimmy nodded his head.

"I expected that. Of course he'd go back later and get it."

"He?" Aunt Hagar raised her eyebrows, and Jimmy looked helpless.

"We're running into the limitations of the English language. To avoid confusion, you'll have to understand that we mean either sex when we speak of the murderer as 'he.'"

"Do you think it was the murderer who was washing his hands?" Judith asked, and Jimmy nodded.

"It's almost certain, I should say. If it were an innocent person, why should the towel have been carried away? The only reason for abstracting it would be to hide blood-stains."

"Then why not look for the towel?" Tony asked quickly.

"We shall, later. If it hasn't already been destroyed, it'll be hidden too well for us to find in a hurry, and we've a lot of ground to cover to-night." He turned back to Aunt Hagar. "About this man you met in the dining room: would it have been possible for him to have passed you in the dark and gone into the butler's pantry?"

"No." She shook her head positively. "In the first place, I'd have heard him. In the second, I'd have felt the draft from the door. He went the other direction, toward the hall."

"In that case, we'll have to take it that the man who kissed you is not the one who was in the pantry washing his hands, and therefore not the murderer."

"Then why in heaven's name doesn't he come forward?" I asked; but Jimmy was studying his notes again and did not answer my question.

"That pretty well settles the question of opportunities," he said. "We've found that everyone in the house had an equal chance to commit the murder, and that the knife might have been taken from the drawer by anyone. We also know that 'Berto went into that room conscious that the person with him carried a knife, and yet not suspecting any danger. By the way," he glanced up from his paper, "did any of you see 'Berto after the game started?"

"I did," Connie admitted. "When we began playing. Tony was 'it.' He caught me, and I gave myself away by giggling—" She stopped, as though appalled by the memory of that happy laughter. "He guessed who I was right away," she went on, a bit unevenly, "and I had to pay a forfeit. My bracelet. Then I was 'it,' and the first person I caught was 'Berto."

"Where?"

"At the foot of the back stairs; but he asked me to let him go because he wanted to get something from his room. He promised to come back right away. But he didn't . . . at least," her voice faltered, "at least I never saw him again. I noticed he wasn't there when the game was over, but I didn't like to speak of it."

"Why not?" Lee asked harshly.

"Because you'd been saying nasty things about 'Berto and me, that's why. Because you'd been telling Mark lies about us. I was afraid, if I said anything you'd make some horrid remark."

"I noticed he was gone, too," Judith interposed hastily. "But I supposed he'd come in later. Then I got so interested in the stories I forgot all about him."

Jimmy was figuring with the blue pencil. "We started the game at eight-fifteen. Tony caught Connie, and Connie caught 'Berto. That means he must have gone upstairs around eight-twenty. At our present figuring, he was in the room, dead, about eight-thirty-five—the time when the murderer was washing his hands in the butler's pantry. That leaves us with fifteen minutes unaccounted for. Did anyone see him during that time?"

Again no one spoke, and Jimmy Lane sighed.

"I suppose we can't hope to cut it any finer, but one thing we can do. Those forfeits are still on the table in the order in which they were posted. By checking them over, we ought to be able to discover if some one was missing from the game for any length of time." He crossed to the table, where the row of oddly assorted objects lay along the edge. "I'll pick them up one by one," he said. "Just sing out when you see something belonging to you. Jot the names down, will you, Phil? To begin with, here's Connie's bracelet, and a seal ring."

"That's mine," said Doug.

"A wrist watch. Judith's. My own cigarette-lighter, and an ivory holder—"

"Belonging to me," Lee spoke up.

"But I didn't catch you, Lee; I caught Lucia."

"Yes," Lucia seemed to come out of a deep abstraction, "that's right, you did. I forfeited a bar-pin, but I didn't put it on the table. It was holding a bunch of jasmine and I pinned it on Aunt Hagar's shoulder so she could enjoy the perfume; then I caught Lee."

"And Lee caught me," Connie contributed. "I turned in my necklace."

"Check. Here it is. A man's watch. Mark's, isn't it?" Mark nodded, and Jimmy's lips twitched as he held up a bit of ribbon and lace. "I'm not sure, but I think this is a garter."

"It's mine," said Connie. "I got caught so often I ran out of forfeits."

"A fountain pen that belong to me. Doug's knife. Judith's beads.' And Phil's Phi Beta Kappa key. Finally, a ten-dollar bill."

"Which is mine," Doug called. "Like Connie, I got caught so many times I ran out of jewelry."

"That completes the list," Jimmy told us, and turned to me. "Will you read the names, Phil?"

I picked up the paper and complied.

"'Connie.
"'Doug.
"'Judith.
"'Jimmy.
"'Lucia.
"'Lee.
"'Connie.
"'Mark.
"'Connie.
"'Jimmy.
"'Doug.
"'Judith.
"'Phil.
"'Doug.'"

"H'm; fourteen catches in twenty-five minutes," Jimmy commented. "Quick work! Now is there anyone whose name isn't on the list?"

"There's 'Berto, of course."

"Anyone else?"

"Wait a minute," Lucia exclaimed, "there's something that isn't there. I said I'd caught Lee, didn't I? Well, I was mistaken. I didn't catch Lee; I caught Tony and he gave me a forfeit; only, I forgot to put it on the table." She fumbled in the pocket of her sweater for a moment, then held up her hand, empty. "Why, I must have lost the thing. It was his cigarette-lighter. Did you find it, Tony?"

Tony shook his head. "Don't try to put it over, Lucia. You're a sweet thing, but a rotten liar." He turned to Jimmy. "Sorry, but as a matter of fact, my name isn't on the list because I didn't feel like playing that fool game. I had other things to think about, so I went out on the veranda to think 'em."

"In the rain?" Lee asked pointedly.

"The rain's coming from the other direction . . . and besides, I was sitting at the north end, where it's glassed in."

"Did you stay out the entire time?" Jimmy inquired, and it seemed to me that Tony hesitated before he answered.

"No; not all the time. . . . After about ten minutes I found I was out of matches. I went in the front door and got some from the dining-room sideboard, then went out again—and stayed until the lights went on. I was the last to come into the living room, and I suppose Lucia noticed it. When she realized I didn't have a forfeit in the pile, being a good little cousin, she tried to cook up an alibi for me. Any old alibi."

"Is that true?" Jimmy asked Lucia, and when she nodded: "Look here, I know you did that thoughtlessly, but you must, all of you must realize that the one thing that will help us now is the truth. We must stick to it no matter whom it hurts. Do you understand?"

There was a murmur of agreement, but I think Jimmy sensed something inimical in the atmosphere, for he abruptly altered his plans.

"I wish you would send for Harker and Mrs. Prill," he said. "I want everybody to stay here in this room while I talk to you, one by one, in the library."

"You mean alone?" Lucia asked.

"Yes; the way you'll be questioned by the police."

I caught a quick exchange of glances; the Conroys seemed to be sharing some secret, unhappy thought.

The Doctor was the first to speak. "We'll do as you say, of course. Only . . . I hope you realize we're all pretty much upset."

"I'm not exactly calm, myself," Jimmy said shortly. "After all, I liked 'Berto, better perhaps than some of the rest of you." His eyes swept around the circle and fell upon Lucia. "If you'll come into the library," he told her, "I'll begin with you. I want you too, Phil, to take notes on what is said."

It is from those notes, jotted down hurriedly in the bewilderment and exhaustion of those early morning hours, that I have reconstructed the interviews which follow.

CHAPTER 8
THE WILL

The library was a great, gloomy room, lined with dusty volumes in age-stained bindings. The windows, which were of the French door type, were not only darkened by the second-floor gallery but were shadowed still further by the hill; even in the daytime it seemed always full of stale, dead air, of the odor of damp earth and moldy leather. To-night, with the rain dripping from the gallery, and the trees thrashing in the wind, it was peculiarly dreary.

Jimmy crossed to the desk, where there was a shaded lamp, sat down, and drew a sheet of copy paper toward him. "What do you think about all this, Lucia?" he asked.

From a low chair by the fire she looked at him helplessly. "What can I think? It's all so terrible."

"Agreed. But hasn't it suggested something to your mind? Something about Sally?"

"Yes," her breath caught in a little sob. "You mean that she was murdered."

"I'm afraid so . . . and by the same man, or woman, who killed 'Berto last night."

"But why should anyone—"

"That's what we've got to find out." Jimmy drew the fat blue pencil from his pocket and poised it over the yellow sheet. "Now who had a motive for killing them both?"

"No one," she said with conviction. "Of course 'Berto was sarcastic and overbearing. He used to have quarrels from time to time—"

"Like the one he had with Lee." Jimmy had evidently forgotten for the moment that Lee was Lucia's brother, but her cry reminded him.

"It couldn't have been Lee! I know he was furious at 'Berto for pouring out that liquor, but that's his way—flashing up in a temper, and then forgetting it immediately. Besides, there was Sally. He'd as soon I have thought of killing me as Sally. Lee didn't do it, Jimmy. Honestly he didn't."

"I'm inclined to agree with you," Jimmy said. "Not that he wouldn't be capable of killing some one in a moment of passion, but he's not the type to plan two cold-blooded murders and carry them through with the finesse we find here."

Lucia sank back with a sigh of relief, which was, I suspected, exactly why Jimmy had reassured her. She would be less on her guard from now on.

"Who else had reason to quarrel with 'Berto?"

"He had a row with Harker," I suggested.

"But there was nothing new about that," Lucia told us. "'Berto could never understand that Henry wasn't a regular servant. They've been quarreling for years. Besides, would anybody be such a fool as to kill him so soon after publicly threatening him?"

"It would seem like the height of something or other," Jimmy admitted. "At the same time, it's possible Harker was crafty enough to count on our arguing exactly that way. I mean that he said to himself, 'Nobody's going to suspect me, because nobody'd believe I'd kill 'Berto so soon after threatening him.'" He paused, then asked: "How about Harker and Sally?"

"It's possible." Lucia was thoughtful, plainly weighing her words. "Yes; Henry might have killed Sally. He's hated all of us for years. The only reason he stayed was because of the will."

"The will?" I could see Jimmy's eyes brighten. "You've spoken of that before . . . something about the property being divided next month. Will you tell me what you meant?"

"Why, yes. Grandfather left a queer sort of arrangement. His estate was to be held in trust for ten years. During that time every one of us must be on the island from September fifteenth to October fifteenth or be cut out of the inheritance."

"But why on earth didn't you take it to court? Surely it would have been easy to set aside a provision as fantastic as that."

Lucia did not answer for a moment; and her reply, when it came, gave me a feeling of disingenuousness. "It wasn't so bad. After all, it was for only ten years—and we like being together."

Jimmy glanced at her quickly, then apparently decided to let the question ride. "So the property is to be divided next month, eh? There's food for thought in that. Obviously, the fewer there are to benefit by the will, the larger the inheritance for each of you."

"You mean you think someone killed 'Berto and Sally for money? Oh, the idea is too horrible!"

"Murder is always horrible," he said gravely. "Do you mind telling me how many are to inherit under the will?"

"Let me see." Lucia checked off the names on her fingers. "There's Judith, Mark, Lee and I. That's four . . . and, of course, Aunt Hagar. She has money of her own, but grandfather put her down to share with us. Then Sally and 'Berto would have inherited if they'd lived."

"That leaves five out of seven." Jimmy jotted down the names, then looked up in surprise. "What about Doug and Tony?"

Lucia sighed. "I suppose I'll have to explain the family relationships. You see, Doug and Tony aren't really Conroys—except by adoption and marriage. Wait." She rose and crossed to the bookcase, where she took a sheet of heavy paper from a large Bible. "So many people try to get us straight that Mark made this family-tree."

Laying the paper on the desk before us, she stood looking over our shoulders.

"Nathan Conroy was my grandfather. He married his cousin, Susan; and Aunt Hagar is his sister. He had five children. Sarah, the eldest, was Mark and Sally's mother. She married Hermann Dietrich, a German scientist. Aunt Mary, the next daughter, was musical and went to Italy to study. She married Count Salvatore Patri, and they had 'Berto. When she died, Uncle Salvatore married another American girl. Tony was her son. You see, he's really not related to us at all. Next came my father Melville. He was killed in the war. Lee and I are his only children. Then, there was Uncle Hugh, who was two years younger than father. He and Aunt Helena had no children, so when his partner died and left a little boy they adopted him. That's Doug."

"Where does Judith come in?"

"Judith was the youngest of grandfather's children. She's not much older than Mark."

"H'm." Jimmy was studying the chart, checking it against the list in his hand. "So the money was to go to Aunt Hagar, Judith, Mark, 'Berto, Lee, Sally, and you—with no provision made for Tony and Doug. Was anyone named to inherit in case all the original beneficiaries were dead?"

THE CONROY CLAN

Nathan Conroy m. Susan Conroy
(1845-1920)   (1855-1916)

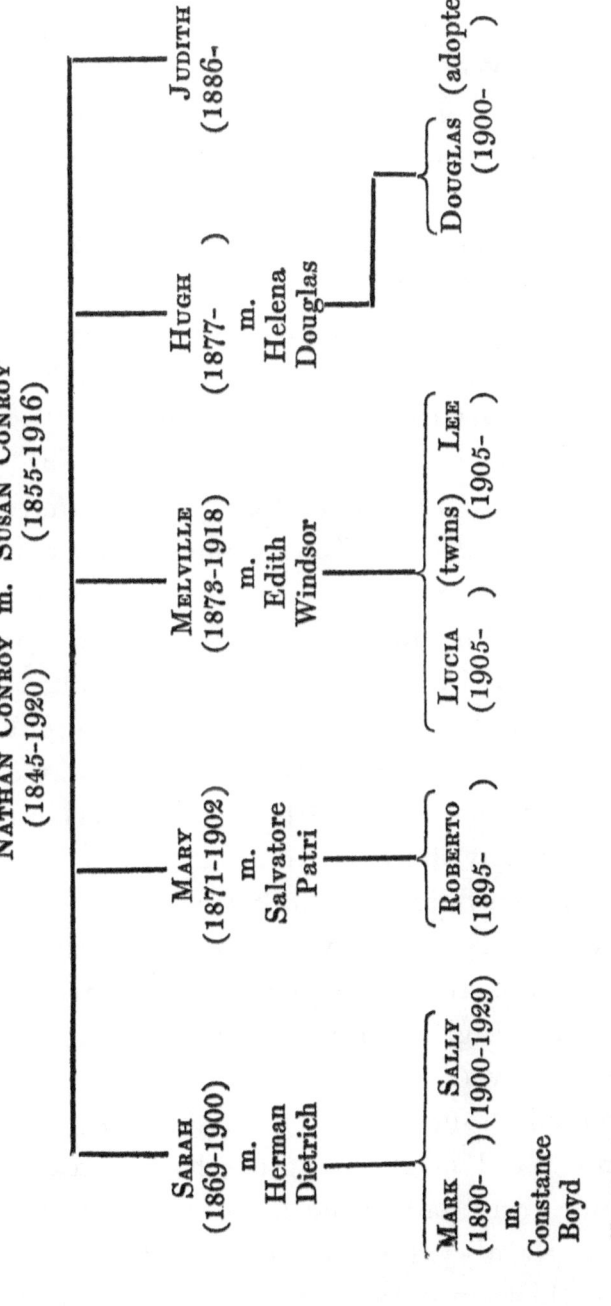

Sarah (1869-1900) m. Herman Dietrich

Mary (1871-1902) m. Salvatore Patri

Melville (1873-1918) m. Edith Windsor

Hugh (1877-) m. Helena Douglas

Judith (1886-)

Mark (1890-) m. Constance Boyd

Sally (1900-1929)

Roberto (1895-)

Lucia (twins) (1905-)

Lee (1905-)

Douglas (adopted) (1900-)

Also in family, but not showing on tree:
Hagar Conroy—(born 1860), sister of Nathan
Antonio Patri—(born 1904), stepbrother to Roberto.

"Yes; in that case the money is to be divided between Prillie and Henry Harker. Besides that, the will gives Henry ten thousand dollars, provided he has stayed on the island and taken care of grandfather's tomb faithfully for the whole ten years."

"Ten thousand?" Jimmy looked surprised. "That's a good deal of money. Do you mind telling me how much there is in the estate?"

"I wouldn't mind, if I knew. We used to think we'd each get from forty to fifty thousand, but with stocks and bonds tumbling the way they are just now, we'll be lucky if we get twenty-five."

Jimmy asked casually: "Since Doug and Tony don't share in the will, why do they come to the island?" Again I suspected an evasion in her answer. "Doug comes on my account, and Tony . . . well, Tony, comes because of 'Berto. You see, Uncle Salvatore, like most foreigners, left almost all his property to his elder son. And even the money that belongs to Tony was in 'Berto's hands to dole out as he saw fit. Oh," she added defensively, "I know Tony ought to have gone out and earned his own living, but he was educated all wrong. Sent hither and thither to Switzerland and to England, and, finally, here to America. Lately he's wanted to settle down, but 'Berto wouldn't give him his money."

"Is that what they were rowing about two days ago?"

"Yes, they were always arguing. Tony hated the way 'Berto kept him dangling. But he was really fond of him, Jimmy. I swear he was."

Jimmy looked thoughtful. "If this had been an unpremeditated murder, I might imagine that the two had got into a row and Tony had killed his brother in the heat of anger. It was plainly planned hours ahead. That means the murderer did it in cold blood, and with some definite purpose."

I had a sudden, horrifying memory of that gay banter on the hill. "Don't you remember? 'Berto said that if they'd both been cave men, Tony would have killed him long ago for his money and his title."

"But that was just a joke!" Lucia cried. "Tony hates the title . . . and as for the property, Uncle Salvatore lost almost everything in the war. All poor 'Berto inherited was a couple of beautiful old places in Taranto, without any money to run them. He was counting on grandfather's legacy to help out."

"That's another thing in Tony's favor," Jimmy mused. "Why should he kill 'Berto just now when, if he waited, a month, he'd stand to inherit a great deal more?"

"Of course." Lucia's voice betrayed relief. "You can see the whole thing's impossible."

"Not impossible, but unlikely, I'll admit. The next is Judith."

"Judith is out, absolutely out," she exclaimed—with almost overemphasis. "Judith is a woman, and, besides, she was fond of 'Berto, and adored Sally. You'll have to forget her."

"O. K." Jimmy spoke lightly, but I knew he would not cease to consider Judith because of anything Lucia had said. "We'll forget her and talk about you and Aunt Hagar. I don't suppose you did it?"

"No," Lucia smiled wanly, "I didn't. And as for Aunt Hagar, what could have been her motive? She has plenty of money, even without grandfather's legacy."

"She said she'd like to murder 'Berto," I pointed out.

"Oh, if you're going to keep remembering what was said on the hill," Lucia exclaimed a trifle petulantly, "you'll have us all murderers, even Doug."

"Speaking of Doug," Jimmy remarked, "did he ever quarrel with 'Berto?"

"Never." Lucia's tone was so positive that it reminded me of the fact that Doug was her fiancé "Doug never
quarrels with anybody, and he hasn't the slightest need for
money."

"I remember Lee called him a bloated bondholder."

"He isn't exactly that; but he does have a natural flair
for finance. After he left college he went into Uncle Hugh's
brokerage office, and it's been thriving ever since. Not
that it matters," she added, "because, of course, he doesn't
inherit under the will."

"Except through you," Jimmy pointed out.

I thought for a minute Lucia was going to protest, but
she seemed to think better of it. "I suppose you've got
to consider that," she agreed. "Somehow, I can't imagine
Doug—"

Neither could I; and neither, apparently, could Jimmy.
"What have you got to say about Mrs. Prill?" he asked.

"Prillie? The idea is just ridiculous! You see, she was
Sally's nurse when she was a baby; then mother died, and
she came to help Judith take care of Lee and me. She's
been with one or the other of us ever since. I really believe
she'd be willing to die for any one of the family. Although,
of course, she'd be particularly New Englandish and unpleasant all the time she was doing it. The way she was
when Sally—" Lucia broke off and bit her lip, as though
sorry she had spoken.

Jimmy pounced at once. "What was it you were going
to say about Sally?"

"It wasn't about Sally," reluctantly. "It was a row Prillie
had with Mark and Connie. Sally'd been living with them
in the old house at home. Connie nagged all the time
and made a perfect slave of her. Mark was too occupied
to notice, but Prillie was down visiting, and she spoke
her mind. It ended with a general row, and Sally took an
apartment by herself."

Jimmy remained silent for a moment, staring speculatively at the curling smoke from the end of his cigarette. "So Connie didn't care for her sister-in-law," he said at length. "That's interesting."

"She'd had a row with 'Berto, too," I suggested. "Don't you remember? She admitted they'd been quarreling on the veranda the other night."

"Yes; and obviously—saving your presence, Lucia—there was some sort of an affair between them."

"I've thought of Connie," Lucia admitted. "She's a vindictive little beast; and, frankly, she's not half so much of a nit-wit as she pretends. At the same time, she wasn't in love with 'Berto, I'm sure of it. She couldn't be in love with anyone but herself."

"Which leaves only Mark."

Lucia reached out and selected a cigarette from a box on the table. As she lighted it I caught the reflection of the flame in her eyes. It seemed to me they held a speculative look.

"What possible motive could Mark have had?" she asked, at length.

"The one Lee suggested—'Berto was making love to his wife."

"It couldn't have been that." Her protest, I felt, was quite genuine. "Mark never worries over Connie's flirtations, and—it may be a catty thing to say—I don't believe he cares enough about her to commit murder. It wasn't the way he felt about Sally."

"Oh, you think he might have done murder for Sally, eh?"

"No . . . yes . . ." She hesitated, then went on with a rush: "There's no use trying to hide it, Jimmy. I do think Mark may have murdered 'Berto—but not because he was jealous of Connie. If he did, it was because he believed 'Berto killed Sally."

"'Berto?" Jimmy looked astonished. "But why 'Berto?"

"Because he and Tony had been over from Italy for several months visiting Mark. Sally'd gone about a lot with 'Berto, and Mark may have thought he'd made love to her and thrown her over, that she killed herself on his account."

"Do *you* think so?"

"No. I can't imagine Sally taking 'Berto seriously. She knew he made love to every pretty woman he met."

"Was Sally pretty?"

"She was beautiful." Lucia spoke softly. "As lovely as a picture. Of course her illness had left her a little worn, but a few weeks on the island would have made her all right again, if only—" Lucia broke down suddenly, and buried her face in her hands.

For a time Jimmy watched her sympathetically, then: "You say she couldn't have taken 'Berto seriously; but there were two other young chaps in the family. . . ."

Lucia raised her head and stared at him with tear-filled eyes. "I suppose you mean Doug and Tony. Of course they both went out with her sometimes, and they were in and out of her apartment a lot, but neither of them made love to her."

"How do you know? Living in New York, you couldn't have had much idea of what was going on at home."

A slow flush stained Lucia's cheek.

"Please believe me, Jimmy, when I say it wouldn't have been possible. Last summer both Tony and Doug were . . . well, interested in me. I suppose it seems funny that such a thing could happen, when we'd all grown up together, but I'd changed a lot in a short time. My first book had just come out, and made rather a hit with the critics. I'd spent six months in Paris . . . anyway, they both wanted to marry me. That's how I know neither of them could have been making love to Sally."

"I see," Jimmy said. And again: "I see." He rose from the desk and strolled thoughtfully across to the fire. I knew his agile mind was fitting together all the bits of evidence he had heard, trying desperately to form some theory that would hold.

Lucia watched him anxiously, twisting her engagement ring around her finger. "What do *you* think?" she inquired, and Jimmy came out of his abstraction to look at her ruefully.

"Hanged if I know. . . You've handed me a pretty stiff problem, Lucia, m' girl. Temporarily, I'm baffled . . . and I don't baffle easily." He reached down, took her under the elbows, and lifted her with an affectionate little shake. "You've been a trump," he said. "Suppose you take a rest, and let me talk to Mark."

"Mark?" She hesitated. "Do you think he killed 'Berto?"

"Not unless he killed Sally, too."

"Why do you say that?"

"Because," he looked immensely solemn and portentous, "because the International Code for Detective Fiction states that only one person may be responsible for *all* the murders."

"But that's nonsense."

"Of course it's nonsense," he said. "But it's the best I've got to offer. Now cut along like a good girl, and tell Mark I'd like him to bring in his medical kit."

Chapter 9
We Question the Family

As usual, the Doctor was composed. His gaze from behind the shining lenses of his *pince-nez* was level, and his voice emotionless. "You wanted me?" he inquired from the door.

"Yes." Jimmy again dropped into the chair at the desk and picked up his notes. "As a physician there are some questions you can settle for us."

Mark crossed to the fire, put down his medical bag and lowered himself carefully into the big chair. He drew a cigar from his pocket, clipped the end with the same precision he might have employed in handling a laboratory specimen, then lighted it and threw both the end and the discarded match into the fire.

Jimmy said suddenly: "First, I want to know what drug it was that killed your sister." If he had hoped to startle the man he failed. Mark merely raised his eyebrows.

"Lucia told you about her death?"

"Yes; everything."

"By 'everything' I suppose you mean the note she wrote in her delirium."

"You're sure she was delirious?"

"Quite sure." Mark rose and walked over to one of the bookcases, drew Webster's *Legal Medicine and Toxicology* from a shelf and brought it to the desk. "The drug she took was chloral hydrate. It's an hypnotic—a bromide—I used

to give her when she suffered from headaches. If you're
interested, you might read this." He opened the book to a
page which was headed "Non-Alkaloidal Organic Poisons,"
and Jimmy read snatches of the printed matter aloud.

"'. . . doses of chloral hydrate, drowsiness and weariness
appear, these symptoms passing, usually, into a state resembling natural sleep . . . in some cases . . . no drowsiness, but,
rather, a period of excitement resembling alcoholic intoxica-
tion—'"

"That is how it affected Sally," Mark explained. "She
went through a period of delirium before she passed into
coma." And, as Jimmy's eyes moved down the page: "You'll
notice that it says the slightly bitter, caustic taste of the
drug is lost when it is in solution in alcoholic beverages.
There was a quantity of sherry in the tea-punch, which
means it might easily have been administered without her
suspecting."

"Upon the other hand," Jimmy suggested, "she might
have felt a headache coming on and have asked some one
to prepare her a dose of the chloral."

"It's possible," Mark said composedly. "In that case,
I would undoubtedly have been the one she would have
asked."

For a brief moment the two were like adversaries measuring their weapons before a combat, then Jimmy closed
the book.

"We'll leave Sally's death for the moment," he said,
"and consider 'Berto."

"Very well." As Mark turned away to replace the book
on the shelf it seemed to me his eyes showed a faint flicker
of relief. "What is there you'd like to know?"

"First," Jimmy selected a question from his list, "would
you say 'Berto's throat could have been cut by a woman as
well as by a man?"

"In view of the fact that his hands were tied, yes."

"Mightn't they have been tied afterward?" I asked.

"No. The bonds were drawn so tightly that they cut into the wrists during his death spasm. That would not have happened if they had been put on later." The Doctor had returned to the fire and resumed his cigar. Now he looked keenly at Jimmy. "You don't mean you suspect one of the women?"

"I don't suspect anyone, as yet. I'm trying to keep myself in the position of a scientist in a laboratory who has a culture containing a thousand different germs and knows that one of them is responsible for a disease. It's only by a process of elimination that he can find the culprit."

Mark smiled a thin-lipped, ironic smile. "You mustn't forget that there are some microbes that defy detection."

"By which you infer . . ."

"Nothing. I was merely carrying on your figure of speech. What more would you like to know?"

"This: could the murderer have cut 'Berto's throat without getting some of the blood on his own clothing?"

"I should say it was not possible. Judging from the wound, they must have been standing face to face. In that case, he could hardly have avoided the spurting blood."

"H'm. That means we can look not only for that towel but the stained garments as well. Also, someone may have noted a change of clothing." Again he referred to the paper. "Next, have you ever had any surgeon's rubber gloves on the island?"

"Yes; I always keep a pair in my bag."

"Do you mind seeing if they are missing?"

The Doctor made a brief examination, then looked annoyed. "They're gone," he said. "Yet I'm ready to swear I saw them two days ago." He was hunting again when Jimmy stopped him.

"It's no use. You won't find them—and *we* won't find any finger-prints, either. Oh, well," he sighed, "I suppose that would have made it too easy." A moment longer he studied his list, then laid it down, and asked, casually: "There's just one more question, Doctor, who do you think killed 'Berto?"

Not a muscle of Mark's face moved. Instead of answering directly, he turned his head and regarded Jimmy with a chill smile. "Are you asking me to guess which microbe?"

"Something like that. After all you're better acquainted with the case than I am. It's possible you know some things I don't."

"Quite possible," Mark admitted. He picked up his cigar from the tray beside him, knocked the ash into the grate, and rose to his feet. "I don't believe I'll answer that last," he said. "Even if I told you what I suspect, it would be only a guess. And guesses are not permitted in the laboratory."

"How about Pasteur?" Jimmy countered. "And Lister? Weren't their first theories little more than inspired guesses?"

"Very true." The Doctor was moving toward the door. "But they didn't tell their wild speculations to the world until they had a chance to prove them."

Mark was gone, closing the door behind him with characteristic precision.

"That is that," Jimmy said ruefully, "and *more* than that."

"Do you think he's guilty?" I asked.

"I wouldn't put it past him. He's devilish cool, and would boggle at nothing. Then there's the question of motive. . . ." He had risen and was pacing back and forth across the room. "We know of at least two reasons Mark might have had for killing 'Berto. First, he may have thought him responsible for Sally's death. Second, he may have been angered by 'Berto's affair with his wife. Still— that makes the whole thing a *crime passionel*. And what I know of the man, I'd say he's not the type to commit murder for emotional reasons." Abruptly, he dismissed the subject and returned to the desk.

"We'll take Connie next," he said. "But remember, Phil, the family don't suspect, as yet, that Sally was murdered. They are under the impression her death was suicidal, so we'll keep off that question for the time being."

Connie was wearing a vivid Chinese coat, its gaudy convolutions of dragons, flowers and butterflies in strange and fantastic contrast to her woebegone countenance. All the rouge had been washed from her cheeks by tears. Her hair was hanging limply about her face, and her eyes were red and swollen. Without looking at either of us, she dragged herself to a leather couch near the desk and sank exhaustedly upon the pillows.

Jimmy crossed and sat down beside her. "I realize how difficult this must be for you," he sympathized, "the shock, the strain. . . ."

His tone had an immediate effect. Connie seemed to remember that he was, after all, a man. She sat up a trifle, pushed the hair back from her face, and patted her eyes with a perfumed handkerchief.

"It's terrible," she whimpered. "No one else seems to care. The Conroys are all so hard. They're sitting in there right this minute talking about music! With 'Berto lying dead! 'Self-control,' they call it. I think it's just plain callousness."

"Of course," Jimmy's voice was on the verge of cooing. "I saw from the first that you were more sensitive than the rest. More perceptive, too. That's why I thought you might have noticed something tonight."

"Noticed what?" She was instantly on her guard.

"Whether any of the men, in fact, whether *anyone* changed clothes while we were playing that game."

She started, and regarded him shrewdly. "I see what you mean! You think the murderer must have got blood on his suit and changed into something fresh. Well, if so, I didn't notice."

Jimmy dropped the question in favor of another. "You remember when we were on the hill the other day, 'Berto said there were three people who had reason to wish him dead? Who do you think he meant?"

"How should I know?"

"Well," I felt his answer was carefully calculated to produce an effect, "Lee seemed to think you were pretty much in 'Berto's confidence."

"Lee!" Connie's voice became shrill, and her expression vixenish. "The dirty cad! To say a thing like that! To go to my husband with that trumped-up tale about seeing us on the veranda Wednesday morning! If you ask me, *he* was one of the three 'Berto meant."

"Was your husband another?"

"The Doctor?" She stopped in mid-speech and studied Jimmy calculatingly. "So that's what's in your mind. Well, you might as well get it out; you're dead wrong. Mark isn't the jealous type. Only thing he cares about is his own work. He'd take the clothes off my back any day to buy new apparatus for his lab. Even if he were jealous, he knew Lee was lying, because at two o'clock—the time he said I was on the veranda with 'Berto—I was in bed. Now I ask you, would he be likely to get jealous over a trumped-up charge like that?"

"No," Jimmy agreed; then, casually: "What was the argument between you and 'Berto?"

"Nothing serious. I just told him I thought he was getting a little too affectionate and he'd have to cut it out, because Lee was making nasty cracks. If only I hadn't said that!" Unexpectedly she lapsed into her former lugubrious mood. Tears began to flow, and she lifted the lace handkerchief to her eyes. "If I'd only kept still," she wailed, "this wouldn't have happened."

"What do you mean?" Jimmy stared at her, and she dropped the handkerchief to return his look.

"Why, it's plain as the nose on your face. Lee was out in the breakfast room taking a drink, and 'Berto found him. They got into a row about his spying on us. Lee got mad, grabbed a knife from the table and cut 'Berto's throat."

"First stopping to tie his wrists and ankles?" Jimmy asked, and she looked nonplused; then:

"I'll bet he worked it somehow," she said. "You can see for yourself he's the most likely one."

"Yes," Jimmy said absently, "I can see that." But his eyes were not upon her face. "What beautiful hands you have," he said admiringly.

"Small, yet strong. They're really clever hands, you know." Connie gave a little, flattered giggle. "They ought to be. I had to earn my living with them before I married the Doctor."

"What did you do?"

"I was a trained nurse. Specialized in surgical cases. That's how I met him. He was recovering from an operation."

Jimmy was silent so long that she waited, then asked:

"Is there anything more you want from me?"

"No; nothing now. You may go." But as she drew herself to her feet and started, swaying upon her high heels, toward the door, he raised his head. "Oh, yes, there is one more question. Do you know anyone in the house who has water colors, or red ink?"

"I don't know of any water colors. There may be some red ink in the desk, or in that closet, where we keep paper supplies."

"There isn't, I've just looked. What I want may not be ink at all. It's a bright red liquid, something like dye."

"There's a bottle of Colorit in the bathroom I use for dyeing faded lingerie. Until it's diluted it's as red as blood. That what you mean?"

"Yes," Jimmy spoke in a voice that showed he was pleased, "yes; I believe that's exactly what I mean."

Connie was succeeded by Aunt Hagar. I believe I have said earlier that of all the disagreeable old beldames I have ever encountered, Aunt Hagar was the most obnoxious. What was true of her in every-day mood was now magnified and raised to the nth degree. She had evidently been pumping Mark and Doug for the gory details of 'Berto's death, and her ghoulish curiosity was still unsatisfied.

It was some time before Jimmy could get her to answer questions.

No; she had not noticed that any one of the men had changed his suit during the game; but then, her eyes were not what they had once been. Men's clothing all looked alike. And why, she demanded, was Jimmy looking only for a suit? Why not a dress?

"You think it was a woman?"

"Of course it was a woman! If you'd eyes in your head you'd see it was Connie Dietrich."

"Connie Dietrich," Jimmy repeated slowly and thoughtfully. "What reason have you to think she killed him?"

"Plenty! To begin with, Connie's exactly the kind that would get us into a mess like this. She simply trapped Mark into marrying her, while he was sick in a hospital. Ever since then she's been trying to ruin him—running up bills, demanding that he take her on trips, flirting with other men. Not that Mark cares," she added hastily. "He hasn't cared for years what she does."

The old lady was running along breathlessly, painting a vivid picture of the family hatred for this alien in their midst. Only the Conroys could have concealed it so perfectly. What other secrets, I wondered, were hidden behind their half-fanatic loyalty?

"Connie's been playing up to 'Berto ever since last year," Aunt Hagar said. "Like as not she had visions of divorcing Mark and becoming a countess." She laughed derisively. "Countess Connie! But they had a quarrel. You heard her admit it."

"She's explained that."

"She would! She'd have half a dozen explanations at her tongue's end—all of 'em lies. What I think happened is this: she found out 'Berto had been making a fool of her and was so furious she followed him into that room and cut his throat."

"How could she have done it without getting blood on her dress?"

"Tush. That's easy," the old lady cackled. "Takes a woman to think of it. Malinda always keeps an old slicker behind the door in the kitchen. Connie put that on while she did the murder."

Jimmy turned to me. "Will you take a look for the slicker, Phil?"

While I was out, Jimmy questioned Aunt Hagar further, but obtained no new information. Her strongest argument seemed to be that Connie looked like all those murdering blondes she saw pictured in the newspapers.

"And being a nurse, Connie wouldn't mind shedding blood," she was saying as I returned.

"The slicker is gone," I told them. "'Not a sign of it."

Aunt Hagar cackled. "*Now* perhaps you'll believe me!"

"I don't know. . . ." Jimmy was plainly weighing the evidence. "Would you say the slicker was large enough for a man?"

"You've seen Malinda!"

"Yes. She must weigh around two hundred. If it fits her, it certainly could be worn by a man as well as a woman."

Aunt Hagar rose angrily from her chair. "You *would* try to figure *that* out. No man living would accuse a blonde of murder if there was anyone else he could shove the crime on."

For the first time Jimmy displayed a flash of humor. Crossing to the door he threw it open and grinned impudently at the old lady. "I don't like blondes," he said, "I prefer black hair."

She glared at him for a moment. "Perhaps it was you who kissed me in the dining room," she snorted, and swept from the room.

"Do you believe all that about Connie?" I asked as he returned to the desk.

"Hanged if I know. It's plain that they all hate her, and that Connie reciprocates in kind. But whether or not Lady Macbeth really thinks she is guilty, I can't say."

Lady Macbeth. With his eye for simile, Jimmy had hit upon something. Back of Aunt Hagar's fondness for mystery stories there was a genuine lust for blood, a ruthless cruelty.

"Mind you, the old lady may be right," he went on. "Connie's a dangerous little puss. If I know anything about blondes—"

"Which you do."

"Which I do, to my sorrow—she'd be a veritable tiger if aroused. Not that I think for a minute she cared anything about 'Berto, but she's far too clever not to know the contempt the family have for her. There's nothing more dangerous than a woman—a man or woman—scorned. Connie's probably been building up resentment against them all for years. The suspicion that 'Berto'd been making a fool of her and that they were laughing might have driven her into a murderous frenzy."

"But what about the bonds on his wrists and ankles?"

"Now you're plagiarizing." He grinned. "That's *my* question. Suppose we see what Judith has to offer?"

Judith seemed more shaken than any of the Conroys, and the very fierceness of her effort at self-control was defeating its own end. Her eyes were sunken, her cheeks unnaturally flushed; the little twitching about her mouth had now become almost continuous. She began talking on the threshold, and talked all the way across the room. What she said was so incoherent it was almost impossible to understand, but it seemed to be a violent insistence that this murder could not, oh, absolutely could *not*, have been done by a Conroy.

"There's just one person who could have killed 'Berto . . . just one. Henry Harker."

"What makes you say that?" Jimmy asked coolly. "Are you hoping to shield your family by hanging a helpless old man?"

"He's not old, not more than fifty-five and they wouldn't hang him. He's mad as a hatter. We could all testify to that. Living alone on the island has made him crazy."

"What other reasons have you for thinking he did the murder?"

"Because he's always hated us. 'Berto in particular."

Jimmy said suddenly: "I remember when they had that row, the other night, 'Berto said something about Harker's having been away from the island. Do you know what he meant?"

"I can guess. According to father's will, Henry was to receive ten thousand dollars at the end of ten years if he had stayed on the island and not left it for more than a week at a time. I believe 'Berto knew he was away last November for a month. Henry was afraid 'Berto would tell the trust company. So he walked around the house while we were playing that game of blind-man's-buff and made some excuse to talk with 'Berto in the breakfast room."

"Can you explain the binding of his hands and feet?"

"Perhaps one of the other boys tied him up, for a joke. 'Berto may have seen Henry passing the window and called him in to cut the bonds. That would explain his remark about the knife."

"Do you think if any of the boys—Lee, or Doug, or Tony—had played such a trick, they'd say nothing about it?"

"It's possible," Judith said slowly. "It would be a horrible thing to confess, under the circumstances, wouldn't it?"

"Yes," Jimmy agreed, "it would," and dropped the subject so abruptly that I knew he had something in his mind.

Further questioning of Judith brought forth nothing of importance. Apparently her only real reason for believing Harker guilty was the fact that she could not bring herself to believe that the murder had been committed by a member of the family. "Nor Prillie, either," she added. "There isn't one of us more loyal than Prillie. She's proved it over and over." But when Jimmy pressed her for particulars, she spoke, vaguely, of Sally's illness and some time when she had nursed Doug's father.

Something in her use of tenses caused Jimmy to glance up quickly. "You speak as though Doug's father isn't dead."

"No," Judith was suddenly on her guard, as though she had let down the portcullis of her mind and was gazing out from behind it, "my brother is alive, but he's ill. He's been in a sanitarium for nearly a year."

"How does it happen that your father passed him up in the will?"

"That's something none of us understands." I felt that Judith was genuinely puzzled. "Because Hugh was the only one of the family father really liked. Perhaps it's because my brother didn't need any more money. He and Doug had so much that the amount they would inherit under the will wouldn't have meant anything to them."

Before Jimmy could question her further she burst out hysterically. Why was he prosecuting them? Couldn't he see that Henry was the only one who could possibly have killed 'Berto? Or was he determined to betray their hospitality? Eat their bread and then turn enemy? There was more, much more of this, all spoken in the tone of one possessed. Coming from old Aunt Hagar Conroy in one of her rages, the tirade would have seemed in character; but from Judith it was unnatural.

Jimmy listened patiently for a time, then, in the midst of a sentence, brought his hand down sharply on the top of the desk. "Stop!" And as she broke off: "I've heard enough. You may go."

Sheer surprise at his abrupt dismissal put an end to her hysteria. She closed her lips tightly, rose from her chair and started for the door; before she reached it Jimmy was at her side.

"Just a minute." Judith was as tall as Aunt Hagar, and as they stood facing each other, her eyes were almost on a level with his. "You don't need to get into such a state," he told her. "I'm not like you, Judith; I don't believe Lee is guilty."

"Lee?" She wet her dry lips. "I don't know what you mean."

"I think you do. Lee is the youngest of your nephews, an orphan that you helped bring up, when you should have been raising children of your own. Now you think he's murdered 'Berto, and this scene you've just staged, accusing Henry Harker, was to protect him."

Judith gave a little gasp, then: "You're right," she admitted. "What I said is true; I can't imagine a Conroy doing this awful thing. But Lee isn't normal just now, I was afraid—"

"I understand." Jimmy patted her shoulder comfortingly. "Just stop worrying, and ask Prillie to come in."

After the hysteria of Judith, Mrs. Prill's impassivity was restful. There was no twitching to her lips; they were firm-set as always; and even her eyes were under control. She nodded curtly to Jimmy from the door, then crossed the room to a straight-backed chair and sat down. Not until she had planted her feet, in their elastic-sided shoes, squarely on the floor and arranged her black skirt primly over her knees, did she turn and look at us.

One monosyllable escaped her: "Well?"

Jimmy asked: "Where were you at eight-thirty?"

"In my room, I finished the dishes a little after seven, then gave Henry Harker his dinner. He'd traipsed out to the dynamo house and tracked mud on the kitchen floor. I made him clean it up before I'd feed him."

"Did he wear a raincoat when he went out?"

"No; he wore a slicker of Malinda's."

"Then the slicker *was* there," Jimmy glanced at me quickly. "What became of it, do you know?"

"So far as I know, it's still there. Henry hung it over a chair to dry when he came in, and it was there when I left for my room. He was still eating in the breakfast room."

"Did you give him anything to drink, any brandy?"

"There isn't any brandy in the house, I know of. Just a little table wine left over from old Mr. Conroy's cellar. The brandy was used up long since."

"Nevertheless, Lee had a bottle of brandy in the breakfast room," Jimmy told her. "Have you any idea where it came from?"

"I can guess. It's that Henry Harker. I've suspected for a long time he was selling Mr. Lee bootleg. That's what I was giving him a piece of my mind about the other evening."

"This wasn't bootleg. It was fine old Three Star."

"Three Star?" Her eyes lighted. "So that's where Mr. Conroy's liquor went. Always did think it was fishy, the way it got used up so fast. He used to have a very fine cellar," she explained. "Dr. Mark told me once it was the best in the state. I'll bet Henry Harker buried a lot of the liquor and has been selling it to Mr. Lee. He'd do anything for money!"

It seemed to me that Jimmy shied away from the question of Harker. "You say you went to your room about seven-thirty?" he asked. "It's on the third floor, isn't it?"

"Yes; at the head of the stairs. Miss Lucia's room is on one side of me, and Mr. 'Berto's was across the hall."

"What happened after you reached your room?"

"Well, at first, I heard a lot of noise down on the second floor. The family were all finishing up their stories, and calling back and forth. Then, along about eight o'clock, everyone seemed to go down to the first floor. After that I didn't notice anything until Mr. 'Berto came up and went into his room."

"'Berto!" Jimmy leaned forward eagerly. "Did you see him?"

"Yes. My door was part way open and I saw him go in. I heard him moving around, opening and shutting drawers. Then a minute later he ran downstairs and met someone on the second floor."

"You're sure of that?"

"As sure as I'm sitting here. I heard him talking."

"What did he say?"

"He said," she sank her voice in unconscious mimicry, "he said, 'All ready for the slaughter.'"

CHAPTER 10
DOUG STARTS SLEUTHING

"All ready for the slaughter?" Jimmy repeated incredulously; and, as Mrs. Prill nodded: "What did you think when you heard that?"

"I didn't think anything. You know how Mr. 'Berto was. Always using silly phrases in that foreign way of his. I thought it was just his manner of speaking."

"That's possible," Jimmy admitted. "It's a common expression. What did the other man answer?"

"I didn't say it was a man."

"You mean it was a woman?"

"I don't know. It may have been either a man or a woman. Whoever it was just whispered something in a low voice, and they went down the back stairs."

"You didn't hear anything more?"

"No; being Saturday night, I decided to take a bath . . . so I closed my door. After that I went to bed. Didn't know anything until they woke me up to tell me Mr. 'Berto had been killed."

"What was your first thought?" Jimmy asked with a suddenness which I knew was intentional.

"To take off my curl-papers."

In spite of himself, Jimmy laughed, and Mrs. Prill said shrewdly:

"I know what you want. To know who I think killed Mr. 'Berto. It'll save time to tell you I don't know . . . and if I did, I wouldn't say. Now do you want to ask any more questions?"

Jimmy recognized the immutability of her decision. He contented himself with a few more inquiries which brought forth nothing new, then dismissed her in favor of Henry Harker.

The caretaker's eyes were bright and alert, darting out glances from beneath wrinkled lids with a suggestion of furtive sharpness that was strangely disturbing, as though a malignant spirit were peering out from behind a mask.

Watching him, I remembered that he had passed ten years in the shadow of a tomb. "To live a life half dead, a living death." Was that Milton, I wondered, or Shake-speare? It seemed to express the life Henry Harker must have led since the body of old Conroy had been interred in the mausoleum on the hill. Might it not be possible that Judith, in her attempt to save Lee, had hit upon the truth? That this life-in-death had touched his brain? In any event, his answers, though surly, were clear enough.

Yes, he admitted, he had worn Malinda's slicker. Left it in the kitchen when he went to his room, at a quarter of eight.

"You've been in your room ever since?" Jimmy asked. And, when he grunted affirmatively: "What about that time you went around the house?"

It was a chance shot, I suspected, but it hit its mark.

"You mean when I looked at the dynamo?"

"Yes. What time was that?"

"A little before nine. The house was all dark down-stairs, and there was a lot of laughing and yelling going on inside. If you don't believe me, you can ask Mr. Tony."

"You saw him? Where was that?"

"At the glassed-in end of the veranda. I know it was Mr. Tony because he was lighting a cigarette, his lighter flared up and showed his face."

"It was a lighter—not a match?"

"Sure it was a lighter. I saw it plain."

Jimmy lapsed into silence.

Harker, sprawled in the chair by the fire, looked not unlike a cadaver that had been propped by some pranking medical student into a gruesome semblance of life. Suddenly, his voice came out of the shadows:

"If you want to know who's guilty . . . it's Mr. Tony."

"Tony?" Jimmy looked up quickly. "What makes you think that?"

"Because he hated Mr. 'Berto, that's why. And no blame to him, neither." Harker's voice was venomous. "Mr. 'Berto was always trying to run everybody, ordering 'em around like dogs. I wouldn't stand for it, and neither would Mr. Tony. They was always fighting."

"Isn't that the best argument for its *not* being Tony? If they were always arguing, why should he kill his brother just now?"

"Because he was going to get married." Harker rasped out the news so unexpectedly that we both started. "I heard 'em jawing about it down by the swamp two days ago. 'Course most of it was in *I*talian, but Mr. Tony sometimes breaks into English when he's mad. I understood enough to know that Mr. 'Berto was going to marry some *I*talian girl. I guess you know what that would have meant: if he got married and had a son, Mr. Tony wouldn't have any chance of getting his title and his property."

"Have you any other reason for thinking he's guilty?"

"You bet I have." Harker leaned forward, his small, pig eyes blinking craftily. "I took a good look at Mr. 'Berto's body to-night, and that shirt he was wearing was Mr. Tony's."

That was the sum and substance of his testimony. Further questioning added only a few details. He knew it was Tony's shirt because he'd noticed it the day they were in the swamp. Tony had caught it on a thorn, tearing a three-cornered piece out of the sleeve, and the tear was still there.

It was impossible to tell whether his accusation was made to save himself, or because he believed in his own words. Obviously he hated the Conroys; but his dislike for Tony was, I gathered, rather less than for the others. He seemed to feel that Tony had done a meritorious thing in relieving the world of 'Berto's presence.

Jimmy dismissed him and sent for Tony. Earlier in the evening the young Italian had seemed in a daze, stunned and bewildered by shock. Now he had recovered his composure, and there was even a hint of flippancy in his attitude. Had he adopted it, I wondered, to cover his natural emotion; or was he really untouched by his brother's death? For a moment he stood in the doorway, his dark, handsome face lighted by his slightly mocking smile, then:

"I'm ready for the slaughter," he told us, and we both started.

"What made you say that?" Jimmy inquired.

"I don't know." Tony strolled to the couch and dropped down on the cushions negligently. "Is there any reason I shouldn't have said it? Oh, I see, you think it's tactless under the circumstances. Perhaps you're right." He shrugged (his one foreign gesture). "It was a pet phrase of 'Berto's, and I didn't think."

Jimmy picked up a cigarette from a box on the desk and joined Tony on the couch. "I'm afraid I've been rather heartless," he said. "I haven't had time to condone with you about your brother's death. I realize what a shock it must have been."

Tony nodded. "Thanks. It has got me down, rather."

"Of course." Jimmy fumbled for matches on a small table and failed to find them; automatically, Tony reached into his pocket and produced a lighter, which he snapped into flame. It was not until he was holding it out that he caught Jimmy's eye and grinned back ruefully.

"A little detective stuff, eh?"

"Something like that. I thought Lucia wouldn't say you'd given her a lighter for a forfeit if the family all knew you didn't own one. Well," it was both a question and a challenge, "with that in your pocket, why did you go into the house for matches?"

Instead of answering directly," Tony dropped back on the pillows and put his hands behind his head. "I know what's in your mind, but you're wrong. Not that I blame you," he added. "The way 'Berto and I slung language at each other, you've a right to think anything—but it wasn't half as bad as it sounded; I was really fond of my brother." (It seemed to me his voice shook, either from emotion or by design.) "It was only that he liked the feeling of power and enjoyed having me beg for money, even money I was entitled to. But everything was patched up two days ago. After that row on the veranda we went down to the swamp and had it out. 'Berto was going to get married next month. I knew his bride wouldn't want me around, so I put it to him to let me have the money that was coming to me—and I'd go to Paris. He roared a bit, at first; but he gave in."

"I see." Jimmy's eyes were half closed. "What enemies did he have on the Island?" he asked suddenly.

"Enemies? Why none, of course."

"Yet, that afternoon on the hill, he said there were three people who had reasons for wishing him dead."

"Oh," Tony was scornful, "that was just one of his jokes."

"Perhaps; but the psychologists say there is usually a truth back of every jest. Whom do you think he might have meant?"

"To begin with, I suppose he might have meant me. You heard his remark about cave men. Second, Henry Harker. Because of that row the other night."

"And the third?"

"Why—Aunt Hagar. You remember, she said she'd choose to murder him *first.*"

"But that was *after* 'Berto's remark."

"*N'importe.*" Tony shrugged again. "He knew the old girl hated him because he never paid any attention to her."

"You mean you think she killed him?" I burst out.

"I'm not thinking, thanks." Tony rose lazily. "I'm leaving that to you and Lane." And to Jimmy: "Have you anything more to ask?"

"Yes." Jimmy's tone was deceptively casual. "How did it happen that 'Berto was wearing one of your shirts?"

"One of my shirts?" If his surprise was assumed it was well done. "Are you sure?"

"I have Harker's word for it. It's light blue, with a triangular tear in the sleeve."

"Then it's mine, all right. But why he should be wearing it is beyond me. Last time I saw it was yesterday. I put it out in the hall for Prillie to mend."

"How did it happen to be stained?"

"Stained? It wasn't that I know of. There was just a tear on the sleeve."

Rather to my surprise, Jimmy did not pursue the question further; and after Tony had left the room he flatly refused to discuss the possibility of his guilt. It was almost four o'clock, he pointed out, and Doug and Lee were still to be interviewed.

Doug proved, on the whole, to be the least helpful of the lot. Not that he was reticent. Far from it. He had been, we gathered, fond of 'Berto in spite of the ragging to which the Count subjected him. His death had not only been a shock to Doug for sentimental reasons, but it upset his orderly sense of things-as-they-should-be. Even his fondness for reading detective fiction had not prepared him; now that he was face to face with murder in real life he seemed as helplessly bewildered as a child.

All that he had to offer was a reiterated insistence that the dastardly deed could not have been done by one of the family, nor yet by Prillie nor Henry Harker. It *couldn't*.

"I'd as soon believe I'd done it myself as to think it was one of them," he wailed.

"Perhaps you did do it," Jimmy suggested, and Doug took him quite seriously.

"Of course I easily could have. I'm telling you I didn't, but if I had done it I'd be sure to lie about it, wouldn't I?"

"Probably," Jimmy grunted; then added curiously: "Just what motive could you have had?"

"Well . . . Doug looked thoughtful, then inspired, "'Berto made fun of me lots of times because I liked sports and didn't care about reading, and his kind of music. I might have got fed up with it and killed him."

"Thanks," Jimmy told him, "I'll make a note of that." And as Doug tiptoed out, swelling a trifle with importance at being added to the list of suspects, he looked after him with grim humor. "I hope the family aren't too engrossed with their troubles to appreciate Doug," he said. "On the hill that day, we decided that every detective story needed a little comic relief. I've a feeling he's cast for the part."

"Then you don't believe—" I was beginning, when an uproar rose in the next room; voices were raised in argument; there was the sound of a chair pushed back and Truffles barking excitedly.

Jimmy threw open the door. In the center of the living room, Lee, planted squarely upon his feet, was declaiming shrilly:

"I won't go in! I won't be cross-examined by that fellow! Who is he anyway? Where'd Lucia get him? Why'd he come here? This isn't the sort of place anyone would come to for pleasure. And that friend of his, that shyster lawyer who keeps him out of trouble—"

"In the name of myself and my friend, I thank you," Jimmy interrupted, stepping into the room.

Lee cringed back for a moment, then stiffened defiantly. "So you were listening at the door? Well, I don't mind telling you what I think! I believe you've no more right to ask questions than I have. You're just as much under suspicion as the rest of us."

"Lee!" Lucia cried. "You don't know what you're saying!"

"You bet I know what I'm saying! I'm telling you we don't know anything about this fellow. He may have killed 'Berto, himself. He may be planning to pin it on us."

"That will do." Mark Dietrich rose from his chair and joined Lucia. His perfect self-control gave an almost inhuman quality to his speech. "We've had enough of your accusations, Lee. An hour or so ago, *I* was the murderer. Now, it's Lane. You'll either control yourself or—"

"You'll put me in a straight-jacket, I suppose?" Lee flung out, and a gasp of horror ran about the circle. "Go ahead! Then, at least, when somebody else gets bumped off, I won't be accused!"

"You believe some one else is going to be killed?" Jimmy regarded him keenly. "Just what makes you think so?"

"I—I don't know," Lee began to stammer; and his hands, which had been raised in a gesture of anger, dropped to his side. The fit of mad excitement was passing; his face, which had been unnaturally flushed and congested, was paling to pasty yellow; all the lines of his body, from the tenseness of passion, slacked into exhaustion. "I don't know," he repeated. "It was just something that came into my head."

"Rather odd, don't you think," Jimmy suggested, "that you should have the idea one murder presupposed another?"

Lee did not answer. He collapsed into a chair, and sat, head hanging, arms limp, as though the violence of his emotion had drained all strength from his body.

Lucia looked at Jimmy with pleading eyes. "It's because of Sally," she said. "He's horribly upset."

"You mean . . . you've told them?"

"Yes. I thought they should know."

Jimmy looked both disappointed and annoyed. Obviously he had intended to break the news himself, and watch the family reaction. But it was too late now.

"They've been trying to remember where everyone was during the afternoon she died," Lucia explained. "I wasn't here, but everyone else was, in and out of the house—swimming, fishing, or sleeping. There isn't a single one who couldn't have committed that murder."

"Which is equally true to-night." Jimmy dropped into a chair with a sigh; his eyes passed from one white, strained face to another. "Except for Lee, I've talked with all of you," he said slowly, "and almost every one had some theory or guess as to who did this murder. As there are only a few who have not been accused by one or more, I shall give you the names." He drew a paper from his pocket and read:

"'1. *Harker.*
"'2. *Mark.*
"'3. *Tony.*
"'4. *Lee.*
"'5. *Doug.*
"'6. *Connie.*
"'7. *Aunt Hagar.*'"

There was an exclamation of surprise at the last two names, and Connie cried out in sharp protest. Aunt Hagar looked pleased, I thought, as though she felt so long as she could be accused of murder she would not be relegated to the wings but might strut her part among the players on the stage.

"The three who escaped accusation were: Mrs. Prill, Lucia, and Judith," Jimmy continued.

"Then one of 'em killed him!" snapped Aunt Hagar. "It's always the one who isn't accused who proves to be guilty."

"But that's perfectly ridiculous!" Connie exclaimed, and Jimmy threw down the paper.

"All of it's ridiculous! There isn't a suggested motive that's strong enough to be convincing. Oh, I'll admit, carried to the nth degree, some of them might have led one of you to kill 'Berto, but Sally. . . . Why, hang it all," he glanced once more around the group with real affection in his eyes, "I know you. I've been with you for ten days, and I'm ready to swear there isn't one of the lot that's capable of killing a sick girl."

In the ensuing breathless silence a strange conviction forced itself upon me. From their averted eyes and a dreadful sort of tension that held them wordless, I knew the Conroys did not agree with Jimmy Lane. In spite of their violent protestations, I felt sure they believed it entirely possible that a member of the family had murdered Sally and 'Berto.

If the same idea had occurred to Jimmy, he gave no sign, but went on, in a matter of fact tone: "If what you say about last year is true and everyone on the island had the same opportunity for killing Sally, we'll do well to drop that problem for the present and try to discover who wrote the last story we read to-night, *Murder in the Conroy Clan.*"

Strange and unaccountable as it may seem, I had forgotten, until that minute, that the whole story of the murder had been written and dropped into the red chest a full
half hour before 'Berto, with his flashing smile, his gay
and insolent eyes, had gone into that darkened room with
a shadowy figure which carried a knife.

CHAPTER 11
THE LAST STORY

The manuscripts were still lying upon the long table, and Jimmy ran through them hurriedly. "They're all here," he said. "As they are unsigned, I'll ask each one of you to call out when I come to your contribution." One by one he read the titles. *Death in the Attic* proved to be by Judith; Lucia, Aunt Hagar, and Mark had written longer narratives; Doug confessed to the short short-story; Connie to the limerick; and Tony to the *risqué* verse. The ninth story in the pile was a brief sketch which Tony insisted had been written by 'Berto himself. Connie, too, had seen the manuscript in his hands. Slowly Jimmy lifted the last, fateful story, *Murder in the Conroy Clan*. "And this," he said, "who will claim this?"

There was silence, a tense silence.

Holding the manuscript under the light, Jimmy scrutinized it thoughtfully. "It's typed on the same yellow paper as the others," he said.

"You'll find a pile of it on the shelves in the closet off the library," Lucia told him. "We always keep a quantity on hand because so many of us do typing."

"How many?"

"Almost everyone. Mark uses a machine for his articles. Connie helps him, and of course I'm typing constantly.

Then, Lee can handle a Corona well enough to get out a respectable letter."

"That describes me, too," Doug spoke up.

"I do my own correspondence—and Aunt Hagar's," said Judith.

"Then Aunt Hagar can't use a machine?"

"No," the old lady shook her head almost regretfully, "I can't. I paid Henry Harker to type my story for me."

Harker nodded sullenly. "That's right enough. I used to do most of Mr. Conroy's letters for him."

"How about you, Mrs. Prill?"

"Never learned. Can't tell one key from t'other."

"Typing is one of the best things I do," Tony said, without being questioned. "I took care of all 'Berto's business letters."

"Then," Jimmy recapitulated, "all of you can type, except Mrs. Prill and Aunt Hagar. At least we can cross them off our list."

Aunt Hagar bridled a trifle, annoyed at being put in the company of Mrs. Prill.

"The next thing is to check the typewriters," Jimmy went on. "How many machines are in the house, Lucia?"

"Two Coronas, an old Remington—in the closet off the library—and 'Berto's portable Bing which he brought from Europe."

"That makes it four," Jimmy counted. "To save time, you might, each of you, write down the machine you used in typing your stories."

While I passed around the paper and pencil, he again studied the manuscript. "The thing I cannot understand," he puzzled, "is how the murderer foretold so exactly all the movements of the evening. It was fairly easy to guess that you would go upstairs, after dinner, to finish your stories. The action of coming downstairs and putting them in the chest could also be foreseen. But how he knew about the game of blind man's buff— By Jove!" His eyes lighted

"Who suggested that game? Can any of you remember?"

They looked at each other blankly, then Lucia cried: "It was 'Berto!"

Why that should have added to the horror of the situation, I cannot say; but its effect was paralyzing. No one spoke until the clock had ticked its way through thirty seconds, then:

"You're sure of that?" Jimmy asked.

"Absolutely." Lucia appealed to the others. "Don't you remember? We were talking about the games we used to play when we were children. 'Berto said blind man's buff was his favorite—"

"Because he could kiss the girls in the dark," Aunt Hagar contributed with relish.

"—and, he suggested we play a game before we started reading."

"I seconded it," Doug spoke up, "because I thought we ought to get a little exercise, and Tony agreed it would be fun."

"But Tony didn't play—" I was beginning, when I caught Jimmy's warning eye and subsided.

The Conroys continued recalling the events leading up to the game. 'Berto had made the first suggestion, which had been seconded almost simultaneously by Doug, Tony and several of the others.

"How could the murderer have known that 'Berto was going to suggest that game?" Lucia asked.

"Perhaps he suggested it to 'Berto."

"But he couldn't be sure 'Berto was going to take the suggestion, could he? What do you think?" She turned to Jimmy Lane who was sitting, lips pursed, eyes vacant, following some line of thought; so engrossed was he that she was forced to repeat her question twice.

"I don't know. I don't know at all. There's something I must work out." For a moment longer he stared at the floor, then rose wearily. "It's almost dawn," he said. "All of you are exhausted. When we've had some sleep we'll be able to tackle this thing with clearer minds."

"Aren't you afraid the murderer may destroy evidence while we're asleep?" Doug protested, and Jimmy threw him a faint smile.

"So afraid, that Phil and I are going through all the rooms before we go to bed."

During the next half hour we conducted a search of the second and third floors, but found no trace of the slicker or towel. At the end of that time, Jimmy ordered the Conroys to bed, and we accompanied Harker to his room, where, again, we drew blank.

Upon our return to the house, Jimmy refused to rest until we had made a second examination of the breakfast room. From Mrs. Prill we had learned two things: that the folded blanket upon the settle was from 'Berto's bed, and the pillow belonged on the couch in the upper hall. Jimmy did not waste time speculating upon their reasons for being there but began to explore the breakfast room and the supply closet; when the object of his search eluded him, he walked over to the window, raised the shade and looked out, then swung back quickly with an exclamation of delight.

I followed him through the kitchen and screen-porch, along the path to a point below the window where he bent down and picked up a glass bottle. This he was wrapping in his handkerchief when I asked him pointedly:

"Aren't you concealing gramma's false teeth?"

He grinned.

"No; just the scalp of a red-headed woman."—And with that I was forced to rest content.

Since our feet were wet and muddy we made our return to the house by the rear gallery.

Dawn was breaking as we climbed the steps, a chill, clammy dawn. The rain had ceased, temporarily, but the branches of the trees were still dripping soddenly. The river had risen and was licking at the grass and bushes on the lower end of the island. In the uncertain light, everything was gray and black. The water, the land, the trees, the house itself, merged into one somber pattern of gloom. Only the lighted tomb overhead seemed to shine with a mocking brightness.

"I'm beginning to hate that building," Jimmy confessed. "The dead have no right to the highest spot on the island while the living huddle below." He glared aloft, then burst out again: "Doesn't it seem to have a look of arrogance? As though, hang it all, as though it were triumphing over us all?" He broke off. "Make me go to bed, Phil. I'm beginning to jitter." We had reached the top of the stairs, and were about to open the door which led to the rear hall, when he stopped. "What's that?"

He was pointing to a rain barrel which caught the water from the eaves, and I saw that the tin cover had been removed and that a bit of grayish fabric was protruding over the edge.

It was Malinda's slicker. With it was the towel from the butler's pantry. Both of them had been soaking for hours in the rainwater and all hope of discovering finger-prints was gone.

I woke at noon, after a scant five hours of sleep, to find the great clock on the stairs striking twelve in almost perfect synchronization with the drip, drip, drip of water from the eaves. A sullen, gray light illuminated the bedroom and fell on Jimmy Lane, deep in work at a table near the window. As I moved and sat up he turned on me eyes that were heavy and ringed from lack of sleep.

"Why aren't you in bed?" I demanded.

"No use. Couldn't sleep. I've been up since eight trying to reduce this chaos to some sort of order."

"Get anywhere?"

"Yes." He gathered eight or nine sheets of paper together, fastened them with a wire clip and brought them over to me. "I'm afraid what I've discovered makes the whole thing madder than ever. I wish you'd cast your eye over this brief summary and see if the same thought occurs to you."

It is surprising to look back now and see how many of the notes Jimmy jotted down that morning proved to have a direct bearing on the solution of the case. For those who wish to refresh their minds as to the sequence of events I am giving them here:

Summary

1. *Nathan Conroy owns an island where he and his family spend their summers. Five years before his death he retires to the island, and remains there the year around with the former manager of his plantation, Henry Harker.*

2. *At his death, in 1920, he leaves a will bequeathing his property to his sister Hagar, his daughter Judith, and his five grandchildren: Mark, Sally, Roberto, Lucia and Lee; but ignoring his only remaining son, Hugh, his adopted grandson Douglas, and his step-grandson Tony. This will requires that the legatees spend the month between September fifteenth and October fifteenth out of every year, on the island. Harker is to receive ten thousand dollars provided he stays on the island for ten years as caretaker.*

3. *In the case of the death of all of the legatees, the money is to be divided between Henry Harker and Mrs. Prill.*

4. *In the summer of 1929, Sally dies a few hours after her arrival on the island, from an overdose of chloral hydrate taken in a glass of tea-punch. The bottle, which previously stood in the medicine chest in the upper hall, disappears and is never recovered.*

5. *At the time of Sally's death, every member of the Conroy family, with the exception of Lucia, is on the island; and all of them have access to the chloral and the tea-punch.*

6. *It is believed that Sally's death was suicidal, until the following summer, when Lucia discovers a note scribbled on the fly-leaf of the book she was reading the afternoon of her death. This says, "Murdered."*

7. *In 1930, the year when the estate is to be settled, the family comes, as usual, to the island. Conditions in the family which may have some bearing on the case are:*

(a) *Lucia Conroy is engaged to her adopted cousin Doug.*

(b) *Lee Conroy has been drinking steadily. It is suspected that Henry Harker is supplying the liquor.*

(c) *Lee quarrels with 'Berto and Tony when they destroy some of his liquor.*

(d) *'Berto flirts with Connie Dietrich and they quarrel.*

(e) *Tony has an argument with 'Berto over money matters.*

(f) *It is reported that 'Berto is about to marry an Italian girl.*

(g) *There is an argument between Mrs. Prill and Henry Harker.*

(h) *There is a row between Henry Harker and 'Berto Patri.*

8. *On the morning of Thursday, September twenty-fifth, the servants leave for a barbecue celebrating the opening of a new levee at the mouth of the river. The family gathers on the hill back of the house and there is a discussion of detective stories in the course of which Aunt Hagar announces that if she were to start on a career of crime the first one she would murder would be 'Berto. This discussion leads to a prize contest for the best detective story.*

9. *In the evening, a terrific equinoctial storm breaks. Truffles, the dog, disappears, and, in searching for him, the whole island is combed— thus establishing the fact that no stranger is in hiding at that time. The storm makes it impossible for anyone to cross the river later that night.*

10. *On the evening of Friday, September twenty-sixth, the detective stories are completed by eight o'clock. They are counted by Jimmy Lane, who finds there are nine manuscripts.*

11. *A game of blind man's buff is suggested by 'Berto, and seconded by several others, including Tony and Doug.*

12. *The game starts at eight-fifteen with Tony as "it." Tony catches Connie, who catches 'Berto, at about eight-twenty. 'Berto asks her to let him off as he wishes to go upstairs. He is heard by Mrs. Prill moving about in his room, and a moment later he joins some one in the lower hall. Mrs. Prill is unable to say whether*

the second person is a man or a woman, but she hears 'Berto whisper, "All ready for the slaughter."

13. At about eight-twenty-five, Lee goes into the breakfast room to get a drink. He is interrupted by the entrance of 'Berto and a second person. He hears 'Berto whisper, "Look out or you'll hurt some one with that knife." Lee slips out of the room by the door into the butler's pantry. At about eight-twenty-seven Doug tries the door from the kitchen into the breakfast room. He finds it locked and a crack of light showing underneath.

14. At eight-thirty Aunt Hagar leaves the living room to get a drink. In the dark dining room she is kissed by some man who has not as yet revealed his identity. Upon opening the door to the butler's pantry, she hears some one at the sink. It is impossible for this to be the same person who kissed her. She crosses and finds the water running and a damp towel lying upon the sink-board. Later the towel is removed.

15. At about eight-forty-five Harker goes to the dynamo room. He sees Tony at the glassed-in end of the Veranda lighting a cigarette by means of a lighter. Later, Tony tells of having gone into the house to get a paper of matches from the dining room sideboard. He gives no explanation of why it was necessary to get matches when he was in possession of a lighter.

16. At eight-fifty the game stops and the family assembles in the living room for the reading of the manuscripts. Judith and Connie both notice the absence of 'Berto Patri, but neither of them comments on it at the time.

17. *At one o'clock, after nine manuscripts have been read, it is discovered that an extra story has been added, probably during the course of the game of blind man's buff. This tenth manuscript is entitled "Murder in the Conroy Clan." Taking the island for its locale, and the Conroy family for its cast of characters, the story is built up about the actual happenings of the day before and through the events of that evening, including the game of blind man's buff. It ends with a description of the game, the reading of the manuscripts, and the discovery that 'Berto Patri is not in the room; it's climax is a vivid account of the discovery that 'Berto's dead body is in the breakfast room.*

18. *At one-fifteen, the story is finished and it is noticed that ''Berto is actually missing. Mark, Doug, Philip Carter and Jimmy Lane go to look for him and find his body in the breakfast room, exactly as described in the story. It is lying on a rug in the middle of the room. The hands and feet are bound with clothesline. The throat has been cut from ear to ear by means of a sharp knife from the kitchen, which is found close by.*

19. *The body wears a shirt belonging to Tony, which (according to Tony's testimony) was placed in the hall for Mrs. Prill to mend. This shirt is not only stained with 'Berto's blood but also with red coloring matter, laid on in irregular splotches.*

20. *A blanket from 'Berto's room is on the settle, also a pillow from the upstairs hall.*

21. *Dr. Mark Dietrich examines the body. He places the time of death at approximately*

eight-thirty, and testifies that 'Berto's throat has been cut in such a fashion that the blood must have spattered upon the murderer.

22. It is discovered that a slicker worn by Henry Harker earlier in the evening, and left over a chair in the kitchen, has disappeared. This is found later with the missing towel in a rain-barrel in the upper gallery.

The notes came to an abrupt end and Jimmy, who had been watching me, asked:

"Do you see where it's all leading?" As I shook my head he leaned over and checked several of the paragraphs with his blue pencil. "These will point the way."

I reread numbers 8, 10, 11, 12, 13, 17, 18, 19, 20 with puzzled interest; then, knowing Jimmy rather likes me to be obtuse, because, in explaining, he not infrequently clears up one of his own doubts and perplexities, I confessed my stupidity shamelessly.

"Wait." He crossed to the table and returned with two manuscripts. The first was a short sketch which Tony and Connie had identified as 'Berto's contribution. The second was *Murder in the Conroy Clan.* "Look," he said, "they've both been typed on the same machine, 'Berto's Bing."

"You mean that 'Berto wrote both stories?"

"Yes. I believe it originated as a hoax which 'Berto planned to play on the family. He purposely started us playing the game of blind man's buff, then slipped that story into the pile on the table. After that, he ran upstairs to his room and put on Tony's torn shirt which he took from the upper hall."

"But why—"

"Wait a minute, you'll see. Then he went downstairs and joined a confederate, some one who was to help him in putting over the joke." His face sobered, and I knew that he was thinking of 'Berto, full of his boyish prank, meeting that sinister figure and whispering gaily, "All ready for the slaughter."

"Then it must have been one of the family," I said slowly.

"Not necessarily. He might have enlisted the service of Harker, or even Mrs. Prill."

"But she overheard them talking—" I began.

"We've only her word for it. Don't misunderstand me, Phil. I have no reason to think it was Prillie. I'm just pointing out that if we are correct and 'Berto typed that manuscript, it puts both Aunt Hagar and Prillie back on our list of suspects. We eliminated them, you'll remember, only because they were unable to use a typewriter."

"Of course!" My mind was working back, testing Jimmy's theory by means of the evidence. I was bound to admit that it held. "That would explain 'Berto's remark about the knife, which Lee overheard."

"Yes; whoever helped him carried the knife to lay on the floor at his feet, as described in the story. As I see it, 'Berto had a tableau all arranged. He got the other fellow to tie his ankles and wrists, then planned to lie down on the settle until he heard the family coming. That explains the pillow and blanket. While they were arranging this, the lights were on and the doors locked, as Doug found them when he came into the kitchen. With 'Berto bound hand and foot, the murder was a cinch. The killer had only to bring that razor-sharp knife across 'Berto's throat. Even the sound of a falling body would pass unnoticed in the scuffle and noise of that wretched game."

"And the slicker—"

"—was put on by the murderer when he went to get the knife."

"But wouldn't 'Berto have thought it odd?"

"Not at all. You see, they were dabbling dye on that shirt, to represent blood."

"So that's why you asked Connie about red coloring matter?"

"Yes. It had been poured into the saucer we found on the sink. It was the empty dye bottle I picked up outside the window. It was probably tossed there by 'Berto himself. That's the reason he took Tony's torn shirt, and why it would have seemed perfectly natural for the fellow who was helping him to put on a slicker to protect his own clothes."

"Then, after killing him, he went into the butler's pantry and washed the dye and blood off his hands."

"Yes." Jimmy rose and began to pace the room restlessly. "The devilish part of it all is that it's so simple. With his hands tied, anyone might have cut 'Berto's throat—the weakest woman as well as the strongest man. In those papers you've got there, you'll find a list of suspects. I've been over it a dozen

times, and I'll be hanged if I can see that any one person is indicated more than another." He nodded at the notes in my hands, and I found a list, headed:

Possible Suspects

Mark Dietrich.

Motives:

    1. Might have been jealous of 'Berto's attention to his wife

    2. Might have believed that he caused Sally's death.

    3. Might wish to increase his inheritance under the will.

Opportunity:

    He was in the game with the rest and was caught but once.

Connie Dietrich.

Motives:

1. Might have discovered 'Berto was going to marry and killed him in jealous rage.
2. Might have wished to increase the inheritance, which she would enjoy through her husband.

Opportunity:

Not so good as most of the others. She was in the game and caught three times.

Aunt Hagar Conroy.

Motives:

1. An extreme dislike for 'Berto.
2. A desire to increase her share of the property inherited under the will. (Not a strong motive since she has money of her own.)

Opportunity:

Was not under observation during the game. Might easily have slipped into the breakfast room.

Judith Conroy.

Motive:

To increase her inheritance under the will.

Opportunity:

Was in the game. Caught twice.

Lucia Conroy.

Motive:

Only the fact that it might increase her inheritance.

Opportunity:

Was in game. Caught but once.

Note: Lucia is practically eliminated because of the fact that she was not on the island at the time of Sally's death.

Lee Conroy.

Motives:

1. Hated 'Berto because he took away his liquor.
2. To increase his inheritance.

Opportunity:

Was in game. Caught but once.

Tony Patri.

Motive:

Might have killed 'Berto in order to get out from under his dominance and to inherit his title and rather small amount of money.

Opportunity:

Was not in the game. Admits he was in the house at least once.

Doug Conroy.

Motives:

1. Might have been annoyed by 'Berto's gibes.
2. Might wish to increase the inheritance which he would gain through his marriage to Lucia.

Opportunity:

Not so good. Was met and caught three times.

Mrs. Prill

Motive:

Would gain by 'Berto's death only if all the other beneficiaries were dead.

Opportunity:
  Very good. Was not in the game. Might have slipped down the back stairs and into the breakfast room undetected.

  Henry Harker.
Motives:
  1. Was known to hate 'Berto.
  2. Would gain inheritance only if all the Conroys were dead.
Opportunity:
  Excellent. Was not seen by anyone during the evening, and admitted being near the rear of the house during the game.

When I looked up, Jimmy was standing at the window, his hands in his pockets, gazing moodily out at the storm. "No chance of getting help from the mainland to-day," he said. "This case will be on our shoulders for another twenty-four hours at least."

"What are you going to do?"

"Oh, the routine things, I suppose. There seems to be nothing else. No use our looking for fingerprints; we haven't the apparatus for testing them even if we found any. We'll have to leave that to the police." His voice was weary, and, for another interval, he remained moodily silent, then burst out with:

"I'm not at all content with things, Phil. I mean with what we got from the Conroys, last night. I have a feeling that they're holding back some knowledge; that something is festering in their minds and paralyzing them with terror."

I knew what he meant, that hint of barely imagined horror which had hung over the family the night before. I, too, had felt it was something quite apart from their sorrow for 'Berto.

"I'm going to make another attempt to discover what it is," Jimmy declared. "I've a hunch, Phil, amounting to an absolute conviction, that when we find what's terrifying them we'll have our hands on the key to this mystery."

As usual, his hunch was right. The fear that was haunting the Conroys was the key; but it was a long, sad time, fraught with pain and bitter tragedy, before he discovered the keyhole into which it fitted.

Chapter 12
The Death Threat

Nothing of any importance was discovered during the afternoon that followed our talk in the bedroom. Jimmy spent the time in a routine search for tangible clews, which produced no results. The slicker, towel, and empty dye-bottle were locked away in the chest in our bedroom, and Jimmy personally nailed up the windows and doors of the breakfast room.

When the storm temporarily abated its fury, Doug, Jimmy and I went over the island, not with any real hope of discovering an intruder but to be able to go on record when the police should arrive. The river had been rising steadily, until all the swampy land was inundated. This did us one good turn: it decreased the area which had to be searched. We took Truffles with us, on this expedition, and he waddled clumsily at the end of his leash barking at startled birds but showing no other sign of interest.

We were, all of us, soaked after our trip; and while we dressed for dinner Jimmy firmly refused to discuss the case.

He was the first to go downstairs, and I found him, a few moments later, in the library studying the books. These were, as I believe I have said, mostly old and mildewed. Obviously the library of their grandfather. But near the, window was a section given over to the books brought, succeeding summers, by the members of the family. A study of these revealed a strange catholicity of taste. Mark had a shelf of scientific reference; Connie a row of cheap and sexy fiction. There were a number of modern novels, in English, French and Italian, belonging to Lucia and the Patris, while at least four shelves were crammed with mystery stories, still in their garish paper jackets.

"Aunt Hagar's cache," Jimmy observed, but I saw that it was not the detective fiction that held his attention it was an amazing selection of works on psychology—both normal and abnormal,—on sex, crime, and insanity that occupied the next shelf. Among them I noted: *Mental Diseases* by James V. May, *An Outline of Abnormal Psychology* by J. W. Bridges, Seabury's *Unmasking Our Minds,* Frink's *Morbid Fears and Compulsions,* Campbell's *Delusion and Belief,* and a number of standard psychologies in French and German.

"Pleasant summer reading," I remarked, and Jimmy nodded agreement.

"Very. Now, I wonder. . . ." He took a volume from the shelf and looked at the flyleaf, "'Judith Conroy,' and opening a second and third, found the same name. "Strange taste for a maiden lady of uncertain years," he said thoughtfully, but before he could make any further comment we were interrupted by the dinner gong.

Judith and Connie were missing, we found, both of them having preferred to remain in their rooms. The rest of the family looked tired and dispirited, but the human contact combined with Mrs. Prill's excellent dinner was comforting. By the end of the meal their faces were a shade brighter and their voices less dreary.

Coffee was served in the living room. As Jimmy Lane settled himself with a cup in a corner of the divan, I noticed Lee watching him furtively. All through dinner he had been sunk in a sort of abstraction, as though he were weighing something in his mind. Now, of a sudden, he seemed to come to a decision.

"Look here," he said in a low tone, "there's something I want to tell you."

"Very well," Jimmy agreed, "as soon as I've had my coffee we'll go to the library." He was stirring his cup when Judith came in from the hall.

She declined coffee, crossed to the piano, and began playing Ravel's *Pavane pour une Infante defunte*. For a little time the lovely music flowed from beneath her fingers, then she seemed to remember that evening when she and 'Berto had played side by side. She broke off in the middle of a phrase and sat, white and still, staring down at her hands.

It was at this moment we heard Connie's heels clicking upon the stairs. For a brief interval she stood in the doorway, effectively posed so that we might admire her dramatic version of mourning—flowing black satin pajamas, with a Russian blouse of georgette that was trimmed with startling white fur. Suddenly she stiffened.

"Look!" she gasped. "There!"

Our eyes followed her pointing finger to the living room table, where the manuscripts had been spread the night before. Pinned to the side of the red leather chest, by means of a small, dagger-shaped paper-knife, was a sheet of yellow paper.

Murder in the Conroy Clan
Chapter Two

Jimmy Lane seized upon it, and we crowded around while he read the contents aloud. It proved to be three paragraphs of typewritten matter. In short, terse sentences it carried on the story we had both read and lived the night before. Beginning with the discovery of 'Berto's body, our interviews with the family, and our search through the various rooms for clews, it ended with one ominous paragraph:

"*Upon Saturday night, as the family drifted into the living room, after dinner, a sheet of yellow paper was discovered upon the table. It was headed "Murder in the Conroy Clean; Chapter Two," and conveyed a warning that Lee Conroy was to die horribly that night.*'"

There was a sharp cry from Lee, and Lucia exclaimed: "It's a joke! It must be!"

Jimmy went on reading: "*In spite of everything that could be done in the way of precaution, in spite of locked doors and windows, only a few hours later Lee Conroy's lifeless body was found sprawled on the steps of the tomb.*'"

For at least five minutes there was no coherence either in our thoughts or in our words. The Conroys, men and women alike, seemed to be gripped by a sort of hysteria which affected them in widely divergent ways. Aunt Hagar was muttering to herself in a corner. Mark sat staring blankly at the floor. Connie was sobbing. Judith lay back upon the divan in a half faint, while Tony relieved his emotions by pacing the room from end to end and swearing under his breath. Only Doug and Lucia kept their heads. With my assistance, they were trying to calm Lee, who was wracked by a terror so cruel, so devastating, that it produced a sort of frenzy.

"I told you!" he screamed. "We've been watching for it all these years. And now it's come! It's come!" His eyes glassy and distended, rolled about the room from face to face. "Which of you is it? Which?"

"Don't, Lee." Lucia threw her arms about him. "Don't, darling. Please be quiet."

Jimmy stopped her, almost sternly. "Let him go on."

But Lee had collapsed against the cushions of the divan. "I'll die," he muttered brokenly. "I'll die, like

'Berto!" He was plainly revisioning the shambles in the breakfast room, and it threw him into a paroxysm of trembling.

Mark came out his dazed abstraction, crossed to the couch and put his hand on Lee's shoulder. "Pull yourself together," he ordered. "Nobody can touch you. I'll watch over you myself."

"You!" Lee shrilled. "How do I know *you* aren't the one who wants to kill me?"

"We'll all watch," Tony promised. "We'll put you in your room—"

"—and lock the doors and windows!" Lee laughed unmirthfully. "That's what it says in that paper. But I'll be found murdered, just the same!"

"It says you'll be found on the steps of the tomb," Doug pointed out. "Nobody's going to get you up there unless you choose to go." The very matter-of-factness of his tone seemed to reach Lee and reassure him.

He lifted his face pitifully to Doug. "That's right. No one can make me go if I don't want to."

Jimmy Lane had been taking no part in this scene; for the past five minutes he'd been standing, apparently lost in thought, but I suspected that he was listening keenly to the half-hysterical talk. Now, his voice cut across the babel.

"One minute. I want to ask you a question. How long before he died was your grandfather insane?"

There was a startled gasp from the group, and Lucia exclaimed:

"How did you know?"

"By adding two and two. You've all obviously been terrified by something. And yet you refused to give me a hint of what it was. When you want to know the truth about anyone, look at his library. That's my pet rule. When I looked at yours, I found a row of books on psychology, with especial reference to insanity. Judith's name was in most of them, but I could tell at a glance that the books had been read thoroughly. I remembered that your grandfather had lived here for five years before his death, alone with Henry Harker. A strange thing in itself. Then there was the matter of the will. Lucia pretended that none of you found it a hardship to come here for a month out of every year. That's absurd on the face of it, especially when it dragged 'Berto clear across the Atlantic. Since a provision as preposterous as that might easily have been set aside, I figured that there must be some reason why you didn't want to bring the matter into court. From that, it was easy to guess that your grandfather was a madman when he died. Am I right?"

"Yes, you're quite right," Mark admitted. "He was insane. Naturally we didn't care to have the fact trumpeted to the world. We preferred to come here every summer."

"And sit watching each other for signs of madness?"

"Oh, it wasn't as bad as that. Personally, I've never believed that his insanity was of the hereditary sort. He was a paranoiac of manic-depressive type. But the symptoms didn't appear until after his fiftieth year. They took the form of *epilepsia tarda,* and were probably the result of a brain lesion or tumor."

"In other words, it couldn't be passed on."

"So I believed until now."

"Now, what do you think?"

"I don't know," the Doctor admitted helplessly. "Of course it's possible that the diagnosis was wrong; such things sometimes happen. Grandfather wasn't a madman, in the accepted sense of the word. He was merely gloomy and given to obsessions, especially about the family."

"What sort of obsessions?"

"That we all hated him. That we were responsible for grandmother's death. She died in a hospital, where the

doctors had ordered her for treatment. He became ob-
sessed with the idea that we'd killed her. The only time he
showed any signs of violence was when one of the family
came near. When he announced he wanted to live here on
the island, the doctors permitted it because it seemed better than an institution. They kept a male nurse with him
at first. But he didn't get along with the nurse, so the last
two or three years he was alone with Henry."

"Were any other members of the family eccentric?" Jimmy inquired, and Aunt Hagar broke into a shrill cackle.

"Eccentric!" she crowed, and Lee echoed her.

"Oh, my God, *eccentric!* Tell him about Aunt Sarah.
About Aunt Mary, and Uncle Hugh! Go ahead, tell him!"

Reluctantly, Mark went on: "I suppose you might say
that *all* of grandfather's children with the exception of
Judith, here, were neurotic, although none of them was
insane. I've always laid it to the fact that grandfather and
grandmother were first cousins."

"Let *me* tell you," Lee interrupted. "Mark will try to
gloss it over, because he cares more for the damned Conroy honor than he does for my life. Aunt Sarah, that was
his mother, was a brilliant chemist; and when her husband made a bigger success than she did, she committed
suicide. Then there was Aunt Mary, 'Berto's mother; she
went abroad to study music and eloped with Count Patri.
After 'Berto was born, she ran away from the Count with
someone else. Two years later, she dropped him and went
into a convent."

"Where is she now?"

"Dead," someone said.

Lee went on: "Then there was my own father—"

Lucia cried out at last. "Lee! You can't say anything
against father. He was splendid."

"Sure he was splendid. Regular motion picture hero.
Died for the glory of his country . . . but he drank like a

fish, and he couldn't hang on to a dollar five minutes. As for Uncle Hugh—"

"Do we have to go into all that?" Tony asked wearily, and Doug answered:

"Of course we don't! It's outrageous."

Lee sprang to his feet and faced them angrily. "That's all right for you two. You haven't any of the rotten Conroy blood in your veins. I'm trying to save my life, and I mean to do it . . . no matter how much mud I have to sling!"

"Better let him go ahead," Jimmy said, and they sank back reluctantly while Lee plunged on:

"Uncle Hugh isn't dead. He's in an asylum." There was a murmur of protest, and he added: "A 'rest home,' they call it, and 'a nervous breakdown.' *I* think he's gone crazy."

"The truth is," Doug explained hurriedly, "my father, I mean my adopted father, you understand, has had a breakdown—from overwork. He's the sort of man who never plays golf or tennis to keep fit." (Doug's passion for athletics could not be forgotten.) "Now he's paying for it with a complete collapse. It's true he's in a sanitarium, under the care of a psychiatrist, but merely as a precaution. All he needs is rest—and he'll be all right."

"That's what *you* tell us!" Lee broke in. "How do we know it's the truth? How do we know he isn't a raving maniac, in a padded cell? None of us has been allowed to see him."

"That's because he has been ordered a complete rest. Dr. Ascher thought it would be better if he didn't see anyone, even the members of the family."

"Like grandfather," Lee jeered. And answered the family's protests mutinously: "It's the truth! And there's somebody else that's like grandfather—somebody who's in this house!"

No one answered; and Jimmy, too, remained silent, his eyes fixed thoughtfully upon the table. I knew that he was weighing this new evidence, considering its relation to the case, and wondering which of that little group by the fire might be secretly insane.

The idea seemed utterly fantastic. Who could picture Dr. Mark Dietrich, with his fine-cut, scholarly face and his slim, surgeon's hands, deliberately taking a human life? Or Judith walking with 'Berto into the breakfast room and running a sharp knife across his throat? The very thought was absurd. And yet. . . . There was Tony. Was it any easier to envision Tony, or Aunt Hagar, in the role? Lee, alone, might have seemed in character, but Lee was marked as one of the victims. That eliminated him from our list. Or did it? A sudden thought struck me, and, glancing up, I caught Jimmy Lane's eye. He shook his head in an almost imperceptible warning and turned to Lee.

"Earlier in the evening you said there was something you wanted to tell me. You remember?"

"Yes." Lee roused himself: from the lethargy into which he had sunk after his outburst. "I don't suppose it's of any importance, now, but it's something that happened night before last, when we were all writing those cursed stories. The house didn't quiet down until around one o'clock, and afterward I couldn't sleep. The river was making such an infernal racket I got to worrying about the bore. I heard it coming about one-thirty, and thought I'd take a look. So I slipped a coat over my pajamas and walked from my bedroom, down the gallery, toward the river. When I reached the south end, just about opposite Doug's door, I happened to look up at the tomb and saw something." He was sitting erect, now. His voice had lost its high, hysterical quality and was hoarse and strained. "I saw someone go up the steps," he said, "up the steps and into the tomb."

"What?" I think all of us cried out simultaneously.

"I know you won't believe it," there was pathos in his voice, "but it's the truth."

"You mean you actually saw him open the door?"

"No; I couldn't see the door, the portico was too dark. But I did see him go up to it."

"What did he look like?"

"I can't tell you. From where I stood, he—it—was only a ghostly shadow."

"Why didn't you tell us this before?"

"Because I was afraid you'd think I'd been drinking. No; that's not the truth." He squared his thin shoulders and drew his weak mouth into a firmer line. For one instant I seemed to glimpse the man he might have been. "The reason I didn't say anything was because 1 thought you'd all figure I was going crazy."

"How did you feel about it yourself?" Jimmy asked, and Lee looked at him with tragic eyes.

"I thought—I thought perhaps I *was* going crazy. But after what happened last night, I've been wondering. . . ."

CHAPTER 13
WE LOOK FOR POISON

The remainder of the evening was spent in a nightmare discussion in which a hundred theories were advanced, only to be abandoned, and wild surmise seemed as credible as sober reasoning. When Jimmy found the conference degenerating into hysteria, he brought it to an abrupt end by asking all the members of the family to find and give up any weapons they might possess.

Pistols, guns, and even pocket knives were locked into the chest in our room, with the exception of two small revolvers which were kept for protection in case of need. In the meantime, Mark and I searched the house for anything which might have been overlooked, or deliberately retained. We discovered only a few kitchen knives, of doubtful sharpness, and an old-fashioned razor in Harker's room, which he surrendered with much grumbling.

Upon our return, Jimmy called the Doctor into the library. "Look here," he said abruptly, "you told us the other evening that if any member of the family was guilty of this murder he had only to come to you, and you would give him something to put him to sleep. From that, I take it, there is poison in your possession."

"There's a certain amount of it, yes. As we are frequently cut off from the mainland by these storms, I always try to keep a complete stock of drugs in the medicine chest.

Then, of course, I have the usual assortment in my case: morphine, chloroform, various antiseptics. . . ."

"My word," Jimmy groaned, "enough to polish off a regiment. Will you go with him, Phil, and collect all the deadly drugs you can find?"

Mark and I cleared out the medicine chest, removing a few germicides, a can of cleaning fluid, and an arsenical face preparation of Connie's. Doug and Tony ranged about the house, seeking other dangerous chemicals. Doug, pleased as a child to be engaged in some activity which was physical rather than mental, collected a rare assortment of nail polish, varnish remover, and blacking, any one of which—he assured us—would prove fatal if taken in large quantities.

"So would water," Tony snapped. "It's called 'drowning.'" Before Doug could produce a suitable retort, Tony disappeared on to the screen-porch and returned with a small, squat tin can, which seemed a most important find, for it was over half full of a commercial cyanide salt used by Harker for spraying the orchard.

Mark next brought his medical kit to the table in the upper hall, where we removed the morphine and two or three other lethal drugs. "How anyone in this family could have the special knowledge to use them, I can't see," he observed.

"There's a book on poisons in the library," I pointed out. "Half the household used it in writing their detective stories." Good manners prevented my adding that he himself possessed the necessary knowledge, but it was impossible to keep the thought out of my mind. It was also borne in upon me that we were forced to take his word for it when he said that he had turned over all of his poisons; then, there was that bottle of chloral which had disappeared after Sally's death, and, also, anyone might have taken a small quantity of cyanide from the can before Tony discovered it.

We locked all the drugs in the chest with the weapons, and, to prevent any possible entry without our knowledge, I sealed the edges with paper tape.

When I returned to the library I found Jimmy deep in gloomy meditation.

"I'm puzzled, Phil," he admitted, "damnably puzzled. The deeper we get into this affair, the murkier it grows. The more facts we learn, the worse off we find ourselves. Take this matter of insanity. You'd think that would prove a help. I Instead, it's a complication. If we accept the theory that one of the Conroys has gone insane and is murdering the others, the search is narrowed down, it's true, but whom do we have on our list of suspects? Only three women, and Mark Dietrich, who strikes me as the least likely of the crowd."

"Why do you say that?" I asked with interest.

"Mark's the wrong type. I mean for our insanity theory, of course. If ever I saw a man who's basically and cold-ly sane, he is that man. Even if he were mad, I couldn't imagine him committing murder in this fantastic fashion. Could you?"

"On second thought, I couldn't."

"That leaves us with Lucia, Judith, and Aunt Hagar."

"Unless we consider Lee," I suggested, and he nodded.

"You mean he murdered 'Berto, then wrote that threat against himself to turn suspicion in some other direction? It's possible, of course. On the face of it, that theory is more plausible than any other. But still . . . I'm not sat-isfied."

I knew what was troubling him, the memory of Lee's face, sick with horror and surprise, as he listened to the reading of that threat. He had seemed half-crazed with fear—or had it been only clever pretense?

"Hang it all!" Jimmy burst out suddenly. "Even the clews are no help. I've been studying that ridiculous *Chapter Two,* and it doesn't tell us a thing." It was the first time I had thought of the internal evidence contained in the paper itself, and I listened with interest as Jimmy lifted the yellow sheet from the desk. "This is the same sort of paper used for the other stories, so that doesn't help us. It was written on the old Remington in there." He nodded toward the door which opened into the stationery closet. "Somebody slipped down and did the typing this morning, after you and I had gone to bed."

"Are you sure?"

'"Dead sure. I looked over the machine last night, and the keys were grimy. Since then, they've been carefully cleaned."

"To eliminate finger-prints?"

"Exactly." He returned to the paper. "This is very short, and could have been typed in five, ten minutes at the most. The walls of the closet are thick enough to prevent any sound reaching upstairs."

"How about the style," I asked, "does that indicate anything?"

"Nothing at all. It's obviously modeled on 'Berto's story, but done rather badly. Also, it's full of errors, both in punctuation and spelling. Which means either it was typed by some one who is not in the habit of writing, or by some one who is deliberately disguising his proficiency."

"Or her proficiency," I added, and he nodded gloomily.

"That's possible, of course. Also, it's possible that it's someone's idea of a joke."

"Then you don't believe Lee is in any danger?"

"I can't believe he's in danger. It's too absurd. If you subtract the murderer, there are still ten of us left to watch over him. And even if there weren't, what possible power could persuade him to go up to the tomb?"

"None, of course."

Jimmy put his hands to his eyes and rose with a sigh of weariness. "In any case, I'm too tired to do any more thinking to-night. I'm going to send the family to bed, and keep watch over Lee."

"You'll do nothing of the sort," I told him firmly. "You've had less than two hours sleep out of the last thirty-six, and in ten minutes you'll collapse. I'll watch over Lee."

In the end, he was forced to agree. It was arranged that Lee take Jimmy's bed in our room, which was at the front of the house; Jimmy moved into Tony's room, directly across the square central hall, while Tony took Lee's at the back.

Since it is important, in view of what happened later, I shall append a sketch of the second floor with the arrangement of sleeping quarters for that night. It will be seen that Doug's room was across the small hall from ours, with a bath in between. Mark and Connie were next to him, Tony slept beyond, and Judith was on the others side of the rear hall, with Aunt Hagar in the front bedroom at that end. All of the rear rooms looked out upon the gallery. Judith's, Tony's, and Doug's had French doors; but Mark's room had no doors opening on to the gallery, only two windows, a fact which made a grim difference later on. Lucia and Mrs. Prill slept on the third floor, and Henry Harker occupied his usual room outside of the house.

Before going to bed, the family assembled in the square hall on the second floor at the head of the stairs. Here, there were chairs and a comfortable cushioned divan grouped in front of an open fireplace; and here, since the evenings had grown chill, we had gathered every night for a glass of mulled wine. This was an old Conroy custom; and I had found it very pleasant, and conducive to sleep.

Prill always mixed the brew, which was cunningly compounded of claret, lemon peel and spices. Just before

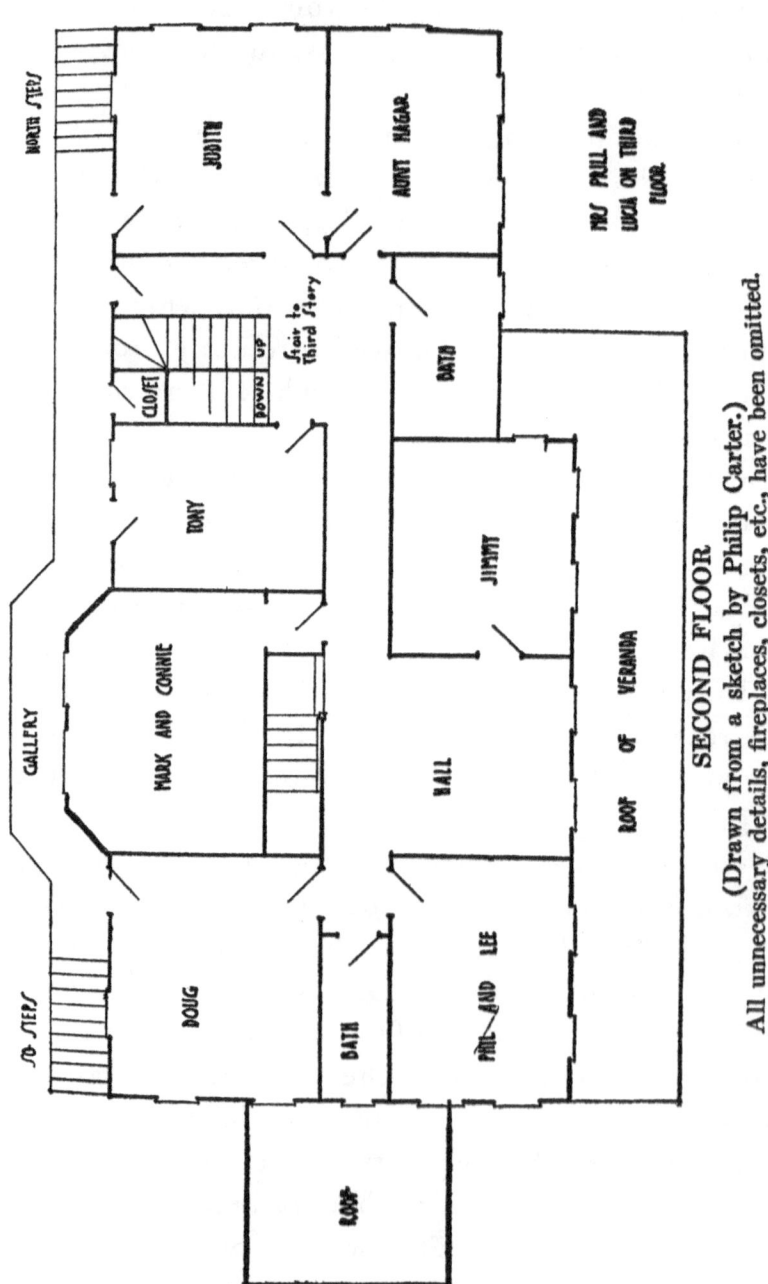

SECOND FLOOR

(Drawn from a sketch by Philip Carter.)

All unnecessary details, fireplaces, closets, etc., have been omitted.

bedtime it was brought up from the kitchen and placed in the coals of the upper fireplace to heat. As it began to steam, sending out a tantalizing odor of cinnamon and clove, the different members of the Conroy clan appeared, in pajamas and bathrobes, to sit cozily around the hearth, sipping and chatting. This had been our nightly routine; and now, in the face of disaster, we clung to it all the more firmly because it seemed to give us a little hold on the realities of life.

It was Tony who brought the kettle up from the kitchen that night, and Judith who added the sugar. Doug watched over the boiling, and Mark passed the tray. All of us accepted cups, except Aunt Hagar, who was allowed only a little port at dinner by her doctor, and Lee, whose habit it was to scorn the brew as "hot lemonade," and sulk because he was permitted nothing stronger.

Before going to bed, Jimmy inspected our room, locking the two windows which opened on to the veranda roof, and bolting the shutters. We left only one, a side window, open. In view of what happened later, I shall state that this window not only looked out on a drop of twenty feet but was covered with a heavy screen. There was no key in the door. In fact, there were only three keys on the whole of the upper floor; one for Judith's room, one for Mark's, and one for Aunt Hagar's. All the locks were the same, we found; and as Connie and Aunt Hagar felt safer with locked doors, we took Judith's key.

After Jimmy had gone back to his room, I locked our door upon the inside and placed the revolver on a table close by the head of my bed. These preparations seemed to cheer Lee, who had recovered some measure of self-control. Doug had talked to him, as he himself described it, "like a Dutch uncle," promising to watch in his room, across the hall, for the rest of the night, and pointing out the absurdity of Lee's supposing that anyone could get at him and force him to go up on the hill. Lee would not have listened, I think, to any other member of the family; but Doug's very lack of humor and imagination, his sturdy dependability, were subtly comforting. It was not until we climbed into our beds and the lights were out that his borrowed courage began to fail.

There was a period, of perhaps five minutes, during which we lay listening to the dismal drum of rain upon the roof, the faint, rustling hiss of water, running down to the river—and the darkness seemed slowly to become full of an evil menace.

Lee asked in a low tone: "Do you believe in ghosts?"

"Of course not," I snapped.

He tried to laugh. "Oh, I'm not serious. It's just that Malinda used to tell us, when we were kids, about a spook that hung around graveyards and tombs. Its arms were two yards long. It didn't have any head. And when it called, you *had* to follow."

That was not a thought for him to fall asleep on, and I told him so, sharply.

"I suppose you want me to think about Santa Claus," he said with bitter humor.

Those were the last words I was ever to hear from Lee Conroy.

Five hours later, at two o'clock, I woke, with the sound of a shot and a scream ringing in my ears, to discover the bed across the room was empty. Lee was gone.

CHAPTER 14
Lee is Found

Upon first waking I snapped on the bedside light, but it took a little time for my dulled brain to realize that Lee was not there. Heavy with sleep, I stumbled across the room to the door. It was still locked, and the key was missing.

By that time my mind began to clear and I caught various sounds in the hall outside. Truffles was barking. There was a muffled pounding and Jimmy's voice urging some one to unlock his door. I could hear footsteps in the hall, and Mark's deep voice calling, "What's the matter?" Again the sounds were blotted out by Truffles' sharp bark.

I abandoned my search for the key and ran to one of the front windows; as I threw it open I noticed, half unconsciously, that it was locked on the inside, exactly as I had left it, and that the bolt was still shot across the shutter. The veranda roof was wet and slippery, but I managed to drag myself along until I reached the window into the upper hall. It was then that my life was actually endangered, for when I pounded upon the glass Jimmy Lane approached with a pistol. Fortunately he recognized me, threw up the window, and I climbed inside.

All of this takes time to write. Actually, it covered less than four minutes.

The square upper hall was a scene of violent confusion. Jimmy Lane was there with Mark, Lucia and Mrs. Prill; Judith arrived a moment later, staggering with sleepiness. As a matter of fact, all of us were like patients coming out from under ether, dizzy and stupid.

Almost immediately, Jimmy demanded: "Where's Lee?"

"He's gone," I stammered.

There was a cry of horror from Lucia: "Gone?"

And simultaneously from Judith: "Where's Aunt Hagar? She isn't in her room."

"And Tony?"

"Call Doug," Jimmy ordered.

It was then we realized that Doug's door was closed, and that Truffles was barking and scratching upon the panels in an attempt to enter.

We hurried across the hall and threw open the door. Inside, the lights were blazing, the French windows wide open, disclosing the rain-swept gallery beyond. In the midst of a shining pool upon the gallery floor, a figure in a plum-colored dressing gown was sprawled grotesquely. It was Aunt Hagar Conroy.

Mark was the first to reach her. "It's only a faint," he announced, relieved, and she stirred, opened her eyes, and struggled to speak.

"Hill," she managed to croak. "Tomb."

Almost at the same moment, Tony called sharply from above: "Mark! Phil! Come here!"

We raced down the slippery steps which led from the gallery to the ground, and up the muddy path toward the tomb. On the hill we found Tony bending over the body of Lee Conroy, which was lying upon the steps, face downward, arms extended; there was no movement except a stream of blood which dripped slowly from level to level of the glistening white marble and disappeared in the sodden grass below.

I think the shock sent all of us a little mad. In my own case, everything went black for a moment, then blazed with a sudden, almost unbearable brightness. There was a roaring in my ears, but through it I heard Tony's voice repeating, over and over, "He was like that when I found him. Just like that." And my own, asking, stupidly, "Why did he come up *here?* Why?"

Only Jimmy Lane kept his head. "Find Harker," he ordered, and I was starting down the steps toward the hill path when I discovered Doug.

He was dressed in pajamas and dressing gown, covered by a dark raincoat. It was this last which, blending with the shadows cast by the shrubbery across the steps of the tomb, had prevented us from seeing him sooner. There was a pistol lying close beside the relaxed fingers of his right hand. He was bleeding profusely from an ugly gash across his forehead and down one cheek. Although he was unconscious, he was still breathing.

While Tony and the Doctor carried the inert Doug down to the house and Jimmy examined Lee's body, I routed out Henry Harker.

He had, apparently, slept through all the hullabaloo, for I was forced to go in and shake him awake. With his assistance, we carried Lee's body into the tomb and laid it upon the improvised bier beside that of 'Berto Patri.

We did not linger in the crypt, but I still have an indelible picture in my mind of the square, white-pillared room with the two sheeted figures, and, beyond, the bronze door that marked the resting place of Nathan Conroy.

On our return to the house, I noticed that Jimmy was carefully carrying some object wrapped in his handkerchief; but as he offered no explanation I asked for none.

We found Aunt Hagar entirely recovered. She had changed her plum-colored garments for a black silk robe, in which she looked more than ever, like that sinister female, Lady Macbeth.

Mrs. Prill, with her usual imperturbability, was building the fire, while Tony comforted Lucia, whose distress was scarcely deeper than Jimmy Lane's.

Jimmy had never really liked Lee, but now he blamed himself with intense bitterness for the boy's death. "I should have watched more carefully," he mourned. "But who could dream he'd go up to the tomb, after that warning?"

"Nobody," I snapped, trying to hide from myself the sick horror that overcame me when I remembered Lee's words: *a sort of spook . . . when it calls, you have to follow.* Nonsense, of course. The superstition of Negroes and of children. And yet . . .

All of us had, by now, donned dry clothing. A motley crew we were, dressed in anything and everything from knickers to bathrobes. Huddled around the hearth of the upper hall, we were like survivors around a campfire on a lonely beach.

The Doctor came out of Doug's room and called Mrs. Prill to take his place. "He's still unconscious," he informed us. "In addition to the blood he lost from that cut, he's been struck upon the back of the head."

"Any fracture?" Jimmy asked quickly.

"No; apparently there's just a very slight concussion. I've put on cold compresses and taken some stitches in the cut. He played into luck there," he added. "The knife plowed across the brow and down the cheek but was deflected by the bone above the eye. He missed blindness by a miracle."

"What sort of knife would you say had been used?"

Mark looked puzzled. "That's what I can't make out. Whatever it was, must have been as sharp as a razor. The wound is as clean as though it had been cut by a surgical instrument."

"Perhaps it was," Jimmy suggested. "How about this?" He produced the object he had carried down the hill and held it out, still in the handkerchief, for Mark's inspection. It was an oddly shaped knife of the finest steel.

"My God!" For the first time the Doctor betrayed real emotion. "That's a scalpel from my bag!"

"I thought so. How does it happen you didn't turn it over to me this evening?"

"I'd forgotten it," Mark said, with an appearance of frankness. "When I looked through my bag tonight, my mind was entirely on drugs. I haven't had occasion to use this for months." He glanced up curiously. "Where did you find it?"

"At the foot of the steps, near Lee's body. Do you think it was used to kill him?"

"It's quite possible," Mark said thoughtfully. "The blade is small, but I think his throat was cut while he was unconscious."

"Unconscious?"

"Yes. When I looked at the body I found a bruise at the base of the skull. I thought, at the time, it was the point where his head hit the steps when he fell. But after examining Doug, I believe Lee was struck down before his throat was cut."

"Which explains why he made no outcry, I suppose," Jimmy mused, then sighed, "Oh, well, we may learn more when Doug comes to himself. In the meantime," he was carefully wrapping the scalpel in his handkerchief again, "I'll keep this for the police. They'll want to examine it for finger-prints."

"They'll find mine, of course," Mark pointed out.

"Not if you haven't handled it for months."

"I didn't say that. I said I hadn't used it for months. It's quite possible in going through my bag I handled it unconsciously."

"Quite possible," Jimmy agreed, in a colorless voice; and, as Mark glanced at him sharply: "Do you know when it could have been taken?"

"It might have been taken any time to-night. After going through the bag for drugs, I left it on the table, here in the hall."

For a time Jimmy stared at the bag as though musing on its part in the scheme of things, then he swung back to the group by the fire. "If we are ever going to get this straight, all of us had better tell what we know. Suppose you begin, Aunt Hagar, and give us your story."

The old lady looked grimly pleased at the preference. She was seated in the huge wing chair by the fire, with Truffles lying spatchcock at her feet. Her sharp old face with its jet-black hair was now visible, now shadowed, by the projecting wing. The play of light gave her an odd appearance, alternately sprightly and fear and sorrow which wracked the rest of the family seemed to have touched her. She accepted Lee's murder as she had accepted the murder of 'Berto, with monstrous relish, as though it were a screen play which was being unrolled for her amusement. Her first words were delivered in a tone of complete and heartless satisfaction:

"This is really getting exciting!" And, at Lucia's horrified protest: "There's no use your shushing me, Lucia Conroy. Lee was nothing but a sot and a wastrel, as bad with women as 'Berto. Maybe worse. You ought to thank your stars he died before he had a chance to disgrace us all."

"Please," Jimmy broke in, "don't keep us waiting. We're all anxious to know what it was you saw that made you scream and faint."

His artful picturing of the group as an eager audience turned Aunt Hagar from the theme of Lee's worthlessness to the saga of her evening, which started with a detailed description of her going to bed.

"After Judith brought my thermos of hot milk, and my glasses, and a book for me to read, in case I didn't sleep, I dozed off and didn't wake up till five minutes of two. I know it was that time because I looked at the clock. Besides, I always wake at two and have a cup of hot milk. I was starting to pour it out when I remembered that Doug had said he was going to sit up all night and watch over Lee. I thought a cup of something hot would be just what he needed, so I put on my bathrobe and slippers and went down the hall."

"Was Truffles with you?"

"No. I left him asleep under my bed. I went down the hall to Doug's room, but the door was closed."

"That's odd," I exclaimed. "He was going to leave it open."

"It was closed," Aunt Hagar repeated, "and locked. I knocked, very softly, so as not to disturb anyone. When he didn't answer, it worried me, so I went back to my room for the key to my door."

"Then the key that's in Doug's lock is yours!" Jimmy exclaimed. "At least that clears up something." He reached into his pocket and brought forth an envelope, carefully folded. "This," he said, "contains another key, which I found in the pocket of Lee's dressing gown."

"Lee's?"

"Yes. Confusing, isn't it? It must be the key to Judith's room, which Phil took to lock their door. Now we find it in Lee's pocket. Oh, well, we'd better not stop to speculate on that now." He turned back to Aunt Hagar. "Did you find the lights on in Doug's room?"

"No, it was dark as a pocket. First I thought Doug had fallen asleep in his chair, but when I turned on the light I saw he was gone."

All of us were leaning forward now, listening intently; and she seemed to gather our attention and enjoy it as she might enjoy the perfume from a bouquet of flowers.

"The French doors were open on to the gallery," she continued, "and everything was blowing about. I was starting over to close them, when there was a call from the hill, and, almost immediately, a pistol shot. By that time, I'd run out on the gallery and was looking up toward the tomb. I saw Lee lying dead on the steps—only then, I didn't know it was Lee, nor that he was dead."

"Did you see Doug?"

"Yes; he was lying at one side, near the foot of the steps. And . . ." her voice rose in shrill excitement, "I saw something bending over him."

"Something?"

She nodded. "I mean exactly that. Some *thing*. I couldn't make out whether it was man or woman. All I saw was a shadowy shape in a sort of cloak that flapped in the wind."

"Did you see where it came from?" Jimmy pressed, and she bestowed upon him a slightly malicious smile. "You won't believe it when I tell you. It came down from the tomb."

CHAPTER 15
THE CALL

In the face of the most rigorous questioning, Aunt Hagar still clung to her story. She had seen that figure, she insisted, and it had come down the steps from the portico of the tomb. In the end, Jimmy Lane dropped the subject, fearing—as he told me later—that she might be led by her fondness for attention to embroider the truth; if, indeed she had not already done so.

The rest of her tale was brief. The dreadful scene she had glimpsed on the hill had been such a shock that she had fainted. The next thing she remembered was coming to herself on the rain-drenched floor of the gallery with the family crowding about her.

Tony's evidence followed. I think all of us had cherished the hope that the figure which Aunt Hagar's imagination had pictured as coming from the tomb was really Tony. But his story, if true, completely exploded that theory.

"I was in bed," he began, "when I heard Doug's yell and then a shot from the hill."

"Were you asleep?" Jimmy demanded.

"Yes . . . no . . ." He hesitated. "I'm not quite sure. I'd been awake a little while before, but I may have dozed off."

"You're certain you recognized Doug's voice?"

"Yes; certain. I'd turned on the light and was half out of bed when I heard Aunt Hagar scream. I grabbed a bathrobe and put it on while I ran out through the French windows to the gallery—" He broke off. "Perhaps I ought to explain that the door from my room into the hall was locked. I'm hanged if I know how it got that way. It was standing half open when I went to bed, and there wasn't even a key in the lock."

He was speaking the truth about that. At least, there had been no key in his door earlier in the evening, when I searched the upper hall. For that matter, there had been none in Jimmy's door, either, and yet he, too, had been locked in.

"My one idea was to get up on the hill and see what the shooting was about. I heard all of you moving around in the hall and thought you'd be after me. I ran out on the gallery and down the north steps, then cut along the back of the house. By the time I reached the hill path I realized the rest of you weren't following. I didn't relish charging up the hill alone, so I decided to get Henry. But his door was locked, and although I knocked fit to rouse the dead I couldn't waken him. Finally I gave it up, and started up the hill full speed. When I got to the top, the first thing I saw was Lee's body lying under the light, in the middle of the steps."

"Did you see any sign," Jimmy searched for words, and decided upon a direct quotation from Aunt Hagar, "did you see 'a shadowy shape'?"

"No; just Lee—although I think I saw Doug, too, without realizing it. He was merely a dark spot, you understand, lying in the shadow of the shrubbery." Mark, who followed Tony, testified that he had been wakened by Doug's call and the pistol shot. Without awakening Connie, he had donned his bathrobe and slippers, unlocked his door and run into the hall.

"Our room has no French windows," he added, "or I should have gone out to the gallery first. When I reached the hall, Truffles was just running down from Aunt Hagar's room, barking and growling. I heard Jimmy pounding on his door and calling that it was locked. There wasn't any key in sight, so I went back and got the one from my room. As I was fitting it into the lock, Lucia and Prillie came down the hall. After I let you out, Jimmy, Phil climbed in the window from the veranda roof, Judith came from her room, and we all went out to the gallery."

Jimmy turned to Connie. "Just when did you waken?"

"Oh, not until everyone was out on the gallery. The racket woke me up, but I was so dizzy I couldn't think. By the time I got out, Judith and Lucia were helping Aunt Hagar into Doug's room, and the rest of you were on your way up the hill." Her speech was glib enough, but her eyes were shifting unhappily. Something was worrying Connie, I decided, worrying her badly. If Jimmy noticed he gave no sign; instead he turned to Lucia, who began quickly:

"When Aunt Hagar screamed, I jumped out of bed and put on my dressing gown. I could hear noises downstairs, Truffles barking, Jimmy pounding. . . ." Like Connie, she was speaking glibly, as though she had something on her mind which she was anxious not to betray in her speech. "I hurried down to the second floor and joined the rest of you."

"Where did you meet Mrs. Prill?"

"She met me coming up the back stairs." A voice came from the open door of Doug's room, where Mrs. Prill had evidently been listening. "I couldn't sleep, and wanted to do a little Bible reading to compose my mind. I'd left my Testament in the kitchen, and when I went down to get it I didn't go right back up again. Thought I'd stop and make myself a cup of hot chocolate on the electric grill. Just as I was pouring out the condensed milk I heard a shot."

"You didn't hear either the call or the scream?"

"No; but that's not surprising. I'm a trifle inclined toward deafness." That was true enough. We had all had occasion to notice it. "The shot frightened me so I was completely kerflummoxed. I got hold of myself, and ran up the back stairs, where I found Miss Lucia just coming down from the third floor. That's all I know." She went back into Doug's room, and Jimmy turned his attention to Judith.

"What can you tell us?" he asked gently, and I noticed for the first time the truly appalling change that had come over Judith Conroy. The emotional upset occasioned by 'Berto's death, the night before, had caused her to break into hysterical speech; that mood had passed. Since this second tragedy, some fear or knowledge seemed to render her almost dumb.

Jimmy was forced to repeat his question twice before she realized he was addressing her; yet her story, when it finally came, differed very little from that of the others.

She, too, had been awakened by the scream or the shot; in the natural confusion of the moment she was not sure which. She, too, had brought herself out of sleep with difficulty, and put on a dressing gown.

"Was your door locked?" Jimmy inquired, and she shook her head.

"No; I let Phil have my key. But I locked the French windows that open on to the gallery. At least," her face wore a puzzled look, "I'm almost certain I locked them. Yet when I woke up they were unlocked."

"That's strange," Jimmy mused. But before he could question her further, Mrs. Prill called from the door of Doug's room:

"He's coming to himself now, Dr. Mark. Will you come in?"

Doug was lying in a huge sleigh bed of dark mahogany, which was pulled close to the old-fashioned fireplace. His eyes were heavy and his face almost as pale as the bandage which covered his cheek and forehead; even his lips were blue, from loss of blood; otherwise, he seemed physically none the worse for his experience. Mentally, it was a different matter. He was plainly suffering from shock. His face wore a dazed expression, and he continually raised his hands to his eyes as though they were troubling him. As we entered, he half drew himself erect and broke into hurried speech:

"What happened?" he demanded. "Tell me, what happened?"

Mark crossed to the bed, put his fingers over Doug's wrist, then nodded to Jimmy. "I think he may safely talk."

Jimmy sat down upon a low chair by the bed, his gray eyes almost on a level with Doug's tortured blue. "Lee has been killed," he said gravely. "We found him dead—on the steps of the tomb. You were lying nearby, unconscious. Some one had struck you on the back of the head, and then slashed you across the face."

"Lee—dead!" Doug dropped back against the pillows, and lay, eyes closed; "I remember now," he said slowly. "It's all coming back."

"Do you feel able to tell us about it? Or would you rather wait until you're stronger?"

"I'll tell you now. My head hurts like the devil, but it's clearing." He opened his eyes again and burst out: "The dreadful part of it is I'm to blame for Lee's death! I said I'd keep watch, and I fell asleep."

"What time was that?"

"Shortly after midnight. As I sat down to watch, the clock in the hall struck twelve."

"Did you have the lights on?"

"I did at first. I was in that big chair near the window, where I could look out at the tomb, and at the same time keep an eye on the door to Lee's room. I had my pistol handy on the table beside me. Oh, I know, I ought to have handed it over when you asked for weapons," he added guiltily, "but it seemed to me I could do more good by holding it back. I'm a crack shot, you know, and in case of trouble—"

"Never mind," Jimmy grunted, "go on."

"For a few minutes I sat there watching. Then it occurred to me that if anyone was coming after Lee he wouldn't be likely to show up while my light was on. The best way to catch him was in the dark, so I snapped off the lamp—and almost at once my eyes began to get heavy. I tried to fight it off, but before I knew it I was asleep."

"What woke you?"

Doug said slowly: "It was a strange sort of call from the hill."

"You mean it actually called Lee's name?"

"No, it wasn't a call in that sense." Doug seemed to grope awkwardly for the right word to convey his thoughts. "It was an eerie sort of wail. Low, but awfully penetrating. It went up and down, then fell in a sort of minor cadence at the end. Like—like— He threw out his hands in a gesture of helplessness. "I'll be darned if it was like anything I've ever heard."

"How many times was it repeated?"

"Can't say, exactly. I've an idea I heard it several times before I was actually awake. First it seemed to be coming from the hill. I thought it was the wind. Then there was quite an interval of silence, and I was dozing off again, when I heard it closer, apparently in the shrubbery at the end of the house. That made me change my mind about its being the wind. I decided it must be a bird."

"Do you still think so?"

Doug shuddered. "After what's happened, I don't dare think."

"What did you do next?"

"For a minute I sat paralyzed, then I really woke up and began to take the thing seriously. I glanced at my watch—

it has a radium dial—and I saw it was one-fifty-two. Then I got to my feet, walked over to the window at the end of the room and looked out. But I couldn't see anything. The shrubbery was as dark as pitch. Besides, the roof of Henry Harker's room cuts off a good deal of the view. While I was there, the call was repeated. This time it seemed to be moving away, toward the hill again. I was just deciding to waken one of you when I happened to look out the French window at the back."

"Wait," Jimmy said. "Was your room still dark?"

"Yes; that made it easier to see outside. The rain was still coming down, but I could see the tomb overhead, and some of the light was reflected on the path between the trees. That's how I saw Lee running up the hill."

"You mean you actually saw him?" Mark asked.

"As plain as I see you. He was in pajamas and a dark dressing gown, with some sort of slippers or moccasins on his feet, and he was rushing madly up the hill, through the rain, toward that hellish tomb."

"What did you do?" At least two of us asked that question.

"I grabbed up my raincoat, rushed out on the gallery and down the steps. I suppose I should have called someone," he stopped to explain, "but I give you my word, I never thought of it. I'd a vague idea he was walking in his sleep. I'd read that people who are awakened too suddenly sometimes go off the deep end, so I didn't want to startle him by yelling out. I just went after—full speed."

"With the pistol?"

"Yes. I'd picked it up when I first went to the window." Doug paused, then continued slowly, as though, approaching some crisis, he wished his account to be exact: "When you're climbing the hill you can't see the tomb because of the trees, and I lost sight of Lee from the time I left the gallery until I reached the top of the path. The last part I clawed up through the shrubbery in a short-cut that brought me out right in front of the tomb. The center of the steps was brightly lighted, and Lee was lying almost at my feet. He was all sprawled out, with his head hanging, and the blood—"

"We know," Jimmy said quickly, for it was plain that Doug was on the verge of collapse. "Never mind about that. Did you see anyone else?"

"No; just Lee. I saw at once that he was dead. I gave a yell. Just then something hit me on the back of the head. I seemed to hear a pistol shot. I suppose I instinctively pulled the trigger, and the gun went off in my hand. Then everything turned black, and that's the last I knew until I woke up in this room,"

"My word. . . ." Jimmy expelled his breath with a little whistling sigh. "What a hideous nightmare!" He rose and walked over to the side window, where he stood frowning into the darkness. "It was here you heard the call?"

"Yes. To the left. Under the window of Lee's room."

"And you didn't hear it, Phil?"

I shook my head. "No. But I wouldn't have heard the crack of doom. I was miles deep in sleep."

"About this business of sleep," Mark exclaimed suddenly, "I've been puzzling over it, and I've come to a conclusion."

"I can guess what it is," Jimmy said, "You think the mulled wine we had last night was doped."

"Sure of it. Nothing else would account for our sleeping so heavily."

"When you went through your medicine kit earlier in the evening, did you miss any morphine or codeine?"

"No. My usual supply was all there. In any case, I don't believe that was used. I'm sure it was chloral."

"Chloral?" Jimmy started. "Then that bottle wasn't destroyed after Sally's death." He was silent for a moment;

all of us, I think, were considering the dire possibilities this opened up. "How much of the stuff was there left? Have you any way of estimating?"

"Only roughly. But there was enough to do a good deal of damage."

Doug had been listening eagerly. "Then if the wine was doped last night, that's why I fell asleep. You've taken a load off my mind." His face showed such relief that I realized his shame at having betrayed his trust had been as great as his sorrow at Lee's death.

"Yes," Jimmy was still cogitating. "I should say there's no doubt but that we were doped. Everyone complained of dizziness upon waking, and the only two who didn't drink the wine—Aunt Hagar and Mrs. Prill—were the two who were awake when the shot was fired."

"Hold on!" I protested. "Harker didn't drink any of that wine, and he slept through the whole thing."

"That's not surprising," Mark told us. "Henry's naturally a heavy sleeper at all times."

"Lee didn't take any, either," Doug pointed out.

Jimmy nodded. "That's probably why he was able to hear the call—while Phil slept through it."

"And how those bedroom doors were locked without our hearing anything," Mark contributed.

"Do you mean to say the doors were locked?" Doug asked.

"Some of them," Jimmy told him. "Judith's was open, but Tony and I were both locked in, and Aunt Hagar found yours shut fast."

"It must have been locked with the key from our room," I said. "There were only three on the upper floor; Mark and Aunt Hagar had the other two."

"You're sure you left the key in the lock when you went to bed?" Jimmy asked, and I nodded.

"Positive."

"Then, unless some one turned it from the other side—which seems unlikely—Lee must have let himself out. You'll remember we found the key in his pocket." He walked to the little hall which separated Doug's room from the one which Lee and I had occupied, and studied the doors intently. "If Lee was answering that call," he said slowly, "he probably went out through Judith's room."

"How do you figure that?" Doug inquired.

"Because the doors and French windows downstairs were all found locked on the inside. On this floor, your room and Tony's were both locked, also the rear hall door, but Judith tells us she found her French windows unlocked when she woke up."

"But why should he have chosen that way?"

"Hanged if I know," irritably. "Any more than I can tell you why he should lock all the doors in the hall, with the exception of Judith's. It's all utterly mad . . . as mad as the question of what took him up to the tomb."

"Could it have been hypnotism?" It was Doug who suggested this, and Jimmy looked annoyed.

"For God's sake, don't bring that up! Things are murky enough now without going in for fantasy. Svengali himself couldn't put a spell on a sleeping man that would take him up a hill through the rain."

"Mightn't the idea have been suggested to his mind before he went to sleep?" Doug was plainly loath to relinquish his theory. "I've heard that a clever hypnotist can order a subject to do something at a given hour, and he'll do it even though the hypnotist isn't there."

"I've heard so, too," Jimmy agreed. "But I've never believed it." He sank into a reverie that held him silent for a time, then: "Have you, as a family, any call?" he asked. "I mean a whistle, or a yodel, peculiar to yourselves?"

Doug said: "Of course, as kids, we had all sorts of calls. But none in the least like what I heard last night."

"Did the voice sound like that of a man or, a woman?"

"I don't know." Doug looked desperately puzzled in his attempt to express what was in his mind. "You see, it wasn't— It was scarcely even human."

"You mean it sounded like an animal?"

"No, not like an animal, either. The intonation was wrong. I mean, an animal doesn't have any expression in the sound it makes. This was eerie, and inhuman, but it seemed to have some thought back of it. It was," again he groped for words, "it was the sort of sound you could imagine being made by a crazy ghost."

Ghost. That was the word I had been dreading. Ever since our grisly discovery of Lee's body on the hill, I had been haunted by the words he had spoken in that darkened bedroom, *a spook that calls you.* Incredible that a silly tale of Malinda's could have anything to do with this tragedy. And yet I found myself telling the story. When I had finished, Doug nodded:

"Yes," he said, "I remember Malinda used to tell us ghost stories when the family was away. Naturally, we had nightmares, and when the grown-ups found out, they put a stop to it. Lee was the youngest, and I suppose the whole business made an extra deep impression on him."

"Do you remember this particular story?" Jimmy asked.

"There wasn't any particular story. Malinda just made them up as she went along. But she did have a pet 'hant' that came out of graves and called. When you heard it you had to go. I say!" He broke off in outraged protest. "You're not taking all that stuff seriously? It couldn't be true, you know."

"Anything can be true." Jimmy's voice was despairing. "After what I've seen and heard to-night, I'm ready to believe in witches, and ghouls, and banshees, hags that ride on broomsticks, and spirits that rise from the vasty deep. What else will explain that 'shadowy figure' Aunt Hagar saw? That call? And the utter, incredible insanity of Lee's going up to the tomb?"

Doug turned and stared at him. "What figure?" he asked, and I was reminded that he had not heard the testimony of the other members of the family. "What figure do you mean?"

"Aunt Hagar saw something," Jimmy explained wearily, "which she swears came out of the tomb and bent over you as you lay near Lee's body." He stopped as Doug broke into a peak of laughter.

"I can't help it!" he choked. "'Member what Aunt Hagar said on the hill—'Plenty of corpses . . . And plenty of chills'!" His shoulders were shaking, his breath coming in gasps. He fell back on the pillow. The Doctor hurried forward, and I ran for Mrs. Prill.

Jimmy joined me in the hall. "He's all right," he said. "Just an hysterical attack from too much talk after that blow on the head." He looked toward the door with an expression of grave perplexity. "Do you know, Phil, it wasn't only Lee who was frightened by that spook of Malinda's. In spite of his protestations, I believe our brave-boy Doug is scared to within an inch of his life."

CHAPTER 16
A MALLET OF CHILLED STEEL

At daybreak Jimmy and I put on oilskins and went up the hill to the tomb, where we found that the force of the rain had washed away all signs of blood; only the outline of Lee's body, where Jimmy had marked it the night before, was visible on the white steps. Nothing could be learned from footprints. Mark, Harker, Jimmy and I had all been on the hill, besides Lee, Doug, Tony and the mysterious murderer. The prints of our strangely assorted footgear, ranging from bedroom slippers to rubber boots, were hopelessly intermingled.

We made one important discovery: in a puddle, about twenty feet from the spot where Doug had fallen, we found the instrument that had struck him down. It was a small, round-headed mallet of chilled steel, with a metal handle less than six inches long, which was usually kept in a closet off the gallery. About the head and handle was wrapped a water-soaked handkerchief.

"Efficient," Jimmy observed, as he swung it in a circle through the air. "Darned efficient. It's small but heavy, and so well balanced that you can take perfect aim."

"But why the handkerchief?"

"At first blush I'd say it was to prevent finger-prints. But why it should be wrapped around the head—" He

broke off, examining the square of blue-bordered linen.
"The initials are L. C."

"Lee Conroy," I said. "He had that handkerchief in the
room last night before we went to bed. I think he put it in
the pocket of his dressing gown."

"Speaking of pockets—this fits into one nicely." He
slipped the mallet into the pocket of his raincoat. "It
could have been concealed easily enough, and that knife,
too." For a moment longer he searched the shrubbery and
grass, then gave it up and turned his attention to the lock
on the door of the tomb. "There's supposed to be only two
keys," he said thoughtfully, "and I had both of them last
night, but of course it's always possible some one possesses
a duplicate." As he spoke he fitted one of the keys into the
lock. "You're going into the tomb?" I asked.

"We're both going in. It's a nasty job but there's no
escaping it. I won't have any peace of mind until I find out
whether that 'shadowy shape' of Aunt Hagar's has left any
earthly footprints."

With a feeling of sick distaste I followed him through
the door and into the entrance hall, where he turned on
the lights and examined the floor. I had hoped to be spared
the horror of the lower room, but Jimmy was inexorable.
Step by step, he went over the stairs; and foot by foot,
scrutinized the walls, searching for a hidden opening.

The upper room was of marble; the crypt cement. In
neither of them was there so much as a crack to mar the
white expanse. The floors and plastered ceilings were
unbroken.

We swung back the doors of wrought metal, which led
into the inner alcove, and discovered a handsome bronze
sarcophagus, raised from the floor by six claw feet. Here
Jimmy not only examined the walls behind the casket but
even the space beneath. In the end, he shook his head.

"We'll have to find some other explanation for Aunt Hagar's figure, Phil. There's no opening here, nor in the room upstairs. I'm convinced of that."

I had been convinced for some time, and thankfully led the way through the crypt to the stairs. On the bottom step Jimmy paused. I saw that he was looking back at the Latin inscription above the doors. Something about the words seemed to fascinate him.

"'*Non vixit quis post mortem non vivit,*'" he read slowly. "Am I wrong, or can that possibly mean what I think it does?"

"'He hath not lived that lives not after death,'" I translated, and he nodded, a growing horror in his eyes.

"That's what I thought." Slowly his glance traversed the room, passing from the inscribed words to the figures that lay, left and right, upon their biers, starkly outlined under the sheets by the cruel flood of white light from above. Suddenly his hand closed on my arm with a convulsive grip. "Let's get out of here," he gasped. "Let's get out of this abominable place!"

With one accord we swung about and half fled up the stairs.

Once in the outside air, we recovered ourselves. Jimmy locked the doors of the tomb and started at a brisk pace down the hill path beneath the moisture-laden branches of cypress and sycamore, but instead of going into the house he turned off toward Harker's room.

"I want to talk with Harker," he explained. "We've not yet had his version of what happened last night."

The caretaker greeted us with sulky reserve. He was still dressed in the sweater and trousers he had donned when I called him the night before. His boots were damp, and his raincoat hung against the wall, its deep cape steaming from the heat of a Franklin stove.

Jimmy's eyes passed quickly from one object to another, and stopped at a wire key ring which hung by the door. I thought he was going to investigate this; but instead, he dropped into a chair near the stove, and held out his hands to the blaze.

"We came to find out if you could tell us anything new about what happened last night." His tone was friendly, but Harker did not respond; he remained standing in the center of the room, his small eyes darting glances of suspicion and dislike.

"Nothing," he growled. "I went to bed about ten o'clock, and fell right asleep. Didn't know anything more until Mr. Carter, here, woke me up and told me what had happened."

"You're sure you didn't hear anything earlier?"

"Not a thing. I'm a heavy sleeper, and when it's cold I pull the covers round my head. Guess it took you some time to wake me, didn't it, Mr. Carter?"

"Yes; I had to come in and shake you."

"'Come in'?" Jimmy echoed. "You mean the door was unlocked?"

"It was closed but not locked—" I broke off. What was it Tony had said? That he had pounded on Harker's door but it had been locked? "That's strange," I was beginning, when Jimmy threw me a warning glance.

"What are those keys by the door?" he asked.

"Two of 'em are for the dynamo room, and one for the boathouse, then there's keys to this room and the house doors, front and back."

"H'm." Jimmy rose and carefully compared the keys with those which fitted the lock of the tomb; even at a distance I could see there was no resemblance between them. Without comment he quietly slipped the ring into the capacious pocket of his raincoat, which already contained the steel mallet, then turned again to Harker. "Were you surprised when Carter woke you and said there had been another murder?"

"Surprised?" The old man's eyes studied us from beneath their pendulous lids. "No. Can't say I was. I wouldn't be surprised at anything that was to happen in this family."

"Why not?"

"Because they got bad blood in 'em," he snarled. "That Conroy blood they're always bragging about. Proud as Lucifer, the whole lot of 'em. Thinking they're God's anointed, smarter, and better than anyone else; pretending they're above morals and laws. Oh, I've heard 'em talking around the dining table—throwing in French and *I*talian just to show off—making fun of everyone and everything. . . ." He was working himself in a paroxysm of rage, and Jimmy fed the flames.

"There's no doubt they're a brilliant family."

"Brilliant!" Harker fairly spat out the word. "Brilliant? They're crazy, every one of 'em! Crazy as bedlam! Except, maybe, Miss Lucia, there isn't one of 'em that isn't wicked-cruel. Take Dr, Mark. They say he does things for the good of humanity. But what is it he does? He's got a laboratory where he keeps live dogs and monkeys. Gives 'em diseases, then watches 'em die. I heard him tell about it—the rest all listening an' relishing it! Then there's Miss Hagar. Always reading about murder. Told me one day she'd worked out ten different ways of killing me without getting found out. 'Perfect crimes,' she called 'em. The old she-devil!" He was lost in his subject now, the ferocity of his words carrying him forward.

Jimmy was watching with grave intentness. Could it be possible, I wondered, that he was taking the man's words seriously? Couldn't he see that Harker was in abject terror of being accused himself, and was striking out against the Conroy family, blindly, viciously, in order to save his own neck?

"Then there's Miss Judith," he went on. "Always reading those psychology books, and asking questions about her father until I'm ready to go nutty. When did I first notice him being queer? How did he look? How did he talk? Do I think he knew it himself? Things like that. If you ask me, I think she's gone crazy, only nobody's found it out yet. And Mr. Tony's no better."

"But *he* isn't a Conroy."

"Not by blood, but he's been with 'em all his life. And look at the way he acts. Always mooning around. Sitting up nights, and sleeping half the day. So crazy about Miss Lucia he went pretty near out of his head when he found she was going to marry Mr. Doug. I heard how he carried on."

"Most of the big scenes of the Conroy family seem to occur in your vicinity." Jimmy suggested ironically, and Harker snorted:

"I can't help it if the island's so small I'm always hearing things! I just happened to be near when Miss Lucia and Mr. Tony were having it out. She told him he was worthless and lazy, while Mr. Doug, even if he wasn't so smart in other ways, had worked hard and made something of himself. Mr. Tony carried on like a crazy man."

"That was last year," Jimmy pointed out.

"Sure . . . but he isn't over it yet. You've only got to look at him to see that. You know how *I*talians are, treacherous and cruel."

"So you think because Miss Lucia threw him over he's butchering the whole family out of spite?"

"I didn't say that," Harker protested sourly. "You're putting words into my mouth. I just said he was bad as the rest. And Mr. Doug's no better. Always out shooting things and bringing 'em in for me to pick. 'Oh, Harker, old man, would you mind doing this? Would you mind doing that?'" His voice cracked on an imitation of Doug's hearty tones. "Always smiling. Always cheerful. But look at that red hair! If you ever refused, like as not he'd pick you up and crack you acrost his knee like a piece o' kindling."

"Whew!" Jimmy looked at him with a slight grin. "You don't seem to have spared anyone, except Mrs. Prill and Mrs. Dietrich."

"Mrs. Dietrich's all right." Harker's voice held contempt but no rancor. "'Tain't her fault she's married to a Conroy. Guess she's been sorry often enough, the way they all look down on her. But Mrs. Prill—she's the worst of the lot!"

"Prillie!" I exclaimed in surprise.

"*Prillie,*" he mocked. "As pious as a bishop. But if you look at what she reads in her Bible, you'll find it's not the chapters about faith, hope and charity—it's the bloody parts, about death and destruction. If you ask me, she'd as lief cut a throat as bake a pie. And if you don't believe *she* had something to do with what happened last night, go see what it was she hid in the gallery closet less than an hour ago."

Chapter 17
Mrs. Prill Tells a Lie

Jimmy sent me ahead to the library while he investigated the gallery closet, which was a cubby-hole on the second floor used as a repository for tools, fishing tackle, and all the other oddments that lacked a regular storage place. None of the family was down, as yet, and I passed through the empty living room, where the pillows were still strewn about the floor, as they had been the night before, when we received warning of Lee's approaching death. It seemed horrible to realize that the slight indentation in the center of the divan had been made by his weight as he sat, head on hand, listening to the family council. To save Lucia pain, I picked up the pillows and smoothed the couch, then went on to the library, where I occupied myself in building a fire.

Jimmy came in with a bundle under his arm, which he put down upon a chair.

"Prillie is getting breakfast," he told me. "She'll serve us alone, in here."

"Did you find what she had put in the gallery closet?"

"Yes." Instead of explaining, he burst out irascibly: "Good God, Phil, this case grows madder every minute! It's like that wretched game we were playing when 'Berto was killed—blind man's buff. I seem continually to be catching suspects in the dark, but before I can identify

them they slip from my hands." He broke off, exhausted
by his own vehemence, dropped into a seat by the fire, and
stretched his feet toward the blaze. "You asked me what I
found in that closet," he said, in a calmer voice. "It was a
raincoat and a pair of rubbers."

"Malinda's slicker?"

"No; a woman's mackintosh, in heather shades. I've
seen it on one of the girls—Connie, Judith, Lucia. Hanged
if I know which."

"But why should Mrs. Prill hide it? There's nothing
incriminating about a raincoat."

"A raincoat *and* rubbers, both damp."

"You mean—someone may have worn them on the hill
last night?"

"It's possible. Anything's possible in this hellish
affair." He rose to his feet, listened intently, then crossed
the room and threw open the door into the rear hall. Mrs.
Prill was standing on the other side with a loaded tray.

If she had overheard our talk, her face gave no intima-
tion of it. Impassive as ever, she carried her burden to the
table by the fire and began to lay our breakfast.

For a time Jimmy watched her, then: "By the way, Mrs.
Prill," he inquired pleasantly, "who asked you to put that
raincoat in the gallery closet this morning?"

Her hands, busy with the dishes, stopped for a moment,
then resumed their steady movement. "Why, nobody, Mr.
Lane. I hung it there myself."

"Oh, then it's your coat?"

"No," coolly, "it's Miss Judith's. I wore it last night
when I went out in the rain to get some wood." She had
turned away, so that her face was no longer visible; but her
tone was candid. "On the way downstairs to make my chocolate, I remembered there wasn't any wood in the kitchen,
and I'd have to get some. I took Miss Judith's coat. It was
hanging just inside her door. I knew she wouldn't mind."

"I thought you told us you went downstairs to get a
Bible, and that the idea of hot chocolate didn't occur to
you until after you had reached the kitchen."

Her wrinkled eyelids fluttered at that, but she recovered herself quickly.

"Well now, I must have spoken without thinking. What
I really went down for was to make some chocolate. I put
on Miss Judith's coat, and went out to the wood pile—"

"In order to make chocolate on the electric grill?"

"I was just going to explain about that. I made the chocolate on the grill, but the kitchen was cold, so I wanted to
build a fire in the stove to warm myself while I drank it."

"H'm." Jimmy's expression was incredulous, "And after
your promenade through the rain to the wood pile, what
did you do?"

"As I told you, I started making the chocolate."

"Still wearing the raincoat and rubbers?"

"Yes. I wanted to get the milk on to boil before I took
them off. While I was pouring it out I heard the shot, and
ran upstairs."

"You weren't wearing the raincoat when you appeared."

"No. I slipped it off and hung it in the rear hall. This
morning I found the wet rubber was making the place
smell, so I took the coat and rubbers out to the gallery
closet."

"Without stopping to wash off the mud?"

"No . . . yes. . . ." She seemed confused. "That is—
there wasn't time."

"Of course not." Jimmy seemed pleased, for some obscure reason. "Thank you, Mrs. Prill, for clearing up a
point that puzzled me."

"You're welcome, I'm sure." She was plainly relieved at
his acceptance of her explanation, and anxious to be gone.

"What is it?" I asked, when she had left the room.
"Don't you believe her story?"

"About as much as I believe black is white." Jimmy dropped into the chair across the table from me. Picking up a cup of coffee, he began adding lumps of sugar absently. "In the first place, it's all eyewash about her going down to make a cup of chocolate. Last night she said plainly that it was an afterthought. In the second, the firewood is not kept outdoors but in a bin on the back porch. I suppose she didn't know I was on to that domestic detail. Third, those rubbers aren't muddy—they've been carefully wiped off."

"What earthly motive—"

"That," he interrupted, "is the thing we've got to figure out. Motive is at the base of this whole damnable business. With 'Berto we found plenty of reasons for his being killed. None of them very convincing, it's true—yet convincing enough for us to admit them as possibilities. Now, we've got to find a motive that will fit the murder not only of 'Berto but of Sally and Lee as well. And that, my son, is going to take some finding."

"But don't you think the murderer is mad?"

"Oh, as to my, thoughts—I've got lots of beauties." The coffee was making him more cheerful. "Like to hear some of 'em?"

I nodded without speaking, and he went on:

"I think there's no doubt but that the murderer—or murder*ess*—is sane. Last night proved that."

"In what way?"

"Because of Doug's injuries. He was struck on the head immediately after Lee was killed. If the murderer had been a maniac, killing only for insane pleasure, he would almost certainly have cut Doug's throat. What do we find? He not only leaves Doug's throat intact but pads the head of a hammer with a handkerchief in order to strike not too hard a blow. All of which suggests that 'Berto and Lee and

Sally were murdered for a motive that was absent in the case of Doug."

"You mean the inheritance, of course."

"Yes; Doug isn't mentioned in the will, but the deaths of the others would increase the inheritance of the remaining legatees."

"But, good God," I was almost childishly repelled, "no one would kill a girl and two men for such a paltry sum,"

Jimmy sighed. '"Better not make rash statements about what men—and women, too—will do for money," he advised. "Burke and Hare smothered a score of poor wretches in order to sell their miserable carcasses for a few pounds apiece. John Williams, the London murderer, killed a man, his wife, a young boy, and a baby for two guineas. And most of Landru's victims were slaughtered for a few hundred francs. Here, the stakes are higher. According to Lucia, the estate is worth in the neighborhood of a hundred and fifty thousand dollars. That would have given the original seven legatees about twenty-one thousand apiece. With three of them out of the way, the remaining beneficiaries stand to receive thirty-six thousand, an increase of fifteen thousand. Not an amount to be sniffed at, Phil."

"It's inconceivable!" I was trying to envision any one of the remaining legatees—Mark, Lucia, Aunt Hagar and Judith—committing murder for such a sum, for *any* sum.

Jimmy caught my expression and smiled ironically. "Nice pleasant prospect, isn't it, trying to fit any of them into the role? But, there's something about money, or, rather, the lack of money, that turns people into fiends, Phil. Remember that Latin Johnny old Green. used to din into us at college? Plautus, wasn't it? Something about gold persuading many men in many matters to do evil? Well, it's true. True as hell. And, here, you've got a perfect set-up for trouble."

"What do you mean?"

"I mean a brilliant, neurotic family, like the Conroys. Not one of 'em has the slightest idea of how to make money, except Doug, and he's not really of their blood; not one of 'em has the slightest idea how to hang on to money after it's made and yet they've been raised in a careless sort of affluence, with ideas of family importance, and a position that has to be lived up to. In addition to that, each one of them has some sort of interest or ambition that needs money to keep it going. Mark has his laboratory. You heard Connie say he'd take the clothes off her back to buy apparatus. Lucia wants to travel, and enough money to support her while she writes stuff that suits *her* instead of the public. Judith wants everything: freedom, clothes, a chance to snatch a little happiness before it is too late."

"You haven't given any motive for Aunt Hagar."

"Because I can't cook up one offhand. Certainly she doesn't need any more money. She already has enough to take care of her in comfort. The only thing that seems to fit her case is madness."

"But you've just proved the murderer was sane."

"Far from it!" For the first time Jimmy gave me the pale ghost of his impish grin. "I merely presented you with *one* of my brilliant theories. Here's the reverse angle: the murderer is most certainly demented; only a madman would send a warning to his victim, and then take the senseless risk of killing him under our very noses."

"But Doug—" I began, quoting his own argument.

"—was saved because Aunt Hagar's scream frightened the murderer away before he had managed to cut his throat. Instead, the knife slipped and made that slash across his forehead and cheek."

"If we accept the insanity theory," I was mentally checking the list of suspects, "I suppose it takes in everyone of Conroy blood."

"Yes; Aunt Hagar, Lucia, Mark and Judith. I'm also inclined to suspect Harker. He may not be a Conroy; but if he hasn't become slightly cuckoo from living on this island alone for ten years with that tomb, I'll eat my panama."

"He's never shown any signs of violence."

"None of them have, except, possibly, Aunt Hagar. Lots of lunatics go about, unsuspected, for years. They're teaching school. Performing operations. Running banks. *Especially* running banks." (Jimmy had suffered sorely in the recent financial upset.) "And nobody guesses the old brain isn't all there until something, frequently something quite unimportant, brings on a crisis."

"What sort of thing?"

He answered seriously, as though it were a point upon which he had put a great deal of thought. "Something like that discussion of murder we had on the hill. I can imagine an incipient madman—one of the manic-depressive type— being influenced by all that talk about killing. Then, if 'Berto chanced to ask that particular person to help him with his mummery, it might be the one thing needed to throw him, or her, over the borderline into active mania. The idea of turning the silly hoax into reality may have become too fascinating to resist; and that, in turn, may have suggested the horrible humor of continuing the story by murdering Lee."

"That doesn't explain Sally."

"I'm not offering it as an explanation. You asked what might bring on madness, and I gave the talk on the hill as an example."

"Then you don't believe it was Prillie who wore that raincoat last night?" I asked out of a brief and thoughtful silence.

"No. I think she's trying to shield some one."

"Judith?"

He nodded. "Judith. I might as well admit that I've had her in mind for some time. I don't like the way she looked when we were all gathered together in the hall after Lee's death. She could easily have put that raincoat over her nightgown, gone out her French windows and up to the tomb."

"What about that call?"

"Hang the call!" Jimmy's voice was fretful. "I can't, I simply can*not* picture Judith wailing like a blooming banshee up and down hills and under windows. The same thing applies to any other member of the family. If you like, we'll say she doesn't go straight up the hill. She stops in the shrubbery and starts whoo-whooing at Lee. For some reason, which we haven't yet discovered, he responds. He gets up without waking you, lets himself out of the room, and locks the door upon the other side. He then takes the key, locks all the other doors in the hall, and goes out through the French windows of Judith's room. If you say all this is far-fetched," he added, "I'll agree with you enthusiastically. I'm not content with any explanation of those locked doors. But that is really another matter. What we're taking up now is the question of Judith. Suppose we figure that Lee followed her siren song up the hill. If Doug hadn't seen him running up the path alone, I'd think they went up together, but if Judith had been with him Doug would have seen her.

"Let's say she met Lee on the steps of the tomb, struck him on the head with the hammer, and cut his throat. Suppose at that moment she heard Doug running up the path, and hid in the shrubbery. While Doug was bending over the body, she wrapped Lee's handkerchief around the head of the hammer—"

"Why should she have had the handkerchief?"

"She probably took it from the pocket of Lee's dressing gown with the idea of wiping the blood from her hands."

"Speaking of blood, why were there no spots on her raincoat?"

"That," Jimmy said, "probably explains the use of the hammer. She'd learned her lesson on 'Berto's murder. This time she knocked Lee out so she could cut his throat from behind, where she was not so likely to be spattered."

I contemplated this horrid suggestion, while Jimmy went on:

"If you ask me her motive, I'll tell you that I don't know. I'd say she was a raving maniac if it weren't for that handkerchief wrapped around the mallet. That looks as though she didn't wish to kill Doug, merely to stun him. Since Doug doesn't inherit, it suggests that increasing her share of the legacy is her real motive."

"How about the gash on Doug's face?"

"Perhaps her first intention was to let Doug off. Afterwards, she began to worry for fear he might have seen her, and changed her mind. Just as she was bending over to cut his throat, Aunt Hagar screamed, and the knife slipped."

"Then you think it was *Judith* Aunt Hagar saw bending over Doug?"

"Yes. She said it might have been either a man or a woman."

"But she said the figure came from the tomb."

"It's possible Judith had some idea of concealing Lee's body in the tomb. Suppose she ran up the steps, found the door locked, and ran down again, just as Aunt Hagar came out on the gallery."

"Could Judith have got back to the house in time?"

"I believe so. Between Aunt Hagar's scream and Judith's appearance in the upper hall there was an interval of a little more than three minutes. She had only to run down the hill and up the north steps, through the French windows and into her room, take off her raincoat and rubbers, put on her dressing gown and join us in the hall."

"But you said there was no mud on the rubbers."

"She probably washed them in the rain barrel. It would have taken only a few seconds. Hang it all, Phil—" He put down his fork and leaned back in his chair, putting his hands to his eyes with a troubled gesture. "It all fits together too well. I'm convincing myself. And I hate to do that. I like Judith."

I, too, liked Judith; but as I followed his reasoning I realized that for some time she had been in the back of my mind. Not only was she the daughter of mad old Nathan Conroy; but also, after her years of virtual slavery with Aunt Hagar, she had, of them all, the most reason to be embittered by life, and the most need for money to aid her in seizing upon a fleeting happiness before it was too late.

Jimmy was continuing his monologue: "I fancy she left the raincoat and rubbers in her room last night. Mrs. Prill discovered them this morning and loyally tried to hide them in the gallery closet."

He finished his coffee, and rose with a sigh. Crossing to the chair, he lifted the bundle he had brought in and unrolled it, disclosing the raincoat and rubbers. "What are you going to do now?" I asked.

"Much as I hate the idea, I'm going to take a look at Judith's room."

CHAPTER 18
In Judith's Room

The Conroys were all at breakfast, so we were able to start our investigations in Judith's room unobserved. This room opened into the rear hall, near the back stairs. Like the rest of the house, it was furnished with shabby but comfortable mahogany of the early Victorian period. The floor was of broad, pine boards waxed until they shone, and before the French windows there was a gay rag rug. Immediately upon entering, Jimmy crossed to this and turned it over.

"Just as I thought. Some one has walked on it with wet feet." He produced one of Judith's rubbers and did some measuring. "Matches up, all right. She was coming from the French window, too. The print on the floor has been wiped up, but it still shows in one or two places." Again he studied the rug, also a cretonne-covered chair which stood before the dressing table. "That wet coat was thrown over this chair. It's still damp on the back. The rubbers evidently stood beside it. Here's the mark on the floor. Now if I can only find something else. . . ."

He crossed the room and opened the door of a small cupboard in which Judith kept shoes and hats. Quickly he began searching the shelves. I was so dazed by the sudden verification of our suspicions that instead of watching the door, as I should have done, I stood stupidly staring at Jimmy.

It was so that Judith found us when she walked in from the carpeted hall. One moment she stood, stricken, before she stepped into the room and closed the door behind her.

Jimmy swung about. The three of us stared at each other, wordless and appalled; then Judith said in a flat lifeless voice:

"I see that you know."

"Yes." Jimmy sounded almost apologetic. "We do— know, Judith."

With an air of almost inhuman detachment, she walked over to a high-backed chair of carved walnut which stood near the French windows, and dropped into it. Her head was tilted back, her eyes closed. The gray light fell across her face and on to her hands, which lay, palms up, in her lap. In the same flat tone she asked:

"What are you going to do?"

"What would you like me to do?"

"I should like you to send Mark to me for a little while."

The implication was plain. Both of us remembered Mark's offer to help any member of the family who was guilty, to a painless end. At the time, the suggestion had seemed hideous. Now, I realized, we were accepting it with a feeling of grateful relief. The thought of Judith in a prison cell, or in an asylum, was intolerable.

"I'll call Mark in a moment," Jimmy promised. "But first, you must tell me the full story—just how you did it, and why."

Judith opened her eyes and gazed at him from tragic depths. "I was hoping you could tell me, because I don't know." She must have read incredulity in our faces, for she cried out: "I'm not trying to say I didn't kill them! I know that I must be guilty. I'm just trying to tell you that my

mind is a blank as to what happened. I suppose," she made
a pitiful attempt at a smile, "that's just what I would tell
you even if I remembered. It's what the murderer always
says, isn't it? That his mind was a blank when he committed the crime?"

"Don't!" Jimmy interrupted. "Don't, Judith! We believe
you. Just try to tell us as much as you can of what happened last night."

"I've already told you what I remember. I went to bed,
and fell asleep almost immediately. It was the shot that
woke me."

"Where were you?"

She looked at him with a faint lifting of the brows.
"That's what I can't understand. I'm *sure* I was in bed. Yet
it seemed to me a moment later I was standing on that
rug, and I noticed my feet were cold. I was leaning with
my hands on something wet that hung across the back of
the chair. At the time, I was so dazed that I didn't stop to
investigate, just threw on my dressing gown and ran down
the hall. But later, after we'd heard about—" her voice
faltered upon the name, "about Lee, I came back into the
room and discovered those French windows on to the gallery were unlocked, my raincoat was lying, soaking wet,
across the back of that chair, and my rubbers were on the
floor beside it."

"Where was your raincoat when you went to bed?"

"It was hanging on that hook near the door."

"Where someone might easily have reached it from the
hall."

"That's sweet of you, Jimmy, but it's no use. You see,
the front of my nightgown was soaking wet, and so were
my hands. I remember wiping them before I put on my
dressing gown." She leaned forward with pathetic earnest-
ness. "Don't try to argue, it only makes it worse. Can't you
see that I must have been the one to do it?"

"I don't see at all," Jimmy looked puzzled. "How could you have done it, Judith, if you were in this room when you heard the shot?"

"But I wasn't," she told him simply. "I merely *thought* I was. It's what the psychologists call 'fantasy.' As a matter of fact, I was, I *must* have been, up on the hill. I've asked the others how long it was before I ran down the hall and joined them. They all say I was the last to appear, except for Connie . . . that means at least three minutes after the sound of the shot, which would give me plenty of time to get down the, hill, take off my raincoat, and put on the dressing gown."

"How do you explain the fact that your rubbers are clean of mud?"

"I suppose I wiped them off when I first came in, and probably my hands, too. There's a washstand behind that screen in the corner. I must have come to myself just after I threw the coat over the back of the chair. I remember being desperately sick and dizzy, exactly as though I were coming out from under ether. Later on, when I heard everyone telling about waking up at the sound of the shot, it was so impressed on my mind that I thought it had happened the same way with me. Oh, that's quite possible," she added quickly. "You've only to read books on abnormal psychology to know." She had been speaking with calmness; now her voice began to sharpen, and a note of hysteria crept into it. "I've known for a long time I was going insane. I watched father when it was coming on, and I saw myself doing the same things."

"What things?"

"Forgetting names, and words, and where I'd put things; having sudden moments of horrible, paralyzing fear, without reason; waking and finding myself places where I'd no idea of going."

"Amnesia," Jimmy murmured, and she nodded.

"Yes. If you've read about it, you know the horrible things that can be done in that state. Wait. I'll show you." She crossed to the table beside her bed and picked up a book which I saw was *The Human Mind* by Dr. Karl Menninger. There was a slip of paper marking a page, and she turned to it quickly. "Here's one of several cases," she said. "A devoted mother who'd been married for fifteen years had a quarrel with her husband, and this is what happened." In a low, tense, voice she read:

> "'*The next morning, while the husband and son were milking, they heard shots. They rushed to the house. There they found the two little girls, shot through the heart, lying in great pools of blood. Their mother lay across the bed, a shotgun in one hand and a bleeding wound in her side. . . . She remained unconscious for several days. When she awoke she could remember nothing about the shooting. When I told her that her little girls were dead she burst into tears and demanded to know what had happened to them. I told her. "But," she cried, "how could I do such a thing? Surely I couldn't! My God! How could I do that?"'*"

Judith closed the book despairingly. "Can't you see how that woman must have felt? How I must feel? Especially since I *knew* I was going insane? I should have told some one. I should have given you a chance to lock me up, after 'Berto's death. But I couldn't believe I'd done it. How could I kill Lee? Why, I loved Lee as if he were my own son," she was sobbing, now, her face buried in her hands.

I longed to comfort her; but what could I say that would not appear forced and insincere? Jimmy seemed less helpless; he took Menninger's book from the table and

studied it for a time, then put it down, and began moving thoughtfully about the room. He regarded the chair
in front of the dressing table with grave intentness. He
moved the screen from before the washstand and examined
the bowl and towels. He crossed to the door which opened
into Aunt Hagar's apartment, and glanced inside. In the
end, he came back and stood looking down at the huddled
figure in the chair.

"Stop crying!" he commanded. "Stop crying, and listen
to me."

Startled by the sharpness of his tone, Judith lifted her
head and stared through her tears. "I want you to answer
some questions," he went on. "First, did you drink any of
that mulled wine last night?"

"Why, yes, I had a full cup."

"Good. Now about your nightgown. You say you found
it was damp. Was that in front?"

"Yes; I suppose the coat wasn't buttoned, and the
rain—"

"Never mind that. Didn't it occur to you that it might
have become damp while you stood leaning against the
chair? Remember, you said when you first came to yourself
you were leaning with your hands on something wet that
was spread over the back of that chair."

"Yes," her eyes widened, "I remember."

"One thing more. Was your hair wet?"

"No," she was evidently groping back in her recollec-
tion, "I'm sure it wasn't. I'd have noticed, wouldn't I?"

"No doubt of it. Have you any hat you could have put
on?"

Before answering, she crossed to her cupboard and
looked through the shelves. When she returned there was
astonishment in her face. "No; I can't find any hat that's
in the least damp."

"I thought not," Jimmy said, and added blithely, "you didn't do those murders, Judith. I'm convinced of it."

She looked up at him, hope warring with stubborn disbelief. "Why do you say that?"

"Because I believe you when you tell me you can't remember."

"That's one sign of insanity," she insisted. "Didn't you understand what I read to you?"

"I did, my dear. But that sort of thing happens only occasionally; not over and over again like this. Remember, you'd not only have to forget killing Lee but you'd also have to forget writing that warning beforehand. You'd have to forget killing 'Berto, and, even before that, helping 'Berto work out that hoax. Then there's the question of your getting that knife out of Mark's bag, the mallet out of the closet. Above all, there's the question of Sally's death. Don't you see that it's grotesque to picture a series of mental lapses which cover a whole year?"

"It does seem incredible. But I felt half crazy last night when I woke up, as though coming out of a trance."

"You'd been drugged. Somebody slipped knockout drops, probably chloral hydrate, into our wine."

"Chloral hydrate? But that was what killed Sally!"

"It was," Jimmy agreed grimly, and left it at that while he picked up the raincoat and looked at it helplessly. "If only we knew which of the women wore this last night!"

"Why do you insist it was a woman?" I asked.

"If you can find a man small enough to cram his feet into those rubbers I'll gladly switch over to the other sex."

"Perhaps the raincoat has nothing to do with the murder."

"Then why doesn't some one step forward and say so?" The words were scarcely out of his mouth when the door flew open with a vigorous swish and Lucia entered.

"Look here!" she said peremptorily. "Prillie tells me you're accusing Judith of this murder because you found her raincoat damp. Is that true?"

"We didn't exactly accuse her—" Jimmy was beginning, when Judith came to his rescue. "I accused myself," she declared.

"But I was the one who wore that raincoat!"

"*You?*" Jimmy stared in astonishment, and she nodded vigorously.

"Yes, I wanted to speak to Lee last night—to make sure he was all right. So after everyone was asleep, I came down from the third floor—"

"Wait a minute," Jimmy interrupted. "Did you drink any of that mulled wine?"

"No. When it was first passed around, I took a cup, but I found I didn't want it and handed it over to Connie."

"All right." Jimmy grunted. "What time did you come downstairs?"

"I didn't look at my watch, but it must have been about one-thirty. When I got on this floor I went straight to the door of Lee's room . . . I mean the room where he used to sleep. I didn't know you'd changed him and that Tony was in there."

"Was the door locked at that time?"

"Yes. I rapped once or twice, and when there wasn't any answer I was frightened. I didn't want to disturb anyone so I went down the hall and through Judith's room, intending to go out on the gallery and call him from there."

"Why didn't you go out the door in the rear hall?"

"Because the bolt was stuck and I couldn't budge it. When I got in Judith's room I saw the gallery was flooded. I was wearing a light negligee and satin slippers. So I put on her coat and rubbers before I went outside. When I reached Lee's room I was surprised to find Tony instead of Lee. He explained about the changed room, and I stayed just long enough to smoke a cigarette, then started back upstairs."

"By the gallery?"

"Yes, by the gallery. You'll remember the hall door was locked, and there wasn't any key. Tony thought you must have locked him in after he went to sleep. I can tell you exactly what time it was when I went back, because I looked at my wrist watch. It was six minutes of two. I'd barely reached my room and climbed into bed when I heard that shot on the hill."

"Why haven't you told us all this before?" Jimmy demanded.

"Because—well, I suppose it was just because I was so upset by Lee's death I couldn't think of anything else."

That had not been her real reason, I felt sure. Something else had held her back. Was it because she feared Doug would misunderstand her being in Tony's room at that hour?

She hurried on: "I never dreamed you'd think Judith had committed the murder, or I'd have told you at once. She couldn't have done it, Jimmy, I saw her lying asleep when I hung the coat over the chair; and, later, after the shot, when I came downstairs she was just putting on her dressing gown."

"You're sure of that?"

"Absolutely certain. There's someone else you can cross off your list, too. While I was in Judith's room, I heard Aunt Hagar getting out of bed. When I went upstairs she was starting down the hall, toward Doug's room, with a thermos bottle and a cup in her hands."

CHAPTER 19
"X MARKS THE SPOT"

Judith and Aunt Hagar were crossed definitely off our list of suspects. This was not done, however, until Jimmy had carefully checked up on all of Lucia's statement and had cross-examined Tony.

He seemed reluctant at first to give any account of Lucia's nocturnal visit, but ended by corroborating her story. He insisted he had no idea of the time of her arrival, yet he was certain that she had left the room by eight minutes of two.

Entering this in his notes, Jimmy looked startled. "Then Lucia must have been in your room at the time Doug heard that call, and on the gallery while Lee was going up the hill path."

Tony agreed, but he claimed it was not surprising they had failed to hear the call. They had both been busy talking. The door had been closed, and the rain pounding on the gallery. As for the rest:

"It would have been impossible for us to have seen Lee," he contended. "The hill path is completely cut off by trees from the north end of the gallery."

Jimmy checked on this and found it was true. The only view of the hill path and tomb was from the extreme southern end of the gallery and the back windows in Doug's room. He also sent Tony in boots and slicker

to walk rapidly down the gallery steps and up the hill to
the tomb. This, we found, took a little over a minute.
Finally he himself tried the experiment of coming down
the stairs from the third floor, and found that it would
have been easily possible for Lucia to see Judith putting
on her dressing gown. Obviously, if Judith was there when
Lucia went upstairs, and there again when she came down,
it would have been impossible for her to be on the hill at
the time of Lee's murder.

Gloomily Jimmy retired to the library. From a locked
drawer of the desk he drew forth the list of suspects which
we had made the morning before.

"There's no doubt about it, Judith and Aunt Hagar will
have to be eliminated," he mused aloud.

"Also Lucia," I suggested.

"And Lucia," he agreed. "Although I am not at all
pleased with that young woman just now."

"What on earth do you mean?"

"I mean that story she told us is as full of holes as
Swiss cheese. In the first place, she knew darned well that
Tony was occupying Lee's room. In the second, if she was
in Tony's room at the time she says, I can't help believing
the two would have heard that call. Then there's her reticence about telling us the story. We'd never have heard it if
Judith hadn't been drawn into the mess by that raincoat."

"But surely that's understandable," I protested. "She's
engaged to Doug, and he's a conventional cuss. Besides,
he doesn't get along any too well with Tony. Naturally
she wouldn't want him to know that she'd been in Tony's
room."

"That's true, too," Jimmy admitted, then sighed. "Oh
well, we'll just forget her for the present. It's obvious she
couldn't have killed Sally . . . and I'm going on the theory
that the murders are all tied together. Let's see who is left
on our list." He brought his blue pencil from his pocket

and drew firm lines through the names of Judith, of Lucia, and Aunt Hagar.

Over his shoulder I studied the remaining suspects.

1. *Mark Dietrich.*
2. *Connie Dietrich.*
3. *Tony Patri.*
4. *Doug Conroy.*
5. *Mrs. Prill.*
6. *Henry Harker.*

"Surely Doug comes off," I protested.

Jimmy shook his head. "Nothing is *sure*. It's just possible that he killed Lee, and that his injuries are self-inflicted. Oh, I'm not accusing your pet Babbitt," he added hastily. "I'm merely pointing out that we've no right to cross him off the list until we've considered all the possibilities." Opening the door, he called to Tony, who was building a fire in the living room. "Do you mind asking Mark to step in here a minute?" He turned back to me. "Aside from what Mark may tell us about the wound, you realize there are a number of other things against the theory of Doug's guilt. In the first place, there is the question of that gun. We know that Doug is a crack shot and that he had a revolver. Why should he go to the trouble of hitting Lee on the head and cutting his throat when a bullet would have settled things much more simply? He needn't have feared to be connected with the gun because, even though the weapon was his, he might easily have claimed it had been stolen by some one else. Then, too, there's the question of motive. So far as I can see, he hasn't the slightest reason for committing murder. Even the fact that he might get some of the Conroy money with Lucia, doesn't count for much because he's the only one of the lot who doesn't need it."

"Then the only thing we have against Doug is that he had the best opportunity of anyone."

"Not quite," Jimmy said. "There was someone who had an even better—"

Before he could finish, Mark Dietrich joined us.

"I've just come from dressing Doug's head," he said; and in reply to a question from Jimmy. "Oh, he's better—almost well, in fact. Only thing that worries him now is the cut. He's afraid it may leave a scar."

"And will it?"

"I don't believe so. Nothing disfiguring, at any rate. He ought to be thanking his stars he didn't lose an eye."

"I don't suppose," Jimmy was watching him warily, "there's a chance the wound might have been self-inflicted?"

"Self-inflicted?" The Doctor stared, then exploded. "Good Lord, no! It's conceivable that he might have struck the blow with the hammer, but no man in his senses would gash himself in such a fashion. Why, I tell you it's a miracle the eyeball wasn't cut in two."

"An even better argument than that has just occurred to me," Jimmy said slowly. "Doug would never have deliberately marred his own good-looks. He rather fancies himself, you know."

"You're right," the Doctor snapped. "Why did you consider such an absurd possibility?"

"Because I'm trying to be thorough," Jimmy explained mildly. "I had already eliminated Doug in my own mind, but I wanted your testimony before I finally crossed his name from the list." As he spoke, his pencil drew a firm line upon the paper and I knew that the number of suspects had been reduced to five.

Mark was scarcely out of the room before we were cold-bloodedly considering his name.

"He's the only one left that has both the motive of the legacy and the possibility of inherited madness," I pointed out. "How about the time element?"

Earnestly we poured over the notes.

"Mark's possible—though far from probable," Jimmy said, in the end. "Doug's call and the shot came at one-fifty-eight. The Doctor was out in the hall unlocking my door about three minutes later. There's a bare chance he might have been able to get down from the hill in that time."

"But what about his clothing? Wouldn't it have been wet?"

"He may have worn a raincoat, and dropped it in his room. I remember Connie looked worried when we questioned her later. Speaking of Connie, suppose we consider her next."

"Connie was sleeping in the room with Mark."

"Very true. But they occupy separate beds. Mark tumbled out in a hurry—she may have been gone, without his noticing."

"Why should she want to kill Lee—" I began, then broke off as a light dawned. "Oh, you mean for the inheritance."

"Right. Connie's fond of money. Devilish fond of it. She certainly didn't marry Mark for his fatal beauty. Probably it was for what she hoped to get out of him. So far, it can't have been much. She must have been looking forward to that inheritance hopefully . . . and to have its value cut in less than half by the depression might drive her to murder."

This was true enough. Connie was exactly the sort of woman I could imagine cutting a throat for a fur coat or a platinum bracelet. It suddenly occurred to me that Connie had been the last to appear after Lee's murder. I pointed this out to Jimmy, who nodded thoughtfully.

"Yes; it's possible she didn't come from her room at all, but that she slipped up the north steps and through Judith's door. There's no doubt she has both the opportunity and the motive. At the same time, you'll have to remember that mulled wine. She certainly drank a full cup. I sat next to her and saw it. Lucia says she drank hers as well, which would explain her outsleeping the rest of us."

"It may also explain her uneasiness," I suggested. "Sleeping like a log all through it, she'd have no way of knowing what Mark, or anyone else, had been up to."

Jimmy agreed cheerfully. "Right-o. Just the same, she stays on our list."

He made a note, then: "The next is Tony."

"But what possible motive—"

"If you ask me that again I'll crown you with a chair. He hadn't any obvious motive, of course. The question of hereditary insanity is out, because he has no Conroy blood, and, now that 'Berto is dead, there is no way in which he can inherit any of the money. But the lack of motive is the only thing that has kept me from suspecting him thus far. When it comes to opportunity he's right at the head of the list."

"How can you say that? Lucia was with him at the time Lee was running up the hill."

"Lucia *says* she was with him. Remember, she lied about having caught him in that blind man's buff game, and she juggled the truth again when she declared she didn't know Lee had changed rooms. It would be quite in character for her to have set forward the time of her leaving Tony's room—in order to supply him with an alibi. Suppose she left at one-forty-five. That would have given him plenty of time to meet Lee on the hill. He was certainly there when we reached the tomb later on."

"But isn't that his best alibi? There was an interval of about eight minutes between the time Lee was killed and the time we found the body. Would any man in his senses have hung around waiting to be caught?"

"He might—if he was smart. Suppose he said to himself, 'If I kill Lee and run back to the house I may or may not be caught coming in. But if I wait here until the others arrive, then pretend I was just ahead of them on the path, they'll be bound to believe my story because they'll argue no murderer would hang around waiting to be caught.'"

That was a new thought, and a meaty one. I sat for a time grappling with it while Jimmy continued:

"It took us some time to get out of our rooms, then Aunt Hagar's faint tied us up for several extra minutes. That may have been longer than Tony expected, and the story of going up the hill the minute he heard the scream would not do without revision. He accounted for the extra two or three minutes by saying he stopped to pound on Harker's door."

"He insisted it was locked." I suddenly recalled the contradictory fact. "Yet when I went down, a few minutes later, I got in without difficulty."

"Exactly. Which suggests Tony was lying. Of course he'd have to take the risk of saying the door was locked in order to explain why he didn't go in and shake Harker awake."

"Yes; but, hang it all—" I broke off helplessly, and Jimmy nodded with complete understanding.

"I know what you mean. You like Tony. You're actually fond of him. You can't believe that anyone you're fond of committed these murders. But you've got to rid yourself of that idea, Phil. No matter how the thing turns out, it's bound to be some one we both like—unless, of course, it should prove to be Henry Harker." He studied his notes. "My word! It's quite possible—"

"What?"

"Don't you see? It may not be Tony's who's lying about that locked door. Perhaps Harker is the one. Say that he was up at the tomb killing Lee and knocking out Doug at the time of the scream. Then, if he locked his door when he left his room, Tony wouldn't have had any answer from inside, for the simple reason that Harker wasn't there. Suppose while Tony charged up the hill, he slipped down through the shrubbery and into his room. That would have given him ample time to take off his wet things, hide them in the closet, and pile into bed."

"Where I found him later." I was well pleased with this new turn of events; Harker had always been my favorite candidate for the halter. "Of course he's guilty. You said yourself he might be crazy—from staying alone on the island so long."

"Yes," he mused, then said slowly: "There's still one person we haven't considered—Prillie. Barring the question of insanity, she has the same motive for committing the murders as Harker. By which I mean, she's due to inherit under the will."

"Only if all the others are dead."

"Exactly." He nodded grimly. "And three are already out of the way. Her opportunity was as good as Harker's. "Instead of making chocolate in the kitchen she may have slipped up the hill."

"How could she have got Lee up to the tomb?"

Jimmy groaned. "Oh, my soul! Ask me anything else. That's what's turning me gray before my time . . . that and the question of the call Doug heard from the shrubbery. I know the two ought to fit together, somehow. That the call was for Lee, and because of some mysterious compulsion he answered it. Yet my mind revolts against the idea of accepting it. Think of it, Phil: a call in the night, a sleeping man compelled to rise and follow. Not straight away, mind you, but first locking doors and juggling with keys. I'd have to take the White Queen's advice and learn to believe six impossible things before breakfast every morning in order to believe that."

I knew from the extravagance of his protestations how much he was distressed by the very idea he rejected. I also understood the helpless, angry sensation of revolt which was induced by the mention of that call, of the figure which Lee had glimpsed entering the tomb the night before his death, and of the ghostly shape which Aunt Hagar had seen coming from the same shadowed portico. It was the protest of a healthy mind refusing to accept anything outside the sane realities of life. And yet. . . . The evidence of a single witness might have been ignored. One might say that Doug had dreamed the call in his drugged sleep, Lee had imagined the figure, or that Aunt Hagar's old eyes had deceived her. But to say that all three were mistaken . . .

"We can't ignore it," Jimmy groaned, and I knew that his thoughts had been paralleling my own. "We've got to fit it all in somewhere, Phil—and do it damned quickly— or there will never be any end to this carnage."

"You mean— You believe there will be more murders?"

"I'm *sure* of it. Figure it out for yourself. If the murderer is mad, there's no reason to believe that his blood-lust is satisfied as yet. On the other hand, if he's sane, and is killing for the sake of the inheritance, there are still several more lives—" He broke off as Mark burst into the room.

At first sight of the Doctor's face, I knew something had happened. All of his urbanity, his callous self-control, seemed to have fallen away, leaving him human, likeable, and afraid.

"Look at this!"

It was a piece of the yellow paper which had been used for so many of the manuscripts. Upon it, drawn crudely in pencil, was a rough map of the Conroy house, the hill, and the tomb. At the top was printed, in straggling block letters, the legend:

Chapter Three

And below, slightly smaller:

X Marks the Spot

Scattered across the face of the map were three crosses done in red crayon. One was in the kitchen wing, approximately at the spot where 'Berto's body had been found. It was labeled: *Saturday. 'Berto.* A second was on the steps of the tomb, and was marked: *Sunday. Lee.* The third was again inside the house, slightly to the left of the place where 'Berto had been killed. It was inscribed: *Monday. Aunt Hagar.*

Chapter 20
The Call is Repeated

The paper had been found by Mrs. Prill in the pocket of the dressing gown worn by Doug on his disastrous trip to the tomb.

"It must have been placed there last night," Mark told us, "while he was lying unconscious."

Jimmy nodded doubtfully. "Perhaps. But why in thunder—" He brooded, frowning, then queried:

"Who has been near that dressing gown besides Doug and Mrs. Prill?"

"Almost everyone," Mark told him. "His raincoat wasn't much protection, and when we brought him down from the hill the gown was soaked. We slipped it off and threw it on the floor, where it lay forgotten until this morning; then Prillie carried it off downstairs and hung it in the lower passage. About half an hour ago she found time to attend to it. While she was emptying the pockets, she discovered this."

"Then the paper may have been put there any time," Jimmy observed. "This morning as easily as last night. By the way," he glanced up suddenly, "we must keep this from Aunt Hagar."

Mark looked rueful. "I'm sorry, but my wife was in the kitchen when Prillie discovered the thing. She was so upset she rushed upstairs and blurted it out."

"How did the old lady take it?"

"She went into one of her rages." Mark was moving toward the door as he spoke. "I ought to go back at once, in case I'm needed."

"We'll go with you."

As we climbed the stairs, we could hear Aunt Hagar at the end of the hall, roaring forth a vigorous jeremiad. At any other time the Elizabethan richness of her flowing abuse might have been amusing; now, it was indescribably shocking to hear the old woman, figuratively and literally in the shadow of the tomb, cursing the members of the Conroy clan, who stood, helpless, about her. They were all there, we found, when we reached the room. Judith was attempting to quiet her, Lucia was helping, and Connie sat whimpering on the bed. Mrs. Prill was bringing *sal volatile* from the bathroom, while Doug, clad in a dressing gown and slippers, was standing at the door with Tony.

"You're a parcel of simpletons!" Aunt Hagar screamed. "A flock of sheep offering your throats to the butcher! If you'd an ounce of brains among you, you'd have had the murderer under lock and key long since. But perhaps you want me killed. That's it!" Her voice rose higher. "You want me killed! You, Judith. You, Mark. And Lucia. You want me dead so there'll be only three of you to share in the money." At this moment her eyes fell upon Jimmy Lane, and she stopped in the middle of her tirade to denounce him roundly as a fool, a nit-wit, a driveling donkey and a bungling imbecile who would stand by, doing nothing, while they were all being slaughtered.

Instead of arguing, Jimmy cheerfully agreed. "I'm lower than the dust beneath your chariot wheel," he told her. "Less than the rust—and all the rest of it. In fact, I'm so disgusted with my own incompetence that I'm perfectly willing to bow out of the case and let someone else take over the job of protecting you."

That brought her up short. "No," she snapped. "I'd rather be in the hands of a fool than a murderer!" She took a sniff of the smelling-salts, blew her nose trumpetingly, and asked, in a more rational voice: "What are you planning to do?"

"First, Phil and I are going on guard and will never leave you, even for a minute. Next, I mean to move you to another room."

Here he struck a snag. Aunt Hagar refused flatly to be moved. One room was as safe as another, she argued. They could lock the doors and put a guard over her, but they could *not* turn her out of her comfortable bed.

Forced into agreement, Jimmy stipulated that all of her meals must be brought up from below, and that she must keep away from the windows. What danger might come from the windows, he himself could not say.

That was the hideous part of the affair. The threat embodied in the crude drawings was so vague that at any other time we might have disregarded it. Following close upon 'Berto's death, and Lee's, it became a grim menace, all the more nerve-wracking that it was impossible to guess from which direction the blow might come.

"It's the utter inanity of the thing that's so infuriating," Jimmy fumed. "Why should anyone use this fantastic method of murder? Why should he warn his victims? Why should his call have the power to drag Lee to the last spot on earth he would want to go? Why should he choose the tomb for the murder? Why any of it? It's grotesque! It's revolting to a sane mind to believe that such a thing can happen. And yet we know it has happened, and that it may happen again."

"We're going to watch over Aunt Hagar—"

"Over *her*, yes. But what about the others? We can't put a guard over each of them. And even if we did set them watching each other, how would we know the murderer wasn't one of the guards?"

We were in our own room, making a few final preparations before taking charge of Aunt Hagar, whom we had left with Lucia, Judith and Mark; it seemed impossible that any harm could come to her while all three were present, and there were things Jimmy Lane wished to say which could be said only in private.

"There must be some reason back of it all," he insisted. "It's impossible anything could be as senseless as this seems."

"Perhaps the very senselessness of it is the explanation," I suggested. "This latest development makes it look as though it must be the work of a madman."

"Madman, yes," he agreed, "but not a gibbering idiot. By a stretch of the imagination I can picture one of the Conroys being coldly, craftily insane. But this goes beyond that, Phil. It's madness in the nth degree. It's insanity in the fourth dimension."

He was interrupted by a knock at the door. Opening it, I discovered Doug Conroy standing in the hall with a small package under his arm.

"Are you alone?" he demanded in a half-whisper, and Jimmy nodded impatiently.

"There's nobody hidden under the bed, if that's what you mean . . . nor in the bureau drawers."

Doug seemed satisfied. He sat down upon a chair and shifted the package from under his arm to his knees. He was looking much better than when we had seen him the night before; color had returned to his face, and his eyes, under the corona of white bandage, had lost their haunted look.

"See here," he began, "what do you think about this new twist? I mean this business of Aunt Hagar."

"I think it's exactly as crazy as all the rest of it," Jimmy told him sourly.

"That's exactly what I want to talk about," Doug said earnestly. "I mean about craziness. Grandfather's craziness." And, as we both stared: "Have either of you thought that he might have had something to do with what's happened?"

"Hardly. He's been dead ten years."

"I know. But isn't it possible he's left some curse that's still going on?" And, as Jimmy snorted: "That sounds idiotic, I know, but I've something important to tell you, if you'll just listen—"

Jimmy subsided. I saw that he was annoyed by the interruption, and was in two minds about listening; but Doug was so desperately in earnest that he had all the persistency of the wedding guest in *The Ancient Mariner*. I think Jimmy knew that sooner or later he would be forced to hear his tale.

"Mark told you how grandfather hated the family," Doug went on. "The only one he ever allowed on the island while he lived here was his son Hugh, that's my adopted father. Dad used to come every month or so to make sure everything was all right and that Henry was taking care of the place. Sometimes grandfather would talk with him sanely, and sometimes he'd be in one of his fits—and he'd rave until the air was blue. Of course dad didn't pay much attention, but I remember he told me once that grandfather had some crazy plan for exterminating the whole family."

"What?"

"It's a fact. He said they didn't deserve to live, and that he was going to wipe 'em off the face of the earth. Of course," he looked apologetic, "I don't suppose it means anything, but I just happened to remember there were some old diaries of his in the library." He unwrapped the package in his lap and brought out three books bound in faded leather. "None of us has ever bothered to look 'em over. Possibly they're just gibberish, but I thought you might be able to get something out of them, something that would help with the case."

"Thanks." Jimmy took the books, not at all gratefully, and dumped them on the bureau. "I'll glance over them if you like, but I doubt if they'll help."

"Maybe not," Doug agreed, "but what I say is, nothing's too small to investigate at a time like this." He let himself out the door, and Jimmy looked after him with a groan.

"Fun's fun," he complained, "and I admit we've got to have comic relief, but when it comes to looking over the ravings of a madman—ten years dead. . . ." He picked up one of the diaries as he spoke, and was turning the pages. Now, he broke off to study some written phrase. After a moment he closed the book

and put it down, then stared thoughtfully at the pile.

"Anything of interest?" I asked, and he seemed to bring himself back from a vast distance.

"No; nothing." But I noticed that he placed the books carefully in one of the bureau drawers before we returned to Aunt Hagar's room.

Dinner was at seven. Jimmy went downstairs first, while I watched over the old lady, who had turned sulky because all of the family were barred from the room and she lacked an audience. She pretended to believe that I was the mute with the bowstring and that it was my intention to murder her while we were alone. When Jimmy returned I left for the dining room with a distinct feeling of relief.

It was my first meal with the family since Lee's death. With the exception of Aunt Hagar, all that remained of the Conroy clan were there. The great table which had once held not only the present group but also 'Berto, Lee, and Sally, seemed too large for the company now gathered about it. 'Berto's chair had been removed, and Lee's, but they still stood against the wall, mutely reminding us of their separate tragedies. All the globes in the chandelier were alight, and Mrs. Prill had added a number of branched silver candlesticks in hopes of brightening the scene. The illumination only served to show the havoc wrought among the Conroys. Their haggard faces, reflected in the somber mahogany surface of the table, were like the faces of ghosts.

There was little conversation. Mark, at the head of the board, sat gloomily staring at his plate; Judith, at the other end, was trembling as though with ague. Connie was frankly in a panic. Tony, after one feeble attempt at humor, lapsed into a silence as deep as Mark's. Only Lucia seemed normal. For a time she talked with Doug about the weather and the possibility of a boat crossing the flooded river. I thought she was showing almost callous lack of feeling, until her eyes met mine; the sick despair I read in their depths left me shaken with pity.

Harker served the meal. If the family perceptibly shrank from him as he put down the plates, it was no more than they shrank from each other. In that lay the peculiar horror of the situation. The Conroys were bound together by bonds not only of consanguinity, but also of real affection, yet now they were forced to suspect each other. Somewhere in that house, closed in by the rain as though by a tangible wall, the murderer of Sally, of 'Berto, and of Lee was to be found. Each of the Conroys knew that at any moment he might look into the face of a cousin, a wife, or a lover and see the familiar features turned into a mask of madness and of death. No wonder they shrank from each other, and yet were drawn together by a common bond of fear.

Lucia said as we finished dinner: "Here's the plan for to-night. We women are going to shut ourselves into the third floor and lock the door on the stairs. The men will spend the night in Mark's room. Not one of us is to leave the others, even for a minute."

"Jimmy and I will watch over Aunt Hagar," I promised.

"The way you watched over Lee?" Connie asked so nastily that the memory of my incompetence on that occasion doubled the precaution with which I prepared Aunt Hagar's dinner-tray.

Earlier in the day Harker had killed three chickens, and Mrs. Prill had made them into a ragout. This spicy mixture had been on the table throughout the meal and everyone had been served from the same covered silver dish. Jelly, potatoes and gravy also came from the common supply; biscuits were selected from a plate which had been passed the length of the board. A bottle of old Nathan Conroy's port was opened in my presence, and several of the family drank from it before I poured a generous amount into one of the beautiful glasses that were standing upon the sideboard. Aunt Hagar was using bottled water, and she cared nothing for dessert, so the only thing remaining was coffee. I carried the tray into the kitchen and watched Mrs. Prill pour a cup from the huge pot on the stove.

"I just made up a fresh quantity," she told me. "So it could be heated if anyone was to want some in the night."

Something in my face must have reflected suspicion, for she chuckled grimly, poured a second cup, and insisted that I watch her until she had drunk the last drop.

I carried the tray up the back stairs to the second floor. These stairs (as may be seen by consulting the floor plan) ascended from a passageway directly off the kitchen and debouched into the upper rear-hall. I had just placed my foot upon the top step when the electric lights suddenly blanked out.

For perhaps thirty seconds I stood helpless, the tray in my hands, afraid to move lest I spill the coffee or wine.

All about me there was movement and the sound of voices calling back and forth. Connie was shrieking hysterically for Mark. Lucia commanded her to stop it; Aunt Hagar's rumbling tones came from her room, followed by a few reassuring words from Jimmy.

Two lights appeared almost simultaneously. One was Tony's cigarette-lighter, which he was holding above his head as he stood in the open door of his room; the other was a match which Mark had struck, in the main hall. The two hurriedly lighted a pair of candles that stood on the highboy, and I saw Connie, Judith and Lucia huddled in the background. At the same moment, Doug came pounding up the front stairs, demanding to know what the row was all about.

It was only then that I realized the trouble was not with the dynamo, for the south end of the house was still brightly lighted; only Lee's room, the hall, Judith's and Aunt Hagar's bedrooms had been affected. That meant, of course, that a fuse had blown out. It might have been caused by the storm but it was equally possible that one of the wires had been deliberately tampered with.

This last was Jimmy Lane's suspicion, we found, when we talked to him through the door. He was convinced that some one had blown the fuse, hoping to enter the room in the darkness. He ordered the family back to their rooms before he cautiously opened the door and allowed me to enter with the tray.

I found a different Aunt Hagar from the one I had left. If she had been startled by the sudden cessation of light, she had bravely recovered, and seemed to be enjoying a sense of pleasurable importance at being the center of interest. While she smacked her lips greedily over the chicken, the biscuits, and coffee, Jimmy slipped out the door, which I locked behind him.

Shortly thereafter, the lights flashed on and when he returned, ten minutes later, he told us he found Harker screwing a fresh fuse in the box on the back porch.

"The fuse was blown, all right," he told us. "But whether it was done by the storm or by a human hand, we'll probably never know. The dynamo wasn't put in, of course, until long after the house was built, and the wires are all exposed along the baseboards in the halls and bedrooms. It would be a cinch to stick a knife or a pin through the insulation and blow out a fuse."

"What was the argument I heard in the lower hall?" I asked. "It sounded as though you and Harker were at each other's throats."

"We were," grimly. "When I told him that all the men were to stay together in the house to-night, he turned ugly. Said we were nothing but a bunch of maniacs and he didn't intend to risk his life. It took strong language to keep him from locking himself in his room. The fellow may really be frightened; on the other hand. . . ." He left the sentence unfinished; and, while she drank her coffee, plied Aunt Hagar with questions about Harker. When had he first come to her brother? What had been his real position? What did she know of his past?

"I see what you're driving at," the old lady told him. "You think Henry's been doing these murders."

"Do you?" he countered, and she nodded thoughtfully.

"It's possible. He hates us. Always has. But I don't know. . . ." She paused to finish her coffee, then picked up her glass of wine and began to sip it slowly. "Personally, I think it's somebody else."

"Who?" we both asked at once.

She shook her head. "I'm not going to tell you . . . at least, not yet."

"But surely—" Jimmy Lane broke off, and I knew he was realizing the cruelty of pointing out that death might at any moment seal her lips.

Aunt Hagar was no fool; "I know what you're thinking," she nodded, "but I'm not afraid. I mean to watch—until I'm sure. No use saying anything before. You wouldn't believe me."

That was all we could get out of her. She insisted that she had passed through a bad day and was tired, that Judith must be called at once to put her to bed. This precipitated another disagreement. Jimmy did not wish to admit anyone into the room.

Aunt Hagar protested that Judith had always put her to bed, and that she wasn't going to let anything upset her routine. She was rapidly working herself into one of her rages, and Jimmy yielded.

Judith was admitted. Deftly she tucked the old lady into the great four poster bed, put a knitted shawl about her shoulders, gave her a book and a reading glass, then departed.

Truffles was whining in the hall, and Aunt Hagar insisted he be allowed to take his usual place on a cushion under the head of her bed. With a good deal of scratching and grunting, he settled himself, his moist nose barely visible under the valance.

After Judith had gone, Jimmy and I barricaded the place for the night. Thoroughly appreciating the absurdity of the performance, we moved a bureau in front of the door which led to Judith's room, and pushed an old-fashioned wardrobe before the window that was next to the bed. Only the end window, which looked out on a drop of twenty feet, was left open, six or eight inches from the top; this was protected by a heavy screen, which Jimmy locked with care.

While we were busy with these preparations, Aunt Hagar watched from the bed, sipping her wine, and throwing an occasional caustic comment in our direction. By the time we were through she was nodding drowsily over

her book; which was, of all weird selections, under the circumstances, Dorothy Sayers' mystery novel *Strong Poison*.

"I wish you'd turn out the light and let me sleep," she
told us; and while I switched off the bedside lamp she
drew the delft blue and white comforter about her wrinkled old throat, then settled herself on the pillow with a
drowsy sigh.

When I returned to the other side of the room, I found
Jimmy Lane seated at the desk with one of old Conroy's
diaries open in front of him. I started to speak, but he
shook his head warningly and glanced toward the bed,
then returned to his reading.

Rather miffed, I established myself in an easy-chair to
watch the window, the door, and Aunt Hagar, who was
already asleep.

Once or twice, at the beginning of the hour, she tossed
and murmured a few words; but later, except for an occasional deep respiration, half gasp, half snore, her sleep was
unbroken.

It was a little after nine o'clock when I turned off her
light. At ten, Jimmy finished the first diary and picked
up the second. At eleven, we heard the family going to
bed. The women ascended the stairs to the third floor;
the men settled themselves in Mark's room. For a time we
could hear them moving about, then silence fell within the
house, a strange, ominous silence.

Ever since the beginning of the equinoctial, the wind
had been from the west, and had thrown the weight of the
storm against the back of the house; now, it had veered
and was coming from the sea. The bore had passed with
the ebbing tide; and the water, piling up against the surf
in the distance, made a steady, guttural roar like the growl
of a beast. I had never noticed it so distinctly before, but
to-night my nerves were keyed to the highest pitch, and

even the soft rustle of a page turned by Jimmy in his reading was enough to bring my heart to my mouth.

There were three hours of waiting; three hours of
wretched starting and staring, of turning to the window
at the tap of foliage against the pane, of moving quickly
to the door at the imagined sound of a stealthy step, or
tiptoeing to the bed for a glimpse of Aunt Hagar, who was
sleeping quietly, now. Her face was turned away, one arm
above her head, the other lying flat along the tufted counterpane. Once I touched her hand, and it seemed cold,
so I threw the edge of the spread over her shoulder, then
returned to watch Jimmy Lane as he plowed methodically
through the little leather book.

It was almost two when we heard footsteps in the hall.
Doug whispered through our locked door that the four of
them were going downstairs for coffee and would bring us
two cups on their return.

For an interval of about ten minutes, I sat listening to
the distant river and the rhythmic breathing from the bed,
then suddenly I heard a commotion below. Tony spoke,
and Mark answered. A door banged; there was a confusion
of running footsteps and voices—broken by a call from the
shrubbery. Low, yet distinct, it was not so much a call as
an eerie wail. Once . . . repeated . . . then again, cutting
across the other night sounds with a hideous insistence.

Before the first note died away, Jimmy had dropped his
book and flung himself in front of Aunt Hagar. Exactly
what was in his mind I do not know. Probably it was some
vague idea of protection; or to prevent her from answering
the call if, through some mad freak, she should attempt to
do so. This last was in my own mind as I rose and stood
defensively in front of the locked door.

The voices below were more distinct, now; and I realized they were coming not from the kitchen but from the

shrubbery outside. Impulsively I was moving toward the window when Jimmy's voice cracked like a whip behind me:

"Come here!"

I turned and ran to the bed.

"Look," he commanded, and lifted the light.

Together we bent over Aunt Hagar.

"Is—is she asleep?" I asked stupidly.

Jimmy's face was a ghastly mask. "No, she's not asleep . . . she's dead." Then, harshly: "In God's name, who is that we hear breathing?"

Chapter 21
More Questions

Aunt Hagar was dead, there was no doubt of it. Her face was cyanosed, her lips blue and distorted. There was not the faintest flutter of the pinched nostrils . . . and yet, apparently from the bed, came the sound of soft, regular breathing.

"Truffles!" Jimmy exclaimed, and reached under the valance.

The hours that followed are mercifully blurred in my memory. I only know that an indeterminate time later we were huddled in the square upper hall, as we had been on the night of Lee's death. We had chosen the upper hall, I think, because it was in the center of the house, and the only windows were at a distance, a fact which gave us a faint feeling of security.

Jimmy had been holding a conference with Mark in Aunt Hagar's room. When he joined us he was carrying a sheaf of scribbled notes, a yellow scratchpad, and the three leather-covered books, which he placed on the table.

Mark made his report with brevity and an apparent lack of emotion; but back of his crispness I sensed a determined self-control. Aunt Hagar had been dead at least an hour when found. She had died of heart failure, in her sleep.

This statement seemed to give the family almost as great a shock as the news of her death.

Doug blurted out: "You mean her throat wasn't cut?"

"No," Mark snapped. "Why should it have been?"

Doug sat back, looking foolish.

There was no reason, of course, except that all of us had mentally pictured that form of murder when the threat against the old lady had first been discovered.

"Then the death may have been natural?" Lucia asked.

Mark said evasively: "That would be possible. She was past seventy. Her heart may have stopped from nervous exhaustion."

The family accepted his statement if not with conviction at least without argument; and only Doug was heard to murmur, incredulously, that it was "damned queer the old lady chose just that moment to die—with that call coming from the shrubbery."

Jimmy Lane broke in with a question: "What about the call? Who heard it? What caused that commotion downstairs?"

Everyone had heard it, apparently.

"We were all in the kitchen getting coffee—" Tony began.

"The four of you stayed together?"

"Yes; that is, practically together. Of course we were in and out of the butler's pantry and the screen porch."

"Which means you weren't together at all," Jimmy growled. "Were you in sight of each other when the call sounded?"

"I don't know," Tony told him. And answered his look of surprise with: "You see, the lights had gone out. Somebody blew the fuse again."

"Not 'again,'" Harker amended. "The kitchen's on a different circuit from the lights up here. The one down there's got the kitchen, screen-porch, breakfast room and pantry on it."

"Were you all in the kitchen when the fuse blew out?" Jimmy asked.

"No," Doug said, "just two of us. I was stoking the stove and Tony was plugging the toaster, at the table near the porch door."

"I was in the butler's pantry," Mark volunteered.

"And Harker was getting wood," Doug went on.

"What happened next?"

"Nothing, for a minute. We were all completely flabbergasted. Then Tony let out a yell, and Mark called in from the butler's pantry to ask if it was dark in the kitchen. I started to find a candle. While I was groping around, we heard that call from outside."

"Where did it come from?"

"The shrubbery at the north end of the house," Mark answered.

Tony nodded agreement. "Our first idea was to catch whoever was giving that call. I beat it out the nearest door, the one into the rear passage. While I was running, the call sounded again. By the time I reached the outside, it had stopped."

Mark interrupted. "It was much the same with me, except that I went out the door of the butler's pantry."

"I made my exit through the screen-porch," Tony contributed, and Harker chimed in with:

"Me, too. But I stopped to get my flashlight out of my coat pocket. By the time I got out, they were all thrashing around in the shrubbery."

Jimmy turned to Doug. "Was the call you heard the same as the one that came the night of Lee's death?"

"Exactly the same—only louder."

"We heard it clear up on the third floor." Lucia shuddered. "Oh, Jimmy, what can it mean?"

Instead of answering, Jimmy rose and crossed to the window, where he stood looking out into the night. The wind had grown stronger and was coming from the sea in a persistent gale which rattled the windows and shook the doors of the old house like an earthquake. As though the storm had helped his decision, Jimmy turned back and spoke to Harker.

"D'you mind helping me for a minute? There's something I want to investigate on the third floor."

They were barely out of sight, in the shadows of the rear hallway, when we heard the slam of a door and the sound of a key turning in the lock, then Harker's voice raised in angry but muffled protest. Doug and I sprang to our feet and were starting to investigate, when Jimmy reappeared, a grim smile on his face.

"I've locked Harker on the third floor," he told us, "There's something I want to discuss with you which I'd rather he didn't hear." He dropped down at the table, where he had placed his notes and the leather-bound books. "First," he said, "you've got to be told that Aunt Hagar's death was *not* natural. It's true, as Mark said, she died of heart failure. But it was caused by a dose of chloral hydrate, administered in a glass of wine. That wine you brought up on her tray, Phil."

"It couldn't have been the wine!" I protested. "It was poured from a bottle we had all used. And it never left my hands until I put the tray down in front of Aunt Hagar."

"It never left your hands," Jimmy agreed. "But for at least a minute and a half you were standing in darkness." He broke off to direct a sudden burst of anger at himself. "Fool that I was! Watching to make sure no one got into the room and not remembering he might have dropped something into the food on the tray during that moment of darkness."

"But who—how—" I began, and broke off, looking around the circle of haggard faces.

"That's what we've got to find out—who could have been waiting in the rear hall when you came up with the tray."

"So far as I know, it may have been anyone—except Mrs. Prill," I said slowly. "She was in the kitchen when I left, and I'm certain there wasn't time for her to get upstairs ahead of me."

"Then at least we can cross her off the list."

"I can alibi Connie and Judith," Lucia told him. "We were all in Mark's room when the lights went out."

"That scratches all the women," Jimmy remarked, "and leaves us with Mark, Tony, and Henry Harker. Doug was crossed off the list on Lee's murder, but we'd better put him back for the sake of thoroughness. Suppose we check up on everyone's whereabouts at the time Phil was arranging and carrying up that tray. To begin with, where were you, Doctor?"

"In the dining room. Immediately afterward, I went upstairs."

"And when the lights went out?"

"I was halfway down the upper hall."

"Which puts you in a tough spot," Jimmy observed, and Mark agreed, without rancor.

"I left the dining room when Mark did," Doug testified, "and went out on the veranda to look at the river. It's been rising steadily all day y'know, and it was so high that it had me worried. I went back to the library to find out when flood tide's due."

"And did you find out?"

"Yes; the bore comes in from the sea in about half an hour—at three-twenty. I was just closing the tide book when I heard a commotion upstairs and ran up the front way to find out; what it was all about."

"And then again, perhaps you didn't go to the library at all," Tony's voice interrupted maliciously. "Perhaps you sneaked up the back stairs and waited for Phil in the upper hall, put out the light, did your stuff, then ran down again, and up the front way."

"I say!" Doug looked unutterably hurt, and Lucia protested, while Jimmy glanced sharply at Tony.

"Why do you say that? Did you see him?"

"No," Tony sighed, "no such luck. I was shut in my room. Went up there directly we finished dinner. I'll save Doug the trouble of pointing out that my door is close to the head of the back stairs, and that it would have been as simple as the deuce for me to be waiting for Phil when he came up with the tray. Truth is, the door was closed, and I didn't open it until after the light had gone out in my room. Then I barged into the back hall to ask what-the-hell."

"In that case," Jimmy said, "any one of you three— Mark, Doug, or Tony—could have blown that fuse by puncturing a wire, either in a bedroom or in the upper hall; and any one of you could have dropped chloral into that glass of wine."

"In the dark?" some one asked, and Jimmy nodded. "It wouldn't necessarily have been dark to the murderer. The light on the gallery is on a different circuit, and a faint glow comes through the glass door into the rear hall. You'll find if you stand with closed eyes for a minute that the lights in a room may be turned out and you'll still be able to see vague outlines, while some one who has kept his eyes open will be totally blinded by the darkness. My theory is this: the murderer was hiding on the stairs of the third floor. When he heard Phil coming up with the tray, he stuck a knife into the electric wire—I can show you the perforation—and blew the fuse. He had been keeping his eyes tightly closed, so, while Phil was blind, he was able to see the faint outline of the tray. There was but one glass— which made the rest easy."

"As you say, any one of us could have done it," Mark echoed him thoughtfully; "And it's equally true that any one of us might have gone out into the shrubbery and given that call."

"Yes," Jimmy; agreed. "Which leaves us exactly where we've been all along. And that is—nowhere."

"Henry Harker!" I exclaimed suddenly. "Of course! He was in the dining room when I filled that glass with wine. After that, I went to the kitchen for coffee, and he would have had plenty of time to run through the rear passage and up the back stairs."

"I've considered that," Jimmy said. "It's possible, of course. But, hang it all, it still doesn't explain everything." He pushed the pad away, rose from his chair, and began pacing up and down the center of the hall, his hands deep in his pockets, a frown on his forehead. Suddenly he stopped and faced them.

"I wish," he said abruptly, "that you would tell me a few more things about your grandfather."

"Grandfather!" Lucia cried, and the others gasped, astonished.

"Your grandfather," Jimmy repeated. "Just how much did you know about him? Did you know, for instance, that the last few years of his life were spent, day and night, in figuring out some means of wiping you from the face of the earth?"

"Good God, no!" Mark exclaimed, and Lucia asked in horror:

"How did you find that out?"

"From his diaries." Jimmy crossed to the table and picked up the little leather-covered books. "Doug brought them to me this afternoon and suggested they might contain something of interest. I didn't take the suggestion very seriously at first, but I spent the evening going over them. One thing is plain: before he died he had, or thought he had, perfected a plan for killing you all."

"Do you—"

Judith's voice shook so that she was forced to start again: "Do you know what it was?"

"Haven't the faintest idea. It was evident that he was afraid the diaries might fall into some one's hands after his death, so he kept all his remarks cryptic and unintelligible . . . but there is some reference to the plan on almost every page." He opened one of the books, turned to the last five or ten pages and displayed an array of cabalistic signs, letters, and figures. "Does this mean anything to you?" he asked.

They passed the book from hand to hand around the circle; one by one they shook their heads. The last to study it was Mark.

"It seems to have something to do with the time," he said, "with months and years."

Doug rose and looked over his shoulder. "And with the equinox. There's the abbreviation *Eqx*, over and over with different dates."

"Yes," Jimmy agreed, "I noticed that. But what possible connection can it have with his scheme? And if, by some wild stretch of the imagination, this massacre is part of his plan, why should he have postponed it ten years?"

"You mean you think he's actually responsible for these murders?" Judith inquired, and Jimmy shook his head ruefully.

"If you'd asked me that question two days ago I'd have heaved a book at you. But now, I tell you frankly, I'm ready to believe anything. Anything!" Again he rose from his chair as though the inquietudes of his mind made it impossible for him to remain seated. "This whole thing is a farrago, a hodge-podge of tangled clews and disjointed motives, all at sixes and sevens. I've struggled with it, trying to bring order out of chaos, until I'm dizzy—and it's still as hopelessly scrambled as ever. Every time I have a theory that seems to be rolling along smoothly, I run into those hellish questions."

"'Why are the warnings sent ahead? What took Lee up the hill? What was the shadowy shape Aunt Hagar saw at the tomb?'" I parroted.

"Exactly." He picked up a slip of paper from among his notes. "And here are a few more:

"'*What did Nathan Conroy have in his mind when he wrote about avenging himself on his family?*

"'*Who kissed Aunt Hagar in the dining room the night of 'Berto's death?*

"'*Where was Truffles when we looked for him Friday evening?*

"'*Why did that call come to-night at least an hour after Aunt Hagar was dead?*'"

He tossed the paper down and shook his head with an impatient gesture. "It's all mad. All without rhyme or reason . . . and yet, I know that nothing can be as disjointed, as meaningless, as this seems. There must be a rhythm back of it somewhere, if we can only catch it."

"Rhythm in a murder?" Lucia questioned, and he nodded impatiently.

"Yes. Every murder, every series of murder, has a definite rhythm, a *leitmotif*, you might call it, which runs through it from beginning to end." This was an old theory of Jimmy's, and a good one, as he has proved upon numerous occasions. "Usually it is easy to catch—as obvious as that tinkly tune 'Berto played the other night. You remember? *Hearts and Flowers?* But in this case, it's vague and obscure. The whole affair is seemingly as chaotic and formless as that Stravinsky thing Doug called 'a dog fight.' You remember, *The Rite of Spring.* I say it's 'seemingly' formless, because we know there's a definite rhythm from beginning to end in that composition. Doug couldn't feel it because he isn't a musician. I caught only a faint impression here and there; but you, as musicians, could discern it easily."

"That's true, of course," Mark said, "but still I don't see—"

"Wait," Jimmy begged. "The analogy is there. And it isn't as far-fetched as you may think. This hideous affair we've been living through is apparently formless, the murders without rhythm or harmony. Yet there must be some reason back of it, some *leitmotif* that ties it all together."

"Perhaps its very unreason is your best clew," I said.

"You suggested that before—that madness was the basis of the affair—and I agree with you to a certain point. Madness, or the fear of madness, seems to be the only thing that runs consistently throughout the whole horrible business. I admit that it looks like the work of a maniac, but, somehow . . . I'm not satisfied. That's why I've been studying those diaries of your grandfather's. Desperately grasping at a straw."

"But how could it have anything to do with this?" Lucia asked. "A threat made ten years ago?"

"God knows," Jimmy said shortly, "I don't." He turned away and walked toward the window, where he stood looking out into the storm. The room behind him was very quiet; all of the Conroys were sitting as silent, as still, as though they had been changed to stone.

Mark, nearest the table, reached out and turned the leaves of one of the diaries. Lucia's fingers twisted in her lap. Suddenly she stopped, her head back, in a listening attitude.

"What's that?" she asked sharply.

We all heard it, then: the sharp, scuffling sound of a body sliding against the house, the crash of a weight dropped into shrubbery, followed by the shrill, piercing bark of Truffles, who had been shut into Mark's room, after Aunt Hagar's death.

"Harker!" Jimmy exclaimed. "He's jumped from a window!"

Doug sprang to his feet, but Tony drew him back. "Oh, let the poor old chap go. If he's afraid to stay in this cursed house, I don't blame him."

"But why should he be afraid?" Jimmy demanded. "Why should he want to go out in this storm?"

We all turned to look at him in bewilderment.

"I—I don't know," Lucia said shakily. "It is strange."

"It's more than strange," Jimmy told her brusquely, and I knew that he was in the grip of some cruel perplexity. "Henry's a cripple. He risked his neck in dropping from a third story. He must have some reason. . . ." For a moment he stood, eyes dilated, then spoke in a low, tense tone. *"What does he know, that we don't?"*

CHAPTER 22
FLOOD TIDE

What does Harker know that we don't? Jimmy Lane had asked, and it was while we sat staring at him, stupefied, that we first caught an ominous sound in the distance. Starting as a dull roar, hardly distinguishable from the rush of the river, it grew rapidly louder. I had thought, at first, that it must be the bore coming up from the sea. Now, I realized this was no ordinary tide; the sound was more threatening than thunder, and was accompanied by a crashing and grinding, as though trees and boulders were being flung together in a great mill.

With one accord we started for the gallery. Doug, Mark, Jimmy and I dragged the women. Tony went to the rescue of Truffles. Fighting our way down the steps and up the hill path, we had barely reached safety when the bore struck the end of the island, foaming and tumbling in a mad cataract across all of the low ground.

For a space, I thought the house was doomed; it was probably no more than sixty seconds, measured by my watch, but at the time, with that wild welter of water boiling below, it seemed hours.

Then, as suddenly as it had come, the bore passed on, sucking away the river and leaving behind it a mass of debris, of crisscross trunks and branches, bits of flotsam and jetsam piled helter-skelter like jack-straws tossed by a giant child.

The house still stood; Harker's room was gone, and a corner of the veranda. The living room chimney was tottering, the south steps to the gallery torn away; but the rise in ground toward the north had prevented further damage. Miraculously, tragedy had been averted.

"Thank God for the levee!" Doug exclaimed. His were the first coherent words I remember; and the others agreed that if it had not been for the new breakwater at the mouth of the river, the house must inevitably have been swept away.

"It's the storm, the moon tide, and the wind from the sea all coming at once," Mark explained and Lucia cried suddenly:

"Where's Henry?"

We had forgotten, for the moment, that Harker was missing.

"Do you suppose he could have been in his room?" Judith asked.

"If so, God help him," Jimmy murmured.

Soberly we started down to search the wreckage below.

No trace of Harker was found in the debris of his room; and although Tony, Jimmy, and I circled the island, fighting our way through wind and rain, we failed to discover his body.

When we returned to the others, we found them in the only available shelter, the portico of the tomb. They had been holding a conference as to whether or not they should return to the house.

The bore would not go out for six hours, Mark argued. Danger from exposure was greater than danger from flood. The only sensible thing was an immediate return to the house.

We all agreed, feeling that the luxury and warmth of. sheltering walls was worth any price.

As we started down toward the house Jimmy lagged behind with Doug. There had been something not quite natural about Jimmy for the last hour; his cheeks had been burning as though with fever, his hands shaking. I had urged him not to accompany Tony and myself in our search of the island, but he had insisted, and had borne the brunt of the difficult expedition. Now, he seemed utterly exhausted. We were scarcely half way to the gallery when he collapsed.

Doug swung him up on his shoulders and carried him down to the house. Mark put him to bed; and Mrs. Prill brought hot water bottles.

Tony offered to stand guard while the rest of the family slept. There was a hint of grim humor in this last, a humor which he was not slow in pointing out: ". . . Unless you're afraid I'll cut your throats. I easily might, you know."

The women were to return to the safety of the third floor. Since Jimmy and I were out of the running as suspects, Doug was to sleep in Jimmy's room while I doubled up with Mark. The theory was, I believe, that we should keep watch on the others. As a matter of fact, we were all so dead for sleep that the trump of doom would not have waked us; even the bore, roaring out down the river to the sea, seemed to have roused only Mark, who started for the gallery to make sure all was well and discovered Tony asleep in the main hall, outraged nature having overcome his self-control and closed his eyes.

The bore was lower than it had been the night before, and did little or no damage. It was after nine, by then, and rain was no longer falling, although the clouds still bulked black and sinister in a threatening sky. It struck Mark, according to his story later, it would be an excellent time to look for Henry Harker before the storm began again.

He returned to the hall and roused Tony. It was undoubtedly careless of them to have left the house without waking someone to take Tony's place, but I can easily understand how it happened. We had, all of us, the feeling that the murderer, whoever he was, would operate only in the dark; and, rather like children, we thought nothing could happen so long as it was daylight.

Right or wrong, they left the house, and were still gone when the family began to awaken, three-quarters of an hour later.

Breakfast was at ten-thirty. Lucia and Judith, unable to bear the expanse of dark mahogany which had once been none too long for the Conroy clan, had removed two leaves, and shrunk the table to a smaller size. The effect was rather worse than before; it made the dining room look large and somber in the gray light, and the empty chairs that stood against the wall seemed still more conspicuous. Sally and 'Berto, Lee and Aunt Hagar. How many of those gathered around the silver coffee urn to-day would be gone to-morrow?

We tried, all of us, to rid ourselves of the grisly thought, to talk determinedly of the storm and its consequences. We were not worried about the absence of Tony and Mark, because Tony had left a note, scribbled upon one of Jimmy Lane's pads. Connie had found it on the table in the upper hall and brought it down to the dining room.

When Tony and Mark returned they had only failure to report.

"There's no doubt about it, Henry's been drowned," Mark told us. "We couldn't find a trace of him."

No one spoke. All of us, I think, were picturing that boiling maelstrom of the night before, with its mass of tossing debris, and, in the midst of it, a man's white face, uplifted for a brief instant, then blotted out by the surging water.

Lucia drew a sobbing breath. "Poor Henry," she said. "I never liked him, but I didn't want him to die."

"Best thing that could have happened," Mark declared. I saw that he was laboring under some excitement.

"What do you mean?"

It was Tony who answered. "He means we can stop worrying, and sleep o' nights. With our simple little brains," he cast a slightly malicious glance at Jimmy, "we've solved the whole business. It was Harker who did those murders."

"That so?" Jimmy was meekness personified. "How d'you figure it?"

"Like this. First, we know his motive. He had an interest in the money if all of us were bumped off. Ten years alone on this island had made him crazy enough to think he could get away with it, Mark says it's one of the symptoms of a certain type of insanity for a man to think he's smarter than anyone else."

"*Folie de grandeur,*" Jimmy murmured, and Mark nodded agreement.

"So much for motive," Tony went on. "Now for how he did it. Sally's murder was easy. He often brought us cold drinks and it would have been a cinch for him to steal that chloral hydrate out of the bathroom and slip it into her glass. 'Berto's murder would have been just as simple. 'Berto probably got him to help in that hoax."

"How about Lee?"

"The theory we have about Lee is the neatest of all. Prillie says Henry was supplying Lee with liquor. Probably swiped from grandfather's cellar. It would be natural for them to have had some sort of a signal."

"You think Harker called Lee from the shrubbery?"

"That's right. Lee'd go anywhere, any time, for a drink." Lucia gave a little gasp, and he glanced toward her quickly. "Sorry, dear, but we've got to get this thing straight."

"Why should Lee have gone up the hill?" someone asked.

"Probably Henry had the stuff cached in the tomb—or Lee thought he had."

"Smart boy," Jimmy murmured, and I glanced at him, puzzled. It had seemed to me at first that he took small stock in this theory. Now I was not so sure. He had picked up the yellow pad, upon which Tony had written his note before going out to search for Harker, and was regarding it intently. "Go on," he said. "How about Aunt Hagar's death?"

"That's easy. Henry was in the dining room when Phil was pouring out that glass of port. While Phil was in the kitchen getting coffee, he ran up the back stairs and waited his chance to blow the fuse and slip the chloral into the wine."

"But why," Judith asked, "why should he have given that call after she was dead?"

"Because," Tony's voice was triumphant, "the call wasn't meant for Aunt Hagar. It was given so that we would all do exactly what we *did*. Rush out into the shrubbery to investigate. You'll have to remember, there were three more people for him to get out of the way: Lucia, Judith, and Mark. Lucia and Judith were upstairs, but Mark was down in the kitchen. I think the whole business was an inspiration of the moment. He saw a chance to get Mark out into the dark where he could do him in. But as it happened, Mark ran out the front way. By the time Henry located him, both Doug and I were there and it was too late. How does that strike you, Jimmy?"

"As very ingenious. What more?"

"There isn't much more. After Aunt Hagar's death, you locked Henry on the third floor while we had that talk down here. I suppose he took it for granted you knew he was guilty. So he climbed out of that window and tried to swim across the river."

"Or went in the rowboat," Mark contributed. "It's missing. It may have been carried off by the bore last night, but, also, it may have been taken by Henry."

"In any event, it means that our troubles are over."

Tony rose and threw his arms wide in a gesture of relief. "I feel as though an elephant had stopped sitting on me."

"Just a minute," Jimmy was staring at the yellow pad, which he still held in his hand. "Just a minute, Tony. Your theory is deucedly clever. But there are one or two things it doesn't cover."

"Yes?" Tony swung around. "What are they?"

"First, if Lee knew Harker kept liquor in the tomb, why was he so startled by that figure he saw coming from the portico the night before 'Berto's death? Second, why did he lock all those doors before he went out? And third, if Harker is guilty, how do you explain this?" he held up the yellow pad.

Upon the white cardboard back, printed with blue pencil, in the same bold letters that had distinguished the last two communications, were the words:

Chapter Four
Judith

CHAPTER 23
"WHY WASN'T I TOLD"

There was no slightest chance that Harker might have written the note. The pad had been placed upon the table at the beginning of the conference which followed Aunt Hagar's death. Tony had seen it there during his vigil; he was ready to testify that the back had been unmarked at that time. He was certain of this because he had used the pad as a makeshift tray for a cup of coffee out of the thermos provided by Mrs. Prill. The faint, circular stain was still there, and the mark of the pencil was over it, proving that the writing must have been done after five o'clock, the hour when Tony had eaten his snack.

"How could anyone have got at it?" he asked in apparent bewilderment. "I never left the spot until Mark came—"

"And found you asleep at the switch," Doug pointed out.

"I suppose *you* didn't fall asleep the night of Lee's death?"

"That was different; I'd been drugged."

"How do we know?" Tony was growing angry. "How do we know that what you tell us is the truth? You may have only pretended to drink that wine. You may be lying when you say you saw Lee go up the path. You may have invented that call. Nobody else heard it."

"I suppose you didn't hear it last night?" Doug flung back.

"Sure I heard it. We all heard it. But how do we know you didn't make it? You'd plenty of time to get out into the shrubbery after the lights went off."

"The same thing applies to you." Doug was plainly trying to hang on to his temper. "You were near the back door and could have sneaked out as easily as I could. As for that note, you were alone with the pad for hours."

They were standing, now, both shouting furiously. They might actually have flown at each other's throats if Judith had not fainted.

It speaks volumes for our state of mind that we had not, until then, considered the threat against her life. All of us were so intent upon tracing the murderer that the cruel terror Judith must have been suffering had not entered our heads. Now, when we saw her lying, a huddled heap, across the arm of the high-backed chair that stood behind the coffee urn, we all jumped to the conclusion that she had been poisoned in the same fashion as Aunt Hagar.

But Mark, after a hasty examination, reassured us. It was only shock. Even as he spoke, she opened her eyes and smiled weakly.

"Sorry to have frightened you," she murmured, and something in her humility touched Jimmy.

He ordered us all out of the room, with the exception of Mrs. Prill. At his request we went into the living room, bleak now, and clammy from the moisture left around its foundations by the flooding river.

It was raining again, with the sullen persistency that had characterized the storm. The far shore line was blanked out by mist, and the island seemed as lonely as that ghostly ship filled with the nescient dead in *Outward Bound*.

Doug and I examined the chimney, decided it was safe, and busied ourselves building a fire. Tony, still fuming, brought the wood. Mark joined Connie, who was bearing the shock very well, I thought; at least she showed none of the hysterical symptoms that had affected her during the first two days. She was quiet, now, and aloof, as though she had ceased to fear any personal danger and was watching the murderer's depredation among the Conroy clan with detached interest.

Lucia was curled on the window seat, sobbing quietly, her head resting on her arm. Her figure outlined against the somber background of stormy water and sky formed a picture of utter despair.

When Jimmy returned, the fire was crackling and a faint warmth was beginning to steal into the room. He had locked Judith and Mrs. Prill into the third floor, he told us. Prillie was armed with a pistol, and the two had a supply of tinned stuff sufficient to last them all day. He had also made an examination of the table in the upper hall, and found no trace of the blue pencil which had been used for writing the threat against Judith.

"But it was there when Mark and I left this morning," Tony insisted. "It was the pencil you used earlier in the evening. Remember? I wrote that note with it—saying Mark and I were going to look for Henry—and left it on the table by the pad." His eye lighted suddenly. "Of course, that means the threat was written after we left!"

"I don't see that at all," Doug argued. "You could have written it yourself, then turned the pad over. Or Mark could have done it while you were asleep."

"Not as easily as you could have written it after we were gone," Tony snapped. "I suppose you got rid of the pencil for fear of finger-prints."

Doug turned to Jimmy. "Look here, there've been a lot of loose accusations thrown around this morning! I think we ought to do something about it. We ought to give each of the bedrooms a thorough turnout and see if we can't pick up some new clews."

"Rot!" Tony exploded.

But Mark seemed to agree with Doug; and, somewhat to my surprise, Jimmy nodded his head,

"O. K. Give me a minute or two with Phil, and then I'll join you."

Once inside the library, Jimmy did not plunge into speech. While I kindled the fire, he paced the room, smoking reflectively.

My curiosity got the better of me. "You have some new theory," I accused.

He stopped and looked at me oddly. "No, on my word. Or—if I have, it only has to do with the method. I haven't the faintest idea as to the identity of the murderer."

"Have you abandoned the madness theory?"

"Not entirely. But of course you realize, with Henry Harker gone, we are narrowed down to Mark. Unless—" He paused, as though struck by some new thought. "Look here, will you be a good fellow and fetch Prillie from the third floor? Let Connie stay with Judith."

When I returned with Mrs. Prill, he greeted her absently and indicated a chair by the fire. It was the same place she had occupied that night after 'Berto's death, when Jimmy had conducted his first examination; then she had been distant and evasive, plainly resentful of our questions, now I sensed a difference in her attitude. The past three days had visibly shaken her, and she was eager to help.

Jimmy's first question had to do with Mark. Had he ever shown any signs of insanity, any eccentricities?

"Not unless you call wanting to be a doctor eccentric," Mrs. Prill told him. "He's wanted to be that ever since he was a little boy. Always reading and studying while the others played."

"Did he have a bad temper?"

"Never." She was positive about that. "Mr. Tony and Mr. Doug used to be fighting all the time. Regular knock-down-and-drag-outs, until Mr. Tony learned he always got licked—then he wouldn't fight any more, except with his tongue. Dr. Mark was always trying to make peace between them. Cold he's always been—and cruel, I guess you'd call it. The things he does to dogs and cats in his laboratory. . . . But I can't think he's the one who's been doing the murdering. Though, of course," she added more slowly, "there's always the chance he might be crazy. I can see he's the only one under suspicion that's got Conroy blood."

"How about Doug and Tony?" Jimmy asked. "I suppose there isn't a chance that either of them might be Conroys after all?"

She considered this gravely, then shook her head. "It's not possible," she decided. "Miss Mary—that was Mr. 'Berto's mother—was dead three years before his father remarried, and Mr. Tony was born long after. As for Mr. Doug, there's never been any secret about where he came from. His father was Mr. Hugh's partner, and he wasn't adopted until he was eight or nine years old."

"I don't suppose Hugh Conroy could have . . ." Jimmy left the sentence suspended suggestively.

Mrs. Prill stared for an instant, then gave a dry laugh. "I see what you're driving at, but you're all wrong. Mr. Hugh's partner had hair the same funny shade of red as Mr. Doug, and the boy was the spittin' image of him."

That was that. None of Jimmy's questions could shake her sincere belief that both Tony and Doug were outside of the Conroy clan and that they were most certainly sane.

Mr. Tony was flighty, she admitted. And would do any-thing to get out of work. But there wasn't an ounce of harm in him—while Mr. Doug used to have a temper to match his hair. But he'd cured himself, and now he was as nice and dependable as you could wish for. Not as bright as the others, maybe; but with a good head for business. And that was *one* thing Mr. Tony hadn't.

"Business or not, both of them are as sane as you and me. Perhaps saner," she added, with a sardonic tightening of the lips.

Jimmy asked one or two more questions, the answers to none of which seemed to give him any particular enlightenment; then sent her to the kitchen for some coffee.

After she had gone, he stood for a moment in the center of the room, his brow knitted into a frown, as though the information he had received disappointed him in some way. In the end, he shook his head, and strolled over to the French windows, where he gazed out into the tangle of trees and shrubbery which filled the narrow space between the house and the hill.

"Damnably dark room for a library," he murmured irritably, "with that gallery overhanging. Why should it have been put there, I wonder? There isn't any view." He broke off with a low whistle and stood so still that, believing he must seen something in the garden, I crossed to his side. "Look here," he asked excitedly, "what age would you estimate these trees? I mean the ones on the lower level."

"Why," I was not unnaturally surprised, "thirty years, I should think. Certainly not more than forty."

"And those up on the hill?"

"It's impossible to say. Over a hundred, at least."

"Fool!" Jimmy chanted. "Idiot! Why didn't I think of it?" Prillie was entering with the coffee, and he turned on her. "Why wasn't I told about the moving of this house?"

She looked astonished. "I don't know that anyone thought of it, Mr. Lane. It all happened so long ago."

"During the time the family was off the island, wasn't it?"

"Yes; 'bout two, three, years before Mr. Conroy died. He got workmen from the other side to do the moving.

It must have been a terrible job. They had to cut it into three pieces, and make a road down the hill. Mr. Hugh was abroad that year, and Henry Harker was always hand in glove with Mr. Conroy, so nobody knew about it until his lawyer happened to come over."

"Was the lawyer coming about a new will?" Jimmy asked.

"Why, yes. How did you know?"

"Never mind that now. What reason did he give for the moving?"

"He said in winter the wind hit it too hard on the hill; he wanted it down where it was sheltered-like. But of course it was just one of his crazy ideas."

"I wonder," Jimmy said softly. And, when she looked at him in surprise: "Doesn't it strike you as strange that he should have had the house moved down to this level, then, almost immediately afterward, have made a will requiring the family to spend a month on the island every year? And isn't is odd that he should have selected the month the fall equinox was due?"

"You mean," a reluctant understanding dawned in Mrs. Prill's eyes, "he *wanted* the storm to come?"

"In the dead of night, when they were asleep," Jimmy agreed. "It all depended upon the flood, the equinox, and a storm from the sea happening to come together with a high tide. That was what he was figuring in the back of that diary—the number of times it had happened in the past, so far as he could discover from records. Of course the hill was always safe, but I fancy this lower beach has been washed over three or four times since the house was built above. The last time must have been between thirty and forty years ago, judging from the size of the trees which have grown up since. Probably he was hoping, gambling upon its coming again during the ten years he named in his will."

"But why," I asked, "did he make it only ten?"

"I imagine he didn't dare try the family's patience for a longer time. He judged their pride would keep them from breaking the will if it was not made too difficult. You can see the old boy had them sized up pretty accurately. He was right about the flood, too. It did come, barely inside of the ten years. One thing he couldn't forsee—the building of the levee. If it hadn't been for that new embankment, the place would most certainly have been swept away last night."

Mrs. Prill said slowly: "I believe you're right, Mr. Lane. But I don't see how it's going to tell us who did those murders."

"Neither do I, at the moment," Jimmy admitted. "At least it clears away some of the fog." He was still at the window, sipping his coffee and gazing thoughtfully up at the hill. "Tell me, where did the house stand original-ly? Never mind," he added quickly, "I think I can guess. It stood north of that big magnolia, where those scarlet cannas are planted—and the tomb is over part of it. Am I right?"

"Right as a trivet. The tomb's built where the kitchen wing used to stand, and the crypt, is the old wine-cellar."

That this fitted with some theory of Jimmy's, I could see plainly, for he nodded, well pleased. "That answers two of our questions, Phil."

"Which ones?" I asked; but before he could answer, Doug knocked impatiently at the door, and asked when we would be ready to go upstairs and start our search for clews.

In view of Jimmy's excitement over his new discovery, I expected him to have changed his mind about the project. But no, he swallowed the last of his coffee and joined the others in the living room.

All of the Conroys were present, except Connie and Judith, who were locked on the third floor. Tony strolled in casually with a cup of coffee, which he said he had taken from the stove in the kitchen. I saw Jimmy was annoyed that he had been allowed to leave the others, but it was too late to protest now, and Doug was as eager to begin our tour of detection as a Basset hound for the hunt.

We began our search in Judith's room. It had been agreed among us that Jimmy, Lucia and I should do the searching while Mark, Tony and Doug looked on and offered suggestions.

Every drawer, every box, every nook and cranny in the various rooms was examined, but without results. Only, two bedrooms were left untouched, Aunt Hagar's and the corner room on the south where Lee and I had slept Saturday night. Both of these had been gone over by Jimmy Lane, then locked, and paper pasted over the cracks and keyholes, so there seemed little chance of their yielding any new evidence.

Our search in Doug's room began rather perfunctorily; we had already gone over it twice before and it had not been occupied since the night of Lee's death.

Doug had been most helpful in our search. When I say that nothing had been discovered, I am excluding his findings: an accumulation of torn paper, buttons, fragments of dried mud, and a rare assortment of hairs—blond, brunette, and indeterminate—that would have delighted Sherlock Holmes. Now that we were searching his room, he tactfully subsided, and stood at one side, waiting for us to finish.

"What's the matter," Tony asked sarcastically, "can't you find any hairs on your own carpet?" As he spoke he strolled across the room to lean against the bureau and watch us at our work. His whole attitude was negligent, but it seemed to me his eyes were darting keenly about the walls and furniture as though in search of something. To mask his interest he lighted a cigarette, and was tossing the match into the grate when he stopped, frozen; for the fraction of a second he stood, hand outstretched, the match still in his fingers, then he glanced about quickly as though to make sure that his preoccupation had not attracted our attention.

That Jimmy Lane had noticed, I felt sure. He cut short our scrutiny of the room and set everyone to examining the hall, at the far end, where the stairs came down from the third floor.

A moment later I realized he had disappeared. Going in pursuit, I found him once more in Doug's room. He was standing on the spot where Tony had stood, bent forward in the same attitude. His eyes were turned in the direction of the fireplace, an old-fashioned affair of painted wood. In the excitement of the last few days the hearth had not been cleaned, and the scattered ashes of a dead fire were still in the grate. He bent over and studied them thoughtfully. I peered over his shoulder, but could see nothing of interest, no charred paper, nor half-burned object to account for the expression that had been on Tony's face. Suddenly he glanced up and gave an exclamation. Following his eyes, I saw that a loop of string was hanging down the flue, its whiteness emphasized by the dark and sooty background. In an instant, he had rolled up his sleeves and reached into the chimney.

"There's a sort of shelf here, made by pulling out three or four bricks," he said. "It goes back into the masonry." Then, almost immediately: "I've got something!" He brought into view a package wrapped in a sooty paper and tied with the string which had hung down, and betrayed its presence. Upon the table, he folded back the wrappings to disclose a blue wax pencil and a medicine bottle labeled: "Chloral Hydrate."

Chapter 24
Lucia Confesses

Like a schoolboy I gaped at the telltale objects on the table, then I saw that Jimmy was regarding them through half-closed eyes, as though attempting to fit their presence in the room with some theory which he had previously evolved.

"'Curiouser and curiouser,'" he quoted *Alice in Wonderland*. "Now I wonder—" He broke off, startled by a cry from the door.

In our intentness over the find, we had thrown all caution to the wind, and Lucia had slipped in unobserved. She was standing, her hands clasped at her breast, her eyes fixed upon the table. Knowing, as I do now, all that was passing through her mind, I am not surprised at her outcry. For one moment she faced what must have been a frightful dilemma, and wavered, undecided. Then, with a sudden, quick movement, she closed the door behind her and came toward us determinedly.

"There's something I ought to tell you," she said.

"Yes." Whatever sympathy Jimmy may have felt, there was no sign of it in his face, only a frowning sternness. "The time you should have confided in us is past, my girl. Earlier, it might have helped. Now, it is unnecessary. I've figured it out for myself."

"About Doug?"

"About you and Doug."

"Then of course you see what it means?"

"I should say it was fairly obvious."

Their cryptic exchange maddened me. I demanded bluntly: "What is it you figured about Lucia and Doug?"

"We're not engaged any more," Lucia told me. "I broke it off almost as soon as I reached the island this fall . . . though how Jimmy guessed, when I was so careful—"

"It was that kiss in the dark," Jimmy explained. "I mean the mysterious man who kissed Aunt Hagar in the dining room, the night 'Berto was killed. I remembered you'd pinned your flowers, fragrant jasmine, upon Aunt Hagar's shoulder, and suspected someone had mistaken her in the dark for you. There was no reason why Doug shouldn't have admitted the fact—which left only Mark and Tony. Mark is hardly my idea of a philanderer, but as for Tony. . . . You'll remember he had a cigarette-lighter in his pocket, Harker saw him using it on the veranda, therefore it was plain he was telling a fib when he said he came into the house to get matches. In addition to that, he'd been enthusiastic about that game of blind man's buff, although he had no intention of playing. I suspected he must have wanted a word with you, and tried to get hold of you in the dark. Later on, when you let slip the fact that he was courting you the summer Sally died, I felt sure there was still some sentiment between you."

"Why should you let the family go on thinking you were engaged to Doug?" I asked, bewildered.

"Because of his wretched pride," Lucia explained. "When I told him I'd made a mistake, and couldn't marry him, he begged me to keep it from the others

until after we'd left the island. He said it was bad enough to lose me without being kidded to death in the bargain. They *do* tease him a lot. So I promised to say nothing while we were here. Please," she added quickly, "please don't get the idea that I'm engaged to Tony. I'm not. He," her voice broke a trifle and I saw that her self-control was slipping, "he's always had a sort of fascination for me, but I know I oughtn't to marry him. I can't stand people who are lazy."

"You've told him you won't marry him?"

"Over and over."

"Which explains that scene Lee saw on the veranda, I suppose."

"Yes; I was having a row with Tony about—oh, about everything. Connie'd been out there earlier, with 'Berto, and left her mandarin coat. It got a little chilly and I slipped it around my shoulders. Lee saw me and thought I was Connie. As soon as I discovered what had happened I explained the whole thing to Mark."

"Where did you talk to him?" Jimmy asked. "In his room."

"Was he at all excited?"

"Not about Connie. He'd known Lee was mistaken because she'd been in bed at two o'clock, the time Lee said she was on the veranda with 'Berto. But he was upset about my being there with Tony. We—we rather argued about it." She was watching Jimmy closely, as though trying to read the thoughts that were passing in his mind. In sudden protest she cried out at something she glimpsed there. "No, Jimmy, honest, Tony doesn't have the slightest idea I'll ever consent to marry him. He still thinks I'm engaged to Doug."

"You're sure of that?"

"Absolutely certain. You see," she hesitated rather pathetically, "I knew if he learned I'd broken things off it would mean more arguments, and that I might weaken. So I let him go on thinking Doug and I were to be married in November."

"But," a thought struck me, "if neither Doug nor Tony believe you're going to marry them, then neither of them can have any hope of gaining that inheritance through you—and we've eliminated their last possible motive for committing the murders."

"Yes," Lucia nodded, and dropped down on the bed as though in relief. "Neither of them could have the faintest reason for doing it."

"But what about those?" I pointed to the telltale objects on the table, and she looked puzzled.

"I don't know. There's no doubt about it, that's the bottle which contained the medicine Mark used to give Sally. I don't suppose anyone could have had it except the murderer."

"No one," Jimmy agreed.

There was silence again while we all stared at the bottle; then Jimmy turned away, crossed to the window, and stood looking up the hill path toward the tomb with grave intentness. Once he opened the French doors and went out to study something from the gallery; once he tried the lock of the door into the hall, as though judging the amount of noise it would make, then he returned.

"The fact that the bottle was found in Doug's chimney doesn't necessarily mean that he put it there," he said softly. "This room hasn't been occupied for twenty-four hours; almost anyone could have slipped in from the gallery, or from the hall."

"Do you mean," Lucia demanded, "that someone is trying to throw suspicion on Doug?"

For an appreciable interval Jimmy did not answer. Then he asked abruptly: "What do you know about Doug's adopted father? Is it true that no one has seen him since he went into that sanitarium?"

"Why, yes." Lucia was plainly bewildered. "The doctor ordered him to be kept absolutely quiet, and no one has seen him, except Doug."

"Then you've no idea of his real condition?" he pressed. "Or what caused it?"

"None. Except, of course, what we've been told." Before she could ask the question that was plainly on her lips, Jimmy drew me to one side.

"Look here," he said, "there's something I wish you'd do for me. It's a nasty job, but you're the only one I can trust."

"What is it?" I asked, glad of a chance for action. "I want you to try and locate the newspaper that came the first day of the storm. Then," he reached into his pocket and produced duplicate keys that I recognized with a sinking heart, "I want you to go up to the tomb. Bring me both moccasins from Lee's feet—and be careful to lose none of the mud that may be on them."

Upon looking back, I believe the afternoon and evening which followed were the most nerve-wracking of any we passed during that entire reign of terror. Inaction in a crisis is always hard to bear, and upon that day it was accompanied by dreadful suspense and a sense of utter helplessness which was almost intolerable. 'Berto was killed Saturday evening. Lee's death occurred a little more than twenty-four hours later, Aunt Hagar's upon Monday night. Only three days, and three lives had been snuffed out by murder, another by accident or suicide. Although the Conroys had never been fond of Henry Harker, he was an integral part of their childhood; and when Truffles ran miserably about, whining for his idol, it added to the nerve-strain. In the end, Jimmy took the dog into the library, where he stayed all day—curled into an unhappy black and white ring—in front of the fire. I had been banished from the room myself, immediately after returning from the tomb with Lee's moccasins.

Going in at seven, to take Jimmy's tray, I found him seated at the desk, flanked by a bewildering array of objects. There was the folded newspaper, which had been brought down from the hill on the day of the storm, and which I had rescued from the screen-porch. There was a pile of yellow paper, evidently, the notes he had been making during the past few days. There was 'Berto's story, *Murder in the Conroy Clan,* and that fatal *Chapter Two,* which prophesied Lee's death; beside it lay *Chapter Three,* with its blue-penciled warning to Aunt Hagar, and the pad that carried the printed words *Chapter Four, Judith.* Beyond, laid in a neat row, were the kitchen knife that had been found at 'Berto's feet, the surgeon's blade from Mark's bag, and the steel mallet we had picked up on the hill, still wrapped in the muddy handkerchief. The chloral hydrate bottle was there, and the blue pencil; even the wrapping paper had been preserved, and was lying, neatly folded, upon the desk. In addition, there were a number of books, opened, or marked with strips of paper: Mark's volume on toxicology; Menninger's psychology, which Jimmy had taken from Judith; *The New Criminology;* and several detective novels, among them: *Hide in the Dark* by Frances Noyes Hart, Van Dine's *The Scarab Murder Case,* and an odd volume of Dr. Fu-Manchu stories.

The room was blue with cigarette smoke. Jimmy Lane, in the midst of the cloud, looked worn and exhausted; his usually ruddy face was pale, and purple smudges ringed his eyes. At sight of me he seemed bewildered.

"It can't be dinner time?"

"It's seven o'clock," I told him, placing the tray on the table near the fire.

He rose and stretched wearily, then crossed to the easy-chair; while I moved up the table, he said dispiritedly:

"I've found the murderer, Phil."

"You've what?" From his air of discouragement and utter dejection, I had been prepared for anything but this.

"I've found the murderer—beyond a shadow of doubt."

"Thank God!"

Jimmy shook his head gloomily. "Forget your pious gratitude until you hear the rest. When I say there isn't a shadow of a doubt, I mean in my own mind. I'm absolutely convinced I know the one who did these murders. But whether I can convince anyone else—well, that's a different matter."

"You must have some proof to offer."

"Certainly I have proof. Any amount of it. But every clew points toward some one other than the real murderer." He paused to munch a sandwich, then burst out: "That's the devilish part of this affair, Phil. The wretch who's done the killing has not only outsmarted us at every turn, but has doctored the evidence so cleverly that it would almost certainly implicate someone else if we offered it in court."

"Then how do you know—"

"By instinct, divination and necromancy," the food was enheartening him, and his conversation was becoming more cheerful, "and because I'm the seventh son of a seventh son. No," he added quickly, "that isn't true. Anyone ought to be able to figure out the answer—even you with your Harvardish, legal mind, Phil."

"I probably could figure it out," I replied tartly, "if I knew all that you know. But you're holding out gramma's false teeth and the scalp of a red-headed woman."

"No; 'pon my word, I'm not. You're in possession of every fact, and you've seen every clew. If you haven't sorted out what's important from what's worthless, it's because you haven't used your brain."

"Suppose you point out a few of what you call 'important' clews."

I studied the slippers, which were standing, as I had left them, upon a square of cardboard. They were of thin leather, rain-soaked and shrunken, so that they presented a leprous, mottled appearance; the fringed tongues were hanging limply over the edge. On the left side, they were heavily coated with

thick mud, which had dried upon the surface and was slowly peeling off in grayish lumps.

"See anything?" Jimmy asked. And, as I shook my head: "All right, then suppose you reconsider that list we made out the first night, after 'Berto was murdered. I mean the order in which the participants were caught in that game of blind man's buff." He was holding out the sheet of yellow paper, and I studied it thoughtfully; but it suggested no new ideas. I said as much, and Jimmy grinned.

"Very well, I'll try you with some additional questions." He handed me a sheet of paper which contained all the questions I had heard before, with a few new ones added.

They were:

Why was the call heard by Lucia on the night of Aunt Hagar's death but not on the night of Lee's?

Why is there mud only on the left side of Lee's moccasins?

Why was the key in Lee's dressing gown pocket?

Why was the mallet wrapped in Lee's handkerchief?

"Upon my word," I said, nettled by my own stupidity, "it's all Greek to me."

"I wouldn't say that. As I remember, you were pretty good at Greek. Suppose you consider the paper we found on that package in the chimney today, the paper and string. Do you recognize them?"

"No . . . yes; I believe I do. It looks like the wrapping that was around Tony's sketch-pad that day on the hill."

"Good! Doesn't that suggest anything?"

It did, but I was loath to admit it. "Anyone might have used the paper," I protested. "If I remember rightly, Tony brought it down from the hill and put it in that drawer in the front-hall table where they keep paper and string. Anyone might have got hold of it."

"Which is true of every object we have. That carving knife was taken from the kitchen, the steel mallet from the gallery closet. The surgeon's knife was in Mark's bag in the upper hall. The pad and blue pencil used in writing that threat against Judith were both lying on the table in the same place. Nothing has been used which was not easily accessible to any member of the family. You can imagine what a defense lawyer would do with those clews."

"Perhaps if you tell me who it is you suspect—"

He shook his head. "No, Phil, not yet."

His reticence hurt me. "I've been known to help you before, in your cases," I blurted out.

"You've helped me this time . . . more, perhaps, than you realize. It was something you said which first put me on the right track. You suggested—not once, but twice—that the very disorder of this affair might be our best clew. It started a train of thought that ultimately led me to the solution—"

"Which you don't intend to tell me."

"Which I don't intend to tell you." He had finished his dinner and pushed away the tray. Now he rose to his feet, crossed to the closet, and produced a raincoat and rubbers. "I'm going out," he told me. "May be gone an hour or so. Your job is to ride herd on the family until I get back. Make 'em stay together, and away from the windows."

His words suggested a possibility so horrifying that I grasped. "You mean there's someone on the island besides the people in this house?"

"That," Jimmy was shrugging into his mackintosh, "is one of the questions I don't care to answer. But you needn't worry," he added, "I'm taking a pistol, and Truffles will go with me." He whistled to the dog, who uncurled

himself, stretched, and stood at attention while the leash
was snapped on his collar. At the French doors, Jimmy
paused to regard me gravely over his shoulder. "Would
you really like to know why I won't tell you what I suspect
about this case, Phil?"

"You know I would."

"It's because," already he was half out the door and his
words were coming from the darkness beyond, "it's because I once saw you play in *Macbeth*."

He was gone.

I stood, the tray in my hands, staring after him.

Macbeth had been given in college, during our Junior
year. I had played Third Murderer in that production.

CHAPTER 25
A CAN OF CYANIDE

It was a full hour before Jimmy Lane returned. The intervening time had been sheer torture, worried, as I was, by his vague hint at an unseen presence on the island. To watch for danger from within was bad enough, but if it might also be threatening us from without . . .

In a tumult of doubt and perplexity, I gathered the family together in the square upper hall, closed and shuttered the windows, then locked all the bedroom doors and those that opened on to the gallery.

The Conroys watched me apathetically and without comment. Mark, Tony and Doug were seated at the table, half-heartedly sampling the sandwiches and coffee that constituted our sketchy evening meal. Connie was curled on the couch with a plate and cup, her appetite apparently unimpaired. Lucia could eat nothing; she seemed unable to remain seated for any length of time, and constantly rose from her chair to fuss with the fire, or listen at one of the windows.

Judith was still on the third floor, guarded by Mrs. Prill. Jimmy's first words when he returned had to do with her.

"I'm going to bring Judith down to this floor, tonight," he said, "where she can be near us."

"Is that wise?" Mark asked. "Surely she's safer up there."

"Safer from some things, perhaps. But how about fire?"

There was a gasp of horror, from Connie this time.

"Oh, but you don't think—"

He cut her short. "I think anything can happen. *Anything.*" Back of his words I sensed some new emotion, and suspected he had made an important discovery on his trip outside. "I mean to put Judith in the center room, the one used by Mark and Connie, with Phil to guard her. The rest of you will spend the night here in the hall under my eye."

There was some small protest, mostly from Connie, who in the midst of death and disaster could still feel resentment at being turned out of her room; but Jimmy won. He himself went up to the third floor, and a few minutes later appeared with Judith, who was taken immediately to Mark's room.

Together, Jimmy and I prepared the defenses for the night. One window sash was left open to admit air; since both windows looked out upon the gallery, we drew the shutters, closed and bolted them on the inside. The door, on Jimmy Lane's orders, was locked immediately after he left the room.

For a time the two of us, Judith and I, sat talking quietly. The day she had passed in the quiet of the third floor, combined with her talk with Jimmy Lane, seemed to have given her new vitality. Color had once more returned to her cheeks, and her eyes had lost the dead, hopeless look they had worn that morning. Now that the moment of real danger was approaching, she was so buoyed up with excitement that she ceased to be afraid.

At a little before midnight, Jimmy knocked on the door; and when I opened it, he stepped into the room for a moment to announce that the family were going to try and snatch some sleep. While he talked, I could see past him into the hall. Connie was occupying the couch, and two cots had been set up for Lucia and Mrs. Prill. Tony and

Doug were in easy-chairs, while Mark was standing guard at the head of the stairs. Only Truffles was missing, and when I asked Jimmy about the dog he evaded answering.

The house had been locked and double locked. The lights were to be left on in every room. Jimmy himself had no intention of sleeping. Judith and I had only to call and he would come. Before departing, he helped Judith arrange a screen in front of the dressing table; and she retired behind it to prepare for bed.

I can still see the room as it looked after Jimmy's departure, cozy and warm, with its shaded amber lights, and the dull, gold screen outlined against the black rectangle of shuttered windows.

There was a small clock on the mantel, a silly Dresden affair belonging to Connie. I picked it up to wind it, and saw that the hands stood at exactly midnight. While I was turning the screw in the back, the clock on the hall stairs struck its first booming note. As though it were a signal, the lights blinked once—then went out. Almost at the same instant, faint and far away, but still unmistakable, the call sounded from outside.

Instantly the house was in a pandemonium. Connie screamed, Lucia cried out. There was the sound of scrambling footsteps in the hall, and Jimmy's voice, raised in a series of sharp orders.

I called to Judith, and was relieved to hear her answer from the darkness: "Don't worry, I'm all right." It steadied me, somehow, and I moved toward the door, where Jimmy was already pounding and calling.

It was here that I made a false move. Undoubtedly, I should have first stopped to strike a light, but Jimmy's voice was so insistent that I took what seemed the simplest course, and left the lighting of a candle to Judith. As quickly as I could, I crossed to unlock the door.

The key was gone.

It seemed impossible, utterly, madly impossible. I my-self had turned the key in the lock less than ten minutes earlier, and Judith had checked on it before she started to undress. Now, grope as I would, I could find only the empty keyhole. It was like one of those mad, suffocating dreams that accompany fever. I had lived through all of this before. The darkness. The sound of voices. The grop-ing for a key. When? Where? Of course—on the night of Lee's death. I'd wakened and he'd been gone. But Judith wasn't gone. She was there, somewhere behind me. *Why didn't she strike a light?*

I called: "Judith!" And again: "Judith!"

This time there was no answer. Only silence. A chill breath seemed to pass through the room. . . .

I think for a moment I went a little, more than a little, mad. I began to pound on the door, calling for Jimmy, who was simultaneously pounding and calling on the other side. How long this crazy exchange lasted, I cannot say. At the time, it seemed endless. Finally my voice, raised now to an hysterical pitch, seemed to carry above the tumult in the hall.

Someone brought a key; it turned in the lock, and the door was thrown open so forcibly that it struck against my forehead and knocked me almost senseless.

The first words I understood, when my head cleared, were from Jimmy Lane:

"Where's Judith?"

Before I could answer, Doug gasped:

"She's gone!"

After that the memories are fragmentary. Some one sprang to the window, and found the shutter at the north end swung open.

"But it was bolted on the inside!"

"Judith must have unlocked it herself!"

"Why should she?"

"That call—I *heard* it!"

All of this in a wild clamor of voices, while the Conroys milled about the room, and Doug stood beside me, staring at the window, and repeating over and over:

"But we were all in the hall together. All of us. *All* of us."

Somehow we formed into two parties, and began a search. Jimmy insisted that the women must not be left alone in the house. He ordered them into coats and boots; and, with Mark as a guard, they took part in the hunt which followed.

When we first started, the two parties consisted of Mark, Connie, Lucia and Mrs. Prill, who were to search the west end of the island; Doug, Tony, Jimmy and myself, who were supposed to look nearer home. As a matter of fact, we soon became separated.

The rain had ceased, and the clouds were beginning to clear, disclosing a sky of midnight blue with a great cold moon that was alternately revealed and blotted out by drifting mist. The trees were still bent with the weight of moisture, and as we moved there were ghostly patterings all around us.

We searched the shrubbery surrounding the house, the dark and funereal cypresses upon the hill. We turned our lights into the great branches of the gum trees, and probed the grisly depths of the tomb. Beating through the brush, losing and finding each other, calling and whispering, we were like mad ghosts in the ghastly light of the fitful moon.

At last, we returned to the house, straggling back one by one, hopeless and exhausted.

Judith was not on the island. She was nowhere on the face of the land. Yet she would not deliberately have jumped into the swollen river, unless something had maddened her, something so horrible, so unexpected, that it had forced her into that waste of water. What it might have been, none of us cared to contemplate, for none of us could forget that everyone had been accounted for at the time the lights went out. And yet, that call, that abominable call, had come from the hill.

We were grouped about the stove drying our shoes when I caught Jimmy's signal and followed him from the kitchen. The lights were ablaze again, and when we reached the upper hall I saw that he was in the grip of overwhelming excitement.

"Come here," he said. "There's something I want to show you."

It was the chest in our room, the heavy oak affair, in which we had locked away all of the knives and poisons that were found on the island. Some one had forced the lock while we were gone; the lid was standing open. None of the objects it contained had been touched, with one exception. The squat yellow can of cyanide was missing.

Jimmy put his finger to his lips. "Hush! Before anyone comes, I want you to go with me."

"But where—"

"I know where it is." He started down the hall, and I followed, past the door to Doug's room, past Mark's and Connie's, to the bedroom that had once sheltered Lee but now belonged to Tony.

As we stepped into the small, white room, with its neat, striped paper and dotted Swiss curtains, it looked exactly as we had left it after our exhaustive search of the afternoon. Exactly as we had left it except—on the blue counterpane and the shiny dark floor, beneath the bed, were four small, white feathers.

In a flash Jimmy crossed the room and snatched up the pillow from the bed. Under the linen slip, the ticking had been hastily ripped, and refastened with a row of small pins. Inside, deep-buried in down, we found the can of cyanide.

CHAPTER 26
THE LEITMOTIF

Ten minutes later the remaining members of the Conroy clan were gathered, by Jimmy's orders, in the library. Without intent, they had formed themselves in a half-circle. Lucia, Doug and Mrs. Prill were on the couch. Mark and Connie occupied the love seat; Tony, the big chair by the fire. I had placed myself, again by Jimmy's orders, between the desk and the door. There was a pistol in my pocket, and I was ready for any emergency.

Most of the objects which had littered the desk earlier in the evening had been removed, and, when we first entered the room, Jimmy himself was missing. As we settled into our places he appeared from the supply closet, where the stationery was kept.

The Conroys observed him with lack-luster eyes. There was no interest, no emotion betrayed by them now. Emotion requires energy, and they were too exhausted by what they had been through to have any strength left. Their faces, as I looked from one to the other, seemed dull and lifeless, as though, already, they were half-resigned to join that ghostly company in the tomb on the hill.

I know, now, that none of them suspected Jimmy Lane held the solution of the mystery in his hands. They believed he had called them together for another futile conference, and they had long since lost all faith in his efforts. Jimmy sensed this, I think, for he stood a moment regarding them gravely, then: "I'm about to tell you the name of the murderer," he said.

It was Mark who first realized the importance of this announcement. "You don't mean you know?"

Jimmy nodded. "Yes; I know who committed these murders, and how they were done." He had their attention, now, all of it.

Doug sprang to his feet. Connie gave a little cry. And Lucia locked her hands in her lap to keep them from trembling. Even Tony sat half-erect, while Mrs. Prill's sharp eyes narrowed and fixed themselves upon Jimmy's face with a piercing regard. If they expected to hear the name of the murderer immediately, they were disappointed.

With a perfect poker face, Jimmy dropped into the chair behind the desk. "I said, last night, that every murder, or series of murders, had a certain rhythm and harmony, like a musical theme. I also remarked that this affair was seemingly as lacking in coherence and form as *The Rite of Spring*. Yet, I was convinced there must be rhythm somewhere, there must be some *leitmotif*—if only we could find it. Phil suggested that perhaps it was insanity, that the very madness, the lack of all reason, was our best clew. I've discovered he was right."

Lucia, all of us, involuntarily glanced toward Mark. "Then he—the murderer, I mean—is mad?"

"No," Jimmy said slowly, "the one who did this is not insane—at least, not in the accepted sense of the word. He is coldly, abominably sane."

"But you said yourself it was undoubtedly the work of a madman," I protested.

"I said it undoubtedly looked like the work of a madman. And that was exactly how it was intended to look." He paused and leaned back in his chair. "Figure it out for yourselves: here's a family under a curse, more or less self-imposed, but still, a curse; two generations have sat watching each other, year in, year out, for signs of insanity. In such a case, if an outsider—some one of entirely different blood—wished to commit murder and avoid suspicion, what would be the first plan that would come into his head? Why, to make the murders seem mad, of course. To make them so bizarre and fantastic they would be considered the work of a demented mind."

"Clever," Mark breathed, "deucedly clever."

"As you say, clever—but not clever enough. The trouble with a scheme like that is the natural tendency to overdo it, to paint the picture in too vivid colors. Which is exactly what happened here. When I took Phil's suggestion, and tried to accept the unreason, the lack of coherence, as of prime importance, I made a discovery. I found that madness as a leitmotif was not convincing. It was like that piece of music 'Berto played for Doug, *Hearts and Flowers*. He exaggerated and burlesqued it, throwing in grace-notes and arpeggios until it was a travesty on the original. This affair was like that. It was madness burlesqued. Insanity parodied. That call, the absurd forewarnings, the hocus-pocus and flummery that went with each murder. All of it was worse than insane. It was silly. And no madman capable of carrying on a massacre like this would be silly.

"No." He returned once more to his point, accenting it with his hand upon the desk. "It was only sham madness, I decided. A counterfeit such as might be attempted by some one with no real knowledge of abnormal psychology."

He paused for a moment, waiting, I thought, for some question. But the Conroys remained silent, as though fearing to betray their thoughts by speech.

"You can see that all this, while it cleared the ground, didn't tell me who was guilty," Jimmy went on. "In fact, it made matters worse, because it enlarged our list of suspects. At the same time, I was getting help in another direction—from Harker."

"*Harker!*"

"Yes. Harker's not dead. Since last night he's been hiding in an underground room, next the tomb."

"Then there *is* another room!" Lucia exclaimed, and Jimmy nodded.

"I suspected as much when Mrs. Prill told about Harker's stealing your grandfather's liquor. She thought he had buried it somewhere, but it seemed more likely that he had some secret chamber that we knew nothing about. Then there was the question of Truffles' mysterious disappearance and the shadowy figure that Lee and Aunt Hagar saw. Two days ago Phil and I searched the tomb and crypt, inch by inch, and could find no opening. But to-day I unearthed the fact that this house was originally built upon the hill and was not moved down to this level until three years before your grandfather's death. That, combined with the flood last night, the will, and the table of figures in the back of his diary, gave me an idea."

"You mean his crazy plans for drowning us all, I suppose," Mark said. "Mrs. Prill has told us about it."

"Didn't that suggest something to you?" Jimmy inquired. And, as Mark sat with raised eyebrows: "Don't you see? Knowing the danger, your grandfather would never have been fool enough to risk his life in this house during a storm. He would have some place on the hill where he could sleep in safety, some place concealed from you so that you would not suspect his plan."

"Of course," Lucia agreed, and Doug burst out:

"Where is it?"

"Under that bed of cannas. As soon as Mrs. Prill told me the crypt was the old wine cellar, I guessed that he'd utilized the rest of the basement to make a room where he could be safe and snug. I also guessed that Henry Harker knew about it and was hiding there."

"You found him?"

"Yes; with the help of Truffles. That evening Truffles disappeared, he'd followed Harker and been locked, by accident, into the room. While we were searching for him, Harker slipped up the hill and let him out. You'll remember, we found him sitting on the front veranda when we got back to the house. When we made our search with Truffles, last night, our mistake was in keeping him on the leash. The minute I took him up to the tomb and released him, he made for that bronze tablet behind the potted cypress in the portico. It's really a door, but it doesn't open into the tomb; it opens into a narrow passage and stairs which parallel the outer wall. The bronze tablet slides quite simply—when you know the trick—only it wasn't so simple this time because Harker nearly shot me when I got inside. He's been afraid for his life ever since the night Lee died."

"Why?"

"Because he was that figure Aunt Hagar saw coming out of the tomb. Naturally, he knew about the danger from storm. He wasn't going to warn the rest of you; that clause in the will giving him half of the property if you all died made him as anxious as your grandfather to have the house swept away. But he wasn't taking any chances himself. Every night, since the storm began, he's gone up to that underground room, and stayed there until the bore passed.

"Of course, he'd no idea that Lee had been threatened. You'll remember, Harker was the only one who wasn't in the house when that Chapter Two was found in the living room. About twelve o'clock he trotted up to the underground room and turned in. He says he was awakened by a noise on the steps of the tomb; a moment later he heard Doug's yell and the pistol shot. He threw on his raincoat and went up to see what had happened, but by the time he reached the steps, both Lee and Doug were down, and there was no sign of the murderer.

"He tells me he knew none of you liked him, and he was afraid of what might happen if he was found with the bodies. When he heard Aunt Hagar scream from the gallery he doubled off down the path, full speed, for his room. By the time he reached there, Tony was pounding on the door. He waited in the shrubbery until Tony had gone up the hill, then threw off his clothes and climbed into bed, forgetting, in his hurry, to relock the door.

"When I locked him into the third floor, last night, he was terrified that the flood might come while he was there. Also, he took it for granted that we thought him guilty, and risked his neck to escape. First he cast loose the rowboat, then hid in that underground room, figuring we'd think he had tried to make the mainland and had been drowned. When I walked in on him he was ready to kill, but when he learned we didn't think he was the murderer, he opened up like a clam in fresh water and told me everything he knew. He helped me with that little comedy I staged to-night."

"What comedy?" Lucia demanded.

"The one that was played at the stroke of midnight. You were all in it. Lights out. Mysterious call from the hill. Judith disappears. . . ."

"You planned *that?*"

"Guilty! I arranged with Harker to turn off the lights at the dynamo house, then give an imitation of that famous wail from the hill."

"Then it was *you* who kidnapped Judith!"

"Yes; or, rather, she kidnapped herself. I arranged with her while I was upstairs this evening to remove the key from the lock in the room, then, while the lights were out, to slip through the window on to the gallery and nip up the hill to Harker. You see," his eyes swept the circle, "I wanted her in a safe place. But, even more, I wanted everyone out of the house for a reason of my own."

The Conroys were quiet now, quiet and watchful, with a tenseness that showed they sensed the approach of a climax; even their relief over Judith's safety seemed swallowed in their dread of what the next few minutes might disclose.

"I wanted everyone out of the house," Jimmy continued, "so that the murderer would have an opportunity to slip back and attend to certain details which I foresaw."

"He did?" It was Lucia who spoke, in a half whisper.

"He did—and it gave me the last bit of evidence I needed."

Again they waited, expecting him to disclose the name; and, again, he disappointed them.

"You see, up to that moment, I had no real proof of his identity. So long as he stuck to his original idea, of imitating madness, I was not even sure myself. Once or twice, I suspected; but the lack of a motive, combined with other things, put me off the trail. It wasn't until he changed his tactics that I began to be sure."

"How did he change?" Tony asked gruffly.

"He stopped throwing suspicion upon a hypothetical madman, and began fixing it on a definite person. When he started planting fake clews in chimneys, I guessed the motive back of the whole affair."

"And it was?"

"Money, partly. But mainly, a woman."

"A *woman?*"

They had been prepared, I think, for anything but this. The announcement was as startling as a pistol shot.

"Lucia!" Connie cried.

Lucia herself said: "Then I was right," in a still voice that seemed to plumb the depths of despair. "Oh, I hoped against hope—"

"That one of your lovers wasn't responsible?" Jimmy asked. "I'm afraid it's true. His plan was to kill as many as possible of the beneficiaries under the will, then throw the blame on his rival."

"You can prove this?" Tony asked, and Jimmy nodded.

"Every word of it. I couldn't have proved it an hour ago, because the murderer had covered his tracks so well that I'd nothing tangible to offer a jury. But with everyone out of the house, I felt sure he would seize the opportunity for hatching more deviltry. And I was right. While we were searching the island for Judith, he broke open the chest in my room and stole enough cyanide to account for the whole family."

For the first time Jimmy rose from his chair and stepped around the desk toward the center of the room. His hand was in his coat pocket and I suspected that it gripped the second revolver. "The cyanide can is in the closet," he said. "Will you fetch it, Doug? I fancy the experts won't have any trouble finding Tony's finger-prints on the tin."

"Tony!" It was Lucia who screamed. She must have feared, of course, that Jimmy would name him. She rose from her seat and stood, eyes distended, fists clenched.

Tony himself betrayed no emotion. He remained sunk in the depths of his chair, hands in pockets, a mocking smile on his lips. "Go on," he ordered Jimmy, "spin your yarn."

Doug had disappeared into the closet, and his voice came to us from its depths. "I can't find the can."

"Farther in," Jimmy told him. "On the shelf by the glass of wine." And to the group: "Phil and I found the cyanide hidden in Tony's room."

"But how did you happen to look?"

"Because," Jimmy's voice rose triumphantly, "because while you were searching the island I watched the murderer hide it."

There was an awful hush, a silence as pregnant as that which comes after the hood is adjusted over the eyes of a doomed man before the trap is sprung. All of us were looking at Tony, who was still sprawled carelessly in the deep chair, his white teeth flashing in a smile.

There was a crash from the closet, the tinkle of falling glass, a gasping moan.

Jimmy stepped quickly to the door, then swung about and nodded to Mark. "Doug needs you," he said, "He's found the cyanide."

CHAPTER 27
THE SKIES CLEAR

Picture the final scene as taking place two hours later in the library, with Tony, the Doctor, Jimmy and myself in front of the fire. Lucia, sick from exhaustion and shock, had been turned over to Mrs. Prill for cosseting. Connie and Judith had expressed a shuddering distaste for details, and only the two remaining Conroy men were present.

"Sorry I had to pull that stuff about your fingerprints on the cyanide can," Jimmy said contritely to Tony. "I wanted some excuse for getting Doug into that closet before I sprung my announcement about seeing him hiding the cyanide in your room. I was afraid he might turn ugly and hurt someone."

"Don't apologize," Tony said. "Matter of fact, you spoke the truth. I was the one who found the can and brought it to you originally, so, naturally, my finger-prints would have been on it."

"Which is true of almost every clew we possess," Jimmy pointed out. "Doug undoubtedly wore those thin rubber surgeon's gloves Mark missed from his case—so that his fingers would leave no prints. You'd used the blue pencil in writing the note before you and Mark went out to look for Harker. You'd also handled the pad. The paper he used around that bottle was from that sketch-book you'd unwrapped on the hill. The afternoon was red hot, and your hands were damp and sticky. It must have been covered with prints."

"But how—why—" I stuttered helplessly, and Jimmy smiled.

"Don't strain yourself. I'll start at the beginning—with Sally's death."

"She *was* murdered?" Mark half rose from his seat, then dropped back again as Jimmy went on:

"Yes. I believe she and Doug were secretly engaged when they came to the island last year. Remember, she'd been living away from home, and none of you had seen much of her. Probably she was waiting to surprise the family with the news when you were all here together.

"In the meantime, she's had an attack of illness and it had left her, I'm told, rather worn and haggard. Lucia came to the island first, and was here a week before Sally arrived. Doug hadn't seen Lucia for some time. She was younger and fresher than Sally. In addition to that, she had just made her first success and was beginning to be known. I think Doug was bowled over by her beauty, and it flattered his vanity to think of having a rising young novelist for a wife. But he knew she adored Sally, and that he wouldn't have a chance in the world of winning her if she suspected him of playing the cad.

"I don't suppose he'd have done anything desperate if chance hadn't played into his hands. But there was Sally trusting him. There was that wretched drug in the closet, and there was the tea-punch, with just enough sherry to hide the taste. The combination was too much of a temptation. Sally no doubt suspected what had happened, and tried to write a note in that book; but before she could make it clear, she passed into delirium."

"Two weeks later," Tony growled, "Lucia and I had a bang-up row—and she promised to marry Doug."

"It didn't stick," Jimmy told him. "Doug came to the island this summer expecting to marry her in November. She confessed that she'd made a mistake and wanted to be released. He begged her not to tell the family until after the summer holidays—hoping, I suppose, that he might win her back again."

"And I gummed the works," Tony interrupted again. "I didn't know she'd broken off with him, but I damn well tried to make her do it. We did a lot of rowing on the q.t."

"And one of the rows took place at two o'clock in the morning on the veranda," Jimmy said. "Lee thought it was 'Berto and Connie. When Lucia discovered he'd been carrying tales to Mark, she marched up and told the truth."

"I remember," Mark agreed. "That was—Thursday."

"Yes; the day before, we had that picnic on the hill. The talk took place in your room, Lucia tells me, and you both were excited."

Mark nodded. "I was afraid she was planning to marry Tony, and I advanced a good many arguments against it." He glanced uncomfortably at his cousin, who grinned back, impudently.

"Not half as many as I could. I'm a lazy beggar, and that's a fact."

"Lucia doesn't agree," Mark said dryly. "She wouldn't hear a word against you."

"And that," Jimmy told Tony, "is what made the trouble. Woman-like, instead of assuring Mark that she had no intention of marrying you, she proceeded to argue. Naturally, her voice rose, and Doug got the gist of it in his room, next door."

"You mean he deliberately planned the murders then?"

"I doubt it. But it must have occurred to him that if you were out of the way his chances of getting Lucia back would be a great deal brighter. I can picture him, after his

success in murdering Sally, dallying with the idea of using
the rest of that poison on you."

"Why on earth had he saved the stuff?"

"Probably for his own use, in case he should ever be
nabbed for Sally's murder, and needed a way out. I fancy
he made that niche in the chimney and hid it there last
year, immediately after her death. Later, he kept it for another purpose. By this summer his marriage to Lucia had
become important for reasons other than sentiment."

"You mean the legacy?"

"The legacy. Doug was desperate for money."

Both Mark and Tony stared at Jimmy in astonishment.

"But he had more than any of us."

"Oh, I've heard all that." Jimmy threw out his hands
impatiently. "That he was a blooming Croesus, the bright
boy of your local Wall Street. But if any of you had the
slightest interest in finance, you'd have heard of a little
thing called 'the depression.'"

"Of course we've heard of it," Tony snapped. "But Doug
wasn't hit by it. He said he'd made money selling short."

"Sure, he *said* so. You don't suppose he'd admit his losses,
do you? He'd lie, and brag, and let you think he was rolling
in coin. He managed to put it over on you—and me, too,
because I wasn't thinking about him, at the time. Later,
when things began to point in his direction, I remembered
that day on the hill. He was reading a newspaper which
had been brought over with the mail. When I asked him if
there was any news he told me 'no.' When I looked at the
paper, later, I found it carried a front page story about a
crash in stocks. It was probably the worst day Wall Street
had seen for weeks. That started me to thinking. Surely, a
man in the stock broking business would have made some
mention of the fact, unless he had a reason for ignoring it.
Also, a normal broker, playing the short side of the market,

would have been in his office and not dallying around on a remote island, even in fascinating company.

"Then, too, I remembered what you had said about his adopted father. You'll note that his breakdown occurred soon after stocks began to crash last year—which may, of course, have been sheer coincidence, but the fact that the family was kept from seeing him made me suspect Doug was deliberately cutting him off, for fear you'd discover the firm was tottering, if not actually insolvent. I've no doubt that when Doug came to the island he was counting on Lucia's legacy to see him through; but, after the news in the paper that day, he must have realized it was imperative he marry her and that the legacy must be doubled or trebled to do him any real good."

"Why should he have thought it necessary to go to such lengths? None of us have much money, but if he'd told us we'd have chipped in and helped him out, somehow."

"There," said Jimmy gravely, "you're touching the real motive back of these murders."

"You said it was Lucia and the money," Mark protested.

"Yes; it was that, of course. But behind that, motivating everything he did, was Doug's tragic inferiority complex."

"Inferiority!" Tony gave a short laugh. "You're not asking me to believe—"

"I see what you mean," Mark interrupted. "His braggadocio was a 'defense reaction.'"

"Exactly," Jimmy agreed. "I've been reading a good deal of psychology lately; I think I understand Doug's state of mind and what led to it. You'll have to start back when you were all children. There was Doug, an only child of eight or nine, with red hair, a temper to match, and a firm idea of his own importance. Suddenly he is orphaned and tossed into the midst of your group, made, willy-nilly, part of the Conroy clan. I don't need to point out what he was up against. He hadn't any brilliant mental qualities; he couldn't play, or sing, or paint, or write. Wasn't even good in school. The only thing he had to offer was a fine physique. Naturally, he went in for athletics. While you were youngsters, he kept his mental balance by beating you at games, or in fights; but as you grew older he lost that release. You got beyond the fighting age, and were all too lazy about physical exertion to care whether he beat you at swimming and tennis or not, so his ego turned to another outlet."

"Money making," Mark suggested, and Jimmy agreed.

"It gave him a chance for bragging, for showing off, and proving continually to himself and to you that he was as clever or cleverer than the rest of the Conroy clan. I doubt," he added, "whether you realize your real basic cruelty to Doug, or how much he hated you. You were so used to considering him stupid and thick-skinned that you made him the butt of all your jokes. His pride was such that he learned to hide what he really felt. Early in this affair, Phil and I were talking about Connie, and I said that the man or woman scorned was always dangerous. I was nearer the truth, at that time, than we knew. Later, when I looked back at the way you ragged Doug on the hill, and at 'Berto's really insulting performance at the piano, I began to get an inkling of his true character.

"It also gave a reason for his engagement to Sally. You see, it satisfied something in him to feel that one of the clever Conroy women was willing to marry him. Later, when Lucia came back, with a newly made reputation, his ego forced him to transfer his affection to her. Losing her to Tony was not only a sentimental shock, but it maddened him to think of what the family would say in ridicule. And the same thing applies to his business. I believe he'd rather have died than taken help from your hands. He'd murdered Sally, and had got away with it, or believed he had.

When he faced the crisis in his affairs, he again became a killer. Oh, I don't mean all at once, or with any completely formed plan. Probably it began with that talk on the hill and 'Berto's crazy hoax. When he asked Doug to help him, he laid the train for what happened later. I don't believe I need to go over 'Berto's murder again. We've covered the ground so many times that you can easily see how Doug could have done it."

"Except for one thing," I put in. "Doug was the only one of us except Connie who was caught three times in that game."

"Exactly," Jimmy agreed. "And if I hadn't been a blind fool, that would have made me suspicious at once. Why should he have been caught so often unless he deliberately put himself in the way of the person who was 'it'?"

"But Connie—" Mark began.

"—had an hysterical giggle which betrayed her. Doug had nothing of the sort. You'll notice, too, that he was caught once at the beginning and twice at the end of the half-hour, which left plenty of time between for the murder. Personally, I don't believe his plans were fully formed at that time, although he undoubtedly hoped Tony would be blamed for 'Berto's death. As I figured it, the way the family, almost simultaneously, began to suspect that one of them had developed old Conroy's insanity suggested the next step. He realized that it would be possible to commit a series of murders and yet avoid detection by doing them in such a fantastic manner that they would seem, at first, to have been the work of a madman. Later on, by planting clews, he could throw the blame on Tony, and so remove him as a rival."

"Good God!" Tony ejaculated, and Jimmy nodded.

"Pretty cold-blooded, eh? But you'd been building it with your own hands, you Conroys, for the past fifteen years. Every time you poked fun at Doug, you drove another nail into 'Berto's coffin, into Aunt Hagar's, and Lee's."

"Lee!" Mark exclaimed, as though the name suddenly reminded him of something. "Hold on! How could Doug have killed Lee? I'll swear that slash across his face was not self-inflicted."

"It wasn't. He got it from Lee."

"What?" All three of us were staring at him now.

"There's no doubt about it. You see, he selected Lee for his next victim because he had more influence over him than over any of the others. He began by sending that warning, which served a double purpose. In the first place, the very idiocy of its being sent ahead fed the madness theory; in the second, it threw Lee into a state of abject terror in which he was suspicious of everyone with Conroy blood. As a matter of fact, the only ones the poor fellow trusted that night were Phil, myself, and Doug.

"The way I have it figured out is this: Doug began by doctoring that mulled wine, probably while it was still in the kitchen, with a little of the chloral hydrate, just enough to insure our all sleeping heavily; then he seized an opportunity to whisper to Lee that he had an idea who was responsible for the threat against his life, but that he must communicate it in absolute confidence. He probably suggested that Lee sneak out of the bedroom after you, Phil, were asleep.

"You'll remember, Doug was with you when Mark went through his bag earlier in the evening, and he undoubtedly marked the scalpel at that time. Later, while we were all asleep, he came out of his room and abstracted it. When Lee joined him in his room, Doug crept up behind and struck him on the head with that steel mallet."

"What?" we gasped, and Jimmy smiled.

"Simple, isn't it? So simple that not one of us saw it . . . yet it's as plain as the nose on your face. The only person to describe Lee running up the hill was Doug. As a matter of fact, he didn't run up at all. He was carried, unconscious, on Doug's back."

"But how did Doug dare?"

"He was in a state of mind to dare anything. Besides, he was sure of practically everyone's being asleep, that is, everyone in the back of the house. So far as he knew, the only two, besides Lee and himself, who had not drunk the drugged wine were Aunt Hagar and Mrs. Prill—both of whose rooms were in front."

"But the locking of the doors—" I began."

"Was done to prevent anyone coming into his room while he was carrying Lee up the hill. As we know, the only place from which the hill path and tomb can be seen is Doug's room—and the stretch of gallery in front of it. He didn't believe that anyone would go out on to that rain-swept gallery; the only thing he feared was some one coming down the hall. The reason, I fancy, that Judith's door was not locked was because she and Aunt Hagar had announced their intention of locking themselves in with Aunt Hagar's key. Doug took it for granted that Judith had done so."

"So his whole story of having seen Lee go up the hill was a fabrication," Mark mused, and Jimmy nodded.

"Just a fairy tale. The explanation occurred to me last night when I was on the hill, walking with Doug. I threw a fake faint to see whether or not he could lift me. I weigh at least twenty pounds more than Lee, but he swung me up as though I were a child." He paused long enough to light a cigarette, and puffed it once or twice reflectively before he went on:

"I imagine his original scheme was to carry Lee up to the tomb, cut his throat on the steps, then leave him there. But when he reached the spot, something happened which upset his plans. In the first place, Lee came to himself.

Possibly the blow on the head hadn't been as hard as Doug supposed, and the cold wind helped to revive him. In any case, I'm certain that he recovered enough to put up a brief fight, because Harker—who was in that underground room—heard some sort of scuffling on the steps. Doug probably had the scalpel in his hand, and in the course of the tussle he was slashed across the forehead and cheek. He managed to get the better of Lee, and cut his throat, as he had originally planned. Only now, you see, he was in a difficult position."

"You mean the slash on his face," Mark said thoughtfully. "It would be hard to explain."

"Exactly, As I see it, his scheme had been to leave Lee on the steps of the tomb, then go back to his room and pretend to have fallen asleep in his chair as though he'd been drugged, like the rest of us. Now, he was forced to change his plans. In a flash he must have seen the possibility not only of covering his steps but also of manufacturing a beautiful alibi. Reconstructing the scene: I believe he first took the mallet out of his bathrobe pocket, where he had concealed it after striking Lee on the head. He was a little squeamish about hitting himself too hard a blow, so he padded it with Lee's handkerchief, then struck himself just hard enough to raise a good bump. He chucked the mallet away, gave that yell for help, shot off the pistol, and dropped down near Lee in a convincing faint. One thing he slipped up on in his excitement. He remembered to drop the knife on the step and to get rid of the incriminating door key by putting it in Lee's pocket, but he didn't think to daub mud on Lee's moccasins in order to make it look as though he had walked up the hill. Only the left side, where his feet hung over the edge of the steps, was coated with mud. If things had not happened so thick and fast he might have rectified the error, but Aunt Hagar came out on the gallery, then Harker appeared from the tomb. He tells me he was carrying an electric torch, and turned it on Doug's face; which explains why Aunt Hagar was able to see him plainly from the gallery, although he was barely visible to us when we ran up the Hill, later on."

"That's all clear enough," Mark said slowly. "And at that point Aunt Hagar screamed and fainted."

"Check!" said Tony. "Then I woke up, ran down the stairs, and began pounding on Henry's door."

"Check!" this time from Jimmy. "Harker ran down the hill, waited for you to clear out then went into his room. A minute later all of us came out on the gallery and discovered Aunt Hagar. You called from above. We rushed up the hill. Found Lee dead, and Doug apparently knocked out, and bleeding convincingly from that wound on his cheek." He glanced about questioningly. "Does that clear up Lee's death?"

"Yes. . . ." Mark hesitated, then: "No, by Jove, there's one thing it doesn't cover. What about that call?"

"There wasn't any call."

"But, hang it all, we heard it," I insisted.

"Not that night. As Tony pointed out this morning, Doug was the only one who heard it the first time it sounded—or, rather, was *supposed* to have sounded. It was pure invention. I believe he got the idea from Lee. Lee talked about that spook of Malinda's, with its hypnotic call, just before he was going to sleep. I don't doubt Doug was listening, either from the hall or the bathroom." Jimmy paused to light another cigarette, then went on, reflectively:

"As I see it, Doug's idea was to make the whole thing as mysterious as possible. It was rather like that children's game, 'obstacle race,' where the one who's 'it' throws all the obstacles he can find in the path of those who follow. Doug's lay was to make the whole affair as inexplicable and fantastic as he could, so that we should be less likely to find the solution. For that reason, he seized upon Lee's absurd spook, and invented a mysterious call, which seemed to come from the hill. Later on, he began to be afraid that I didn't believe his story, so he bolstered it up by slipping out the night of Aunt Hagar's death and giving that wail in the shrubbery where we all could hear it."

"Let me see," Mark mused, "where was Doug when Phil took up Aunt Hagar's tray?"

"He claimed to have gone out on the veranda to look at the river, and I don't doubt that he did. But instead of going back into the library, as he said, I believe he went on through the lower passage and up the back stairs. The rest was just as we figured it out before: he waited on the third-floor stairs until Phil reached the hall with his tray, then blew the fuse and dropped in the chloral. He had plenty of time to slide down the rear stairs and noisily up the front way while Tony and Mark were striking lights."

"Check!" Tony repeated. "Then all he had to do was to stick with the gang and trust to luck that Aunt Hagar'd be finished off by the chloral. Even if she weren't, there'd be nothing tying it to him."

"Nothing," Jimmy agreed. "Following that, came the little prank of blowing the fuse in the, kitchen, then slipping out and giving that banshee wail from the shrubbery. Incidentally, that made me look at you with suspicion, Tony, because, according to Doug, you were handling the electric toaster at the time. That meant you could have blown the fuse more easily than anyone. It started me on your trail."

"Which is exactly what Doug wanted."

"Yes. It was about there, I fancy, he began trying to turn suspicion in your direction."

"But why did he wait so long?" Mark asked.

"Because if he'd directed attention toward Tony earlier we'd probably have locked the boy up, which would automatically have proved him innocent when Doug committed more murders."

"I see," Mark nodded, and I burst out:

"But why did he plant those clews in the chimney of his own room?"

"That," Jimmy informed us, "was one of the smartest things he did. If he'd put that package in Tony's room, nine chances out of ten we'd have suspected the plant. By hiding it in his own chimney, with the string hanging down in the obvious fashion, he made it look as though it had been put there for the express purpose of planting evidence against him."

"That," Tony said grimly, "is why I kept my mouth shut when I saw the string in the chimney. I knew darned well if I said anything you'd think I was pointing it out deliberately."

"But the cyanide," I protested, "was found in Tony's room."

"Exactly. That little farce I staged to-night—lights out, the call, Judith's mysterious disappearance—must have shaken Doug's confidence badly. He knew something was up, but he wasn't quite sure what. Just as I planned, he decided to hurry events. While we were out of the house, he sneaked back to plant a final and definite clew that would lead us to Tony. I had no way of knowing exactly what it would be, but I watched, and wasn't surprised when he broke open that chest. He knew, with the cyanide gone, we'd go over every inch of the house with a fine-tooth comb, and, sooner or later, we'd find it, apparently concealed with the greatest care, in Tony's room. And then—"

"Gallows for Tony," that young man suggested cheerfully.

"Gallows for Tony," Jimmy agreed, and there was an interval of thoughtful silence. "I should have been quicker on the trigger," he said regretfully. "As I look back, I can see a dozen places that screamed the truth aloud. But I was fooled by the fact that you all inferred that Doug was a nit-wit. If I'd used my brains, I'd have realized he couldn't be as stupid as you believed. He wasn't brilliant, it's true, but he had a certain smartness—the tricky smartness of a man who has spent his time in making a business success. What you Conroys don't realize is, that it takes brains, of a kind, to make money. Doug had that sort of brains. Another mistake we made: we gave the murderer credit for laying his plans ahead and foreseeing with uncanny astuteness every eventuality. I know, now, we were mistaken. Doug merely started a train of events, then waited and seized upon the chance of the moment to carry them through.

"He sent those warnings, then watched for an opportunity to make good on them, knowing he'd lose nothing by failure. As it happened, luck played into his hands.

"He took a chance on being able to entice Lee out of his room, and Lee came.

"He took a chance on finding some way of putting the chloral hydrate into Aunt Hagar's food; and when he saw you pour out the wine, Phil, it suggested the next step.

"Lee's mention of Malinda's ghost stories gave him the idea of a wailing voice.

"Aunt Hagar's tale about seeing the shadowy shape coming from the tomb made him bring me those diaries of your grandfather's.

"By leaving his plans fluid, open to change at any moment, he was able to seize upon every opportunity that offered, and make the most of it—which is, after all, exactly the method of a modern business man."

"But the originality—" I began, and he chuckled.

"Nothing he did was original. Shrewd, I'll admit; but almost every move he made was taken from one of these detective stories of Aunt Hagar's. In *Hide in the Dark* you'll find a man murdered in the midst of a game. In *The Scarab Murder Case* you'll find the double twist of a murderer planting clews against himself in order to throw suspicion upon another. The very words he used in describing that weird call, 'an eerie wail . . . low but penetrating . . . falling into a sort of minor cadence at the end,' you'll find in one of Sax Rohmer's Dr. Fu-Manchu stories." Jimmy rose and stretched himself as though released from a strain.

"There's nothing startling, nothing unbelievable about this affair," he said, "if you take it from the psychological standpoint. The great difficulty with the world at large is that it thinks people eccentric and insane when they're only running contrary to the general herd of mankind. Sometimes a man's abnormality takes the form of an exaggeration of the so-called human virtues. When a man overdoes the cult of bodily well-being, as Doug did, when he makes a god of success, then look out, there's something wrong somewhere. What it is, the psychologists can't agree. Freud will tell you it's sex. Flügel, that it's environment. Schlapp, like as not, that it's glands. Speaking of Schlapp. . . ." He picked up a copy of *The New Criminology* from the desk and began turning the pages.

"Schlapp and Smith have this to say:

> *"'These are the glands that make for aggressiveness and strong physical activity. They are the glands of that idol of modern mediocrity, the go-getter, and it is not beyond the truth to say that this kind of criminal is usually no more than a go-getter gone wrong.'"*

He laid down the book and nodded to us over his cigarette. "In other words, beware of the Babbitts. If they don't get you one way, they will another." He crossed to the window and threw open the shutters. The dawn had come; the sky was no longer black but flushed a delicate pink. Already the hill above was touched with gold from the rising sun, and the trees were a tender, misty green.

"The storm is passed," Jimmy said softly. "We can look for help from the mainland."

"Now that we no longer need it," Mark put in. "I think you've explained everything."

"Not *everything*." A thought struck me and I rose to my feet, in somewhat belated indignation. "You haven't explained what you meant when you said, last evening, that you wouldn't tell me your plans because you'd seen me play the Third Murderer in *Macbeth*."

Jimmy turned back from the window. His head was outlined against the cheery light, and I saw once more his flashing, impish smile. "I meant, old dear, that I didn't dare trust you with the family if you knew the truth—even a child could have read it in your face. You see, I once watched you *try* to act."

FEAR OF FEAR

FLORENCE RYERSON
COLIN CLEMENTS

Also Available

Coachwhip Publications

CoachwhipBooks.com

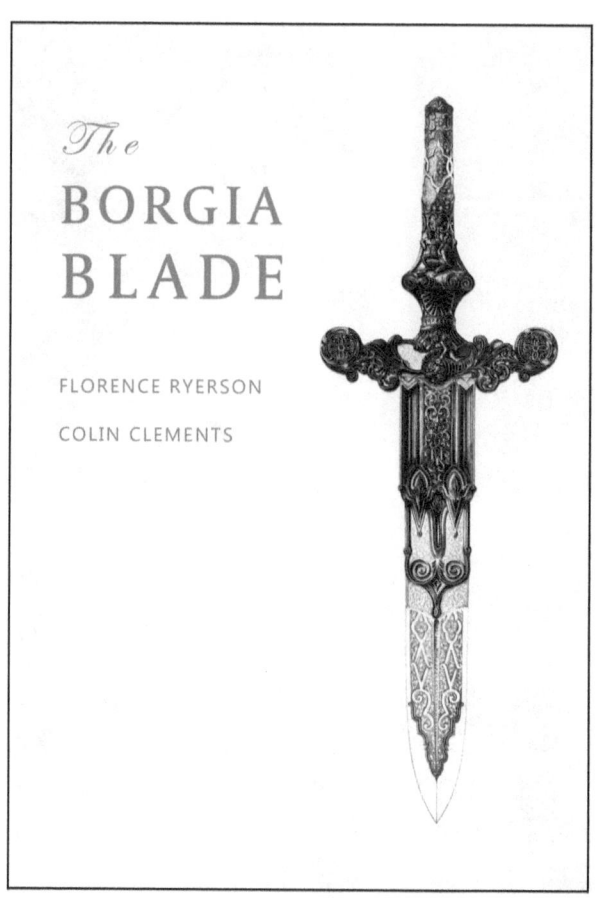

The BORGIA BLADE

FLORENCE RYERSON

COLIN CLEMENTS

Also Available

Coachwhip Publications

CoachwhipBooks.com

SULTAN'S HAREM MYSTERY

Drink the Green Water
The Milkmaid's Millions

HUGH AUSTIN

Also Available
Coachwhip Publications
CoachwhipBooks.com

Jack Dolph

MURDER MAKES THE MARE GO

Also Available

Coachwhip Publications

CoachwhipBooks.com

Also Available

Coachwhip Publications

CoachwhipBooks.com

Also Available

Coachwhip Publications

CoachwhipBooks.com

NO FACE TO
MURDER

EDITH HOWIE

Also Available

Coachwhip Publications

CoachwhipBooks.com

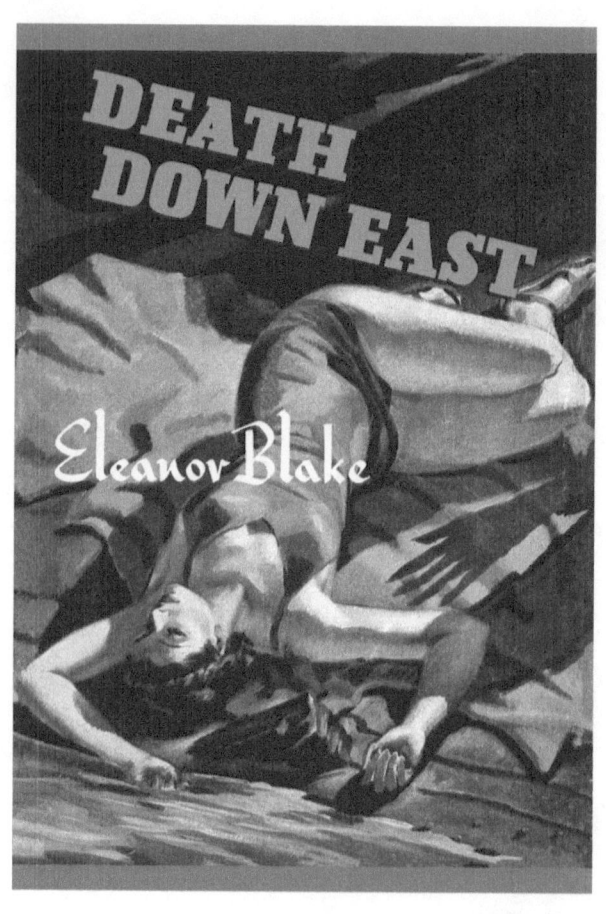

Also Available

Coachwhip Publications
CoachwhipBooks.com

MURDER
ON THE
BLUFF

ESTHER TYLER

Also Available

Coachwhip Publications
CoachwhipBooks.com